RETIREMENT HOMES
ARE MURDER

This Large Print Book carries the Seal of Approval of N.A.V.H.

RETIREMENT HOMES ARE MURDER

MIKE BEFELER

WHEELER PUBLISHING
A part of Gale, Cengage Learning

Detroit • New York • San Francisco • New Haven, Conn • Waterville, Maine • London

GALE
CENGAGE Learning™

Copyright © 2007 by Mike Befeler.
Wheeler Publishing, a part of Gale, Cengage Learning.

Wheeler Publishing Large Print Cozy Mystery.
The text of this Large Print edition is unabridged.
Other aspects of the book may vary from the original edition.
Set in 16 pt. Plantin.
Printed on permanent paper.

LIBRARY OF CONGRESS CATALOGING-IN-PUBLICATION DATA

Befeler, Mike.
    Retirement homes are murder / by Mike Befeler.
       p. cm. — (Wheeler Publishing large print cozy mystery)
    ISBN-13: 978-1-59722-494-9 (pbk. : alk. paper)
    ISBN-10: 1-59722-494-4 (pbk. : alk. paper)
    1. Murder — Investigation — Fiction. 2. Retirement communities — Fiction. 3. Memory disorders in old age — Fiction. 4. Retirees — Fiction.
    5. Large type books. I. Title.
PS3602.E37R47 2007b
813'.6—dc22   2006102218

Published in 2007 by arrangement with Tekno Books and Ed Gorman.

Printed in the United States of America
3 4 5 6 7   13 12 11 10 09
ED084

To my wife, Wendy, and my kids,
Roger, Dennis,
and Laura.

ACKNOWLEDGMENTS

Many thanks for the assistance from Wendy, Laura, Kasey, and Dennis Befeler; suggestions from John McIntosh, Barbara Graham, Wanda Richards-Seaman, Phil Enger, Stuart Bastin, and Jodie Ball; and editorial support from Denise Dietz and John Helfers.

CHAPTER 1

Where was I?

I gasped for breath and felt beads of sweat form on my forehead. I surveyed a room I didn't recognize.

There had to be something to jog my memory. Somewhere.

What looked familiar?

The dresser. I bought it in 1968 and later lugged it to the two different houses Rhonda and I lived in. But what happened to Rhonda? She used to be with me.

An ache of loneliness constricted my chest. She died. Cancer. I now lived alone.

I tried to find something else recognizable in this strange place. In the dim light my eyes focused on a gold aloha shirt, lying in a crumpled pile on a chair. Rhonda bought that for me on Maui in 1990. What a vacation. We went there after our son was grown and I had retired. Just the two of us. Like a honeymoon all over again.

Now I was alone here. Wherever the hell here was. It appeared to be some kind of apartment.

I swung my creaky old body off the mattress and peeked out the curtains. The sun illuminated trees below, some laced with red flowers. White clouds puffed across a bright blue background.

But I didn't recognize the building. I squinted at the distant sheer slope of a mountain draped in dark green. It looked like Hawaii. I had to think. Yes! I'd moved to Hawaii in 1995.

It still amazed me that I ended up in Hawaii. I was the original landlubber and didn't like the ocean. It scared the shit out of me.

The squeak of a door opening interrupted my thoughts.

"Good morning, Mr. Jacobson," an attractive young woman said. She wore an orange hibiscus in long black hair that cascaded down over a bright blue and green muumuu. The aroma of pikake perfume permeated the air. I pictured her slender fingers fluttering in a graceful hula.

"You always visit gentleman while they're still in pajamas?" I asked. "Who are you?"

She smiled, showing even white teeth. "Oh, Mr. Jacobson. You're such a card. I'm

Melanie. I have your pills."

"Pills?"

"Yes. Now be a good sport and take your medicine." She handed me a glass of water and a small paper cup with three pills.

I hefted the cup as if it contained lead shot, uncertain whether or not to trust her. "I hate taking pills. You're not trying to poison me, are you?"

"No." She laughed and her eyes scrunched up. "Your doctor wants you to take your medication twice a day."

"What's the medicine for?"

She clicked her tongue, and a wry smile crossed her face. "We discussed this yesterday afternoon."

A fog of uncertainty swept through my addled brain. I had once prided myself on my good memory. Why couldn't I remember talking to her yesterday? Why couldn't I recognize my surroundings? My head jerked up. "Yesterday afternoon?"

"Yes."

"Where am I?"

She sighed. "You're at Kina Nani."

"What the hell is Kina Nani?"

"It's a retirement home."

That stopped me faster than hitting a brick shithouse. I could feel my jaw drop.

She must have decided to take advantage

of me standing there with my mouth open. "Now be good and swallow your pills."

This didn't look like the type of place I would ever pick. Even with Rhonda gone, I wouldn't move into a tiny room with a bird's-eye view of trees. Or a place where strange young women barged in. I gulped down the pills with the hope they would help rejuvenate my memory. But still — "How'd I get here?"

"Your son told me you might not remember. He moved you in yesterday. We're glad you decided to join us. You'll love it here." She gave me one last smile and then turned and made a quick exit.

No, my son Denny would never have done this to me. He knew how much I valued my independence. But still . . . Think.

I pushed my palms against my forehead, trying to squeeze some memory out of my foggy brain.

There had to be something I could remember.

I started with the basics. I am Paul Jacobson. Born September 20, 1921, in San Francisco, now living in Hawaii. After a pause and a deep breath, I still didn't recognize this apartment that I'd supposedly moved into the day before.

What else?

My stomach growled.

Where could a guy get some grub around this joint? I'd have to get dressed and look around.

I put on Bermuda shorts, a polo shirt, and tennis shoes.

This place still didn't look the least bit familiar, but the things in it did. There was my old television set, a picture of Rhonda and me on our wedding day, a golf trophy I won in 1997. Boy, did I putt well that day. Within three of shooting my age. Some things a person never forgot.

Combing my full head of neatly trimmed gray hair, I looked at myself in the mirror and patted my flat stomach. Not bad for an old fart. Still had all my good white teeth, strong limbs, no arthritis, face not too badly wrinkled. I had been alive for at least eighty years but could have passed for a young fellow in his seventies.

I reached for the door handle, and my hand grazed a set of keys dangling from the knob. Must have been my keys. I thrust them in my pocket, stepped out, and closed the door.

Outside, I looked at the number by the door — 615. A nameplate showed "Paul Jacobson." Damnation. This had to be where I lived. But it didn't look at all familiar.

Wandering down the hallway, I spied two elevators, side-by-side. I'd have to head down.

After an interminable wait, the door of the left elevator slid open, and I stepped in. I stood face-to-face with a swarm of old people. Several walkers. Crap. This place was full of old fogies. "Where does a guy get some breakfast around here?" I asked.

A woman in a yellow muumuu gave me a skeptical look. "Second floor, of course."

"Second floor," I mumbled to myself.

After a bumpy ride punctuated by stops on two other floors, the elevator door opened. I was swept out as the limping horde moved through an entryway and into a large room, brightly lit by overhead lights and floor-to-ceiling windows. Sure enough, it looked like a feeding trough for the decrepit, a room crammed with tables, seating two to four geezers and geezerettes.

I sniffed. The mingled aroma of papaya, fried eggs, and sausage tickled my nose. Dishes clattered in the background, and I could sense the heat of sweaty old bodies.

I tried to figure out where to sit.

A young woman with black hair tucked in a bun grabbed my arm. "This way, Mr. Jacobson."

She steered me to a table with two other

men. One reminded me of a cross between a bald gnome and a Buddhist monk in an aloha shirt. He shoveled food into a wrinkle-lined cavity above a recessed chin.

The other one stood up and appeared to be approximately my size, probably five-eleven, with white hair and a full white beard. Reminded me of a skinny Santa Claus. He gave me a welcoming smile and waved me to a chair.

"I'm Paul Jacobson," I said.

"I know," the white-bearded man said. "We met yesterday."

"Yesterday?"

"Sure. You arrived here yesterday."

"Who are you?" I asked.

"I'm Meyer Ohana. We had a pleasant dinner together yesterday."

"You keep talking about yesterday."

"Don't you remember our conversation?"

"Nope," I said. "This is all new ground for me."

"I didn't realize it yesterday, but you must suffer from short-term memory loss."

"Yeah. That's my big problem. You could ask me anything about 1940, but yesterday is a big blank."

"So how was your memory before you started having problems?" Meyer asked.

"That's the strange part," I said. "When I

15

was in business, I could remember the exact facial expression of a customer from the last time he entered my store or the precise words the daughter holding his hand had spoken."

"You had a photographic memory," Meyer said.

"I guess so. I can even picture what I've seen today and could repeat our conversation, so far, word for word. But yesterday's a blank. That's why this place is a mystery to me."

"You'll get used to it," Meyer said.

"Maybe. What do they have you in here for?"

Meyer gritted his teeth. "I'm still mobile and have all my mental faculties. But I'm starting to lose my sight because of macular degeneration. Although I can make out general shapes pretty well, I can't read books anymore."

"You like this place?"

He shrugged. "It isn't bad. The food's acceptable."

"Looks like he enjoys it." I pointed to the bald troll who ignored us as he stuffed eggs, sausage, and hash browns in his mouth like he had to get the manure wagon loaded in two minutes.

"That's Henry Palmer. He was a world-class mathematician. Henry, do you remember Paul from yesterday?"

Henry stopped with a fork full of oozing eggs inches from his lips and then popped it in his mouth.

"Henry's single-minded. A.S."

"What's A.S.?" I asked.

"Asperger's syndrome. It's difficult to connect with Henry sometimes, unless you're interested in one of his projects. He likes collecting coins and is an expert on baseball statistics. Ask him anything about baseball."

"Okay," I said. "Henry, who hit the most home runs for the 1958 Chicago Cubs?"

"Ernie Banks." He didn't even look up but kept reaching for the food. "Forty-seven. Most in the National League and Majors. Mantle only had forty-two in the American League."

"I'll be damned," I said. "No memory problem with him."

"No," Meyer said. "He's sharp as a guillotine. But he's not very good around people."

"How so?" I asked.

"Henry lacks some of the basic social graces," Meyer said. "He'll insult you all the time. He doesn't mean any harm. It's the way he is."

"How's he handle it when people insult him back?"

"Why don't you try it?"

I scrutinized both of them. Meyer smiled, and Henry worked away at the trough.

I squinted at Meyer. "You setting me up?"

He shrugged and chuckled.

"I'll bite," I said. I looked at Henry's large forehead and wrinkled face and thought of a polished peach with chunks removed. "Henry, were you born that ugly or did you get in the middle of a fight between two rabid beavers?"

Without even looking up, Henry said, "Paul Jacobson, you're an idiot, have the memory of a slug, and your shoes don't match."

I inspected my feet. "Hell," I muttered. I was wearing two different tennis shoes. "How'd he notice that?"

"He sees things others don't," Meyer said. "Henry is very focused."

"I'm convinced, Henry. You want to be hired as my valet?"

"You need more than a valet," Henry said without lifting his head from his food. "A nursemaid."

I laughed. "I'm going to like this dive. I get to sit with a blind guy who escaped from the North Pole and one of his weirdo elves.

18

What more could I want?"

"You could go live somewhere else," Henry said.

Ignoring him, I turned toward Meyer. "What's there to do around this place?"

"Opportunities abound: bingo, shuffleboard, balloon volleyball, bridge, concerts. . . ."

"Sound like things for old people."

"Exactly."

"But I'm still alive," I said. "Anything more active?"

"There's a swimming pool."

"A swimming pool at my manor?"

"Yes, and we have a Jacuzzi."

"I hate swimming," I said, "but I could use a nice soak in a hot tub."

"The temperature's not kept very high," Meyer said.

"Too bad," I said. "That would be a good way to dispatch some of the inmates."

After breakfast I returned to my apartment and scanned my new domain. I still couldn't believe I had been here since yesterday. As I strolled through the kitchenette, I sniffed the aroma of stale beer. Looking down, I noticed a bag of trash containing bottles and cans. Why was this here? It looked like I'd had a party

19

the previous night. I sure didn't remember anything about it.

I stuck my head out the front door, looked both directions, and saw a cleaning lady down on her hands and knees, scrubbing the hallway carpet.

"Where do you get rid of trash around here?" I asked.

She looked up at me, pointed and said, "Toward the elevator. Trash chute."

I picked up the bag, headed in the direction she had indicated, and found a metal door. I pulled the cold steel handle toward me, jammed the bag inside the opening, and waited for the clinking of falling trash.

No sound.

The top of the bag still showed. I pushed on the bag, but it wouldn't go down.

"Damn!" I shouted. "Something's clogging the chute."

I removed the bag, placed it on the floor, and then peered into the chute. Couldn't see a blasted thing. I stood up on my tiptoes and leaned over as far as I could.

Still nothing. Too dark.

I returned to my apartment and took a gander to see if I could spot a flashlight. I found one up on a kitchenette shelf.

When I returned to the end of the hall, I flicked on the flashlight, leaned into the

opening, and aimed the light beam downward.

A bloody face peered vacantly upward.

CHAPTER 2

I gasped and juggled the flashlight, catching it at the last moment, before it would have fallen onto the face. My heart pounded, and I slumped to the floor. This was awful. What was a body doing in the garbage chute? Who was it? What had happened? I had to do something. I raised myself up and stumbled toward my apartment. The only person in sight was the cleaning lady.

"Call someone," I shouted. "There's a body in the trash chute."

She squinted at me. "What you mean?"

"Go tell your boss. There's a body stuffed in the trash chute. I'm phoning 9-1-1."

I lurched into my apartment. My hand trembled as I reached for the phone. I dropped the receiver, and it tumbled to the rug. Reaching over, I picked it up like a hot potato and punched in the three digits. I waited with my stomach doing more somersaults than an Olympic gymnastics team during floor exercises. It wasn't good for old guys to go through things like this.

Within minutes a siren sounded in the distance.

I dashed out into the hallway, took a deep breath to calm myself, and marched to the trash chute. I paced back and forth, waiting for someone to show up.

Finally a policeman lumbered toward me. He stood approximately six feet tall with a firmly set jaw and a nose that, at least once, had encountered something hard.

"It's in the garbage chute," I said, pointing.

"You the one who made the call?" he asked.

"Yeah, I was trying to throw away some trash."

He took a handkerchief out of his pocket and carefully pulled the handle to open the chute. Then, with his other hand, he whipped a flashlight from his belt, directed the beam into the opening, and leaned over to peer inside.

A moment later his head emerged. With a scowl he reached for a cell phone attached to his belt and made a call. "Suspected homicide. Body in the trash chute, sixth floor of the Kina Nani retirement home. Notify Saito and send a medical examiner.

We'll also need rope and a harness to pull it out."

He extracted a roll of yellow police tape from his pocket and roped off the trash chute. Then he turned to me. "Okay. Please give me your name and tell me what happened."

He stared at me with cold gray eyes, and I felt my throat tighten. I gave him my name and explained the sequence of events while he took notes on a small pad.

"Anyone else around?" he asked.

"A cleaning lady." I turned my head and surveyed the hall. "She isn't here anymore."

He shone his flashlight at the bag of bottles and then bent down to look more carefully.

"You wait over there," he said, motioning me toward the side wall.

Just then two men and the cleaning lady came toward us. One of the men, a tall drink of water in a blue suit a size too large, introduced himself as Alexander Farns, the retirement home director. He looked like Ichabod Crane with a corncob up his ass. The other, a short, rotund, jovial man in a baseball cap, identified himself as the facilities manager. Compared to the stuffed shirt, he looked like a real human being. He even had dirt under his fingernails.

The policeman said, "I'd like to get a list of all your residents and any employees who have been in the building in the last twenty-four hours." He turned to the facilities manager. "Tell me about your trash disposal system."

The facilities manager reached up and tweaked his baseball cap. "One trash chute on each floor. Doors stay locked from eleven at night till seven in da morning. Fo' keep down noise, you know."

"So someone would have been here at both times to lock and unlock the door?"

Farns stepped forward, elbowed the facility manager to the side and cleared his throat. "That's correct. We have a very consistent process and excellent staff."

More people began to arrive. One man uncoiled a rope while another snapped pictures of the chute and leaned inside to photograph the face.

"I can clear the trash out of the way," I volunteered, pointing to my garbage bag on the floor.

The policeman clenched his fist and stared at me. "You leave it right there!"

"Okay." I raised my hands. "Only trying to be helpful. You can have it."

After much effort, the police extracted the body, a withered old man I didn't recognize.

He couldn't have been more than five feet tall. They laid him on a tarp that had been spread out on the floor.

"It's Mr. Tiegan from apartment 630," the cleaning lady said.

The name didn't mean anything to me. I regarded the body more carefully. Only someone that skinny and light could have been crammed into a trash chute.

"All of you move away," the policeman said.

The group of gawkers stepped back, and I continued to watch as the photographer snapped more pictures and a man wearing rubber gloves bent over to examine the corpse.

Later I overheard this man saying, "Early indication is death occurred between one and five A.M."

It took an hour before the body was removed. My bag of bottles had also disappeared.

I continued to watch as one of the police technicians used a brush to dust the handle of the trash chute with black powder. Then he placed a strip of tape over the powdered handle, pressed it down, removed it, and attached the tape to a card.

A short, stocky man in his thirties, with dark slacks, oriental eyes, and well-groomed black hair approached me. He reminded me of a fire hydrant. I smelled stale cigarette smoke. He held out a badge, and I noticed tobacco stains on his fingers. "Mr. Jacobson, I'm Detective Saito. I need to speak with you."

"Sure. We can go into my apartment."

I sat on the couch, and he pulled up a chair to face me. "Mr. Jacobson. You reported finding a body?"

"That's right. I was getting rid of a bag of garbage and saw a face in the trash chute."

"And what time was that?"

"I don't know exactly, but right after breakfast. I called 9-1-1 immediately."

"And the contents of the bag you were throwing away?"

"I found a bunch of bottles in my kitchenette. Tried to get rid of them."

"And where did the bottles come from?"

"That's a good question. I have this memory problem. I have no clue about the bottles."

"How convenient," he said.

I looked at him in disbelief. "What are you suggesting?"

"I'm surprised that you know nothing about what you tried to throw away."

"Look, I woke up this morning not knowing where I was. I've been informed that I moved here yesterday. I found this bag of bottles and was disposing of it. That's all."

"So the first night you're here, a murder takes place?"

"If you mean the body in the trash chute, I know nothing about that. Don't even recognize him."

He stared at his notepad. "That's interesting, Mr. Jacobson. I've been informed that there is some pending litigation between the two of you."

"What?" I lurched up from the couch.

"My information indicates that less than a month ago, Mr. Tiegan, the victim, sued you."

"I don't even know Mr. Tiegan," I said, slapping my palms to my forehead, trying to shake loose any memory.

"The court records indicate otherwise."

Stopping to think, I still couldn't associate the shriveled body with anyone I'd met before. I gave up and plopped back down on the couch. "Look. I have this short-term memory problem. Even if I'd seen Mr. Tiegan the other day, I wouldn't remember him, because yesterday is a blank."

"What were you doing after midnight last night, Mr. Jacobson?"

"Sleeping, I guess."

"Can you be more specific?"

"I would imagine I was in bed, because that's where I am at night. But since my memory is shot, I can't say for sure."

He grunted and wrote a note on his pad.

"I need to ask you to give me a set of fingerprints."

I shrugged. "Okay with me."

He brought out a small kit and proceeded to ink my fingers and press them on a card.

"I look like a refugee from a tattoo parlor," I said, admiring my hands. "Kind of like your tobacco-stained fingers, Detective."

"It'll disappear with a good washing using soap and hot water," Detective Saito said. "May I have your permission to look around your apartment?"

"Sure, why not?"

He lumbered to his feet and strolled around, scrutinizing my kitchenette, dresser top, and bookshelf. He leaned over and inspected a small object on a shelf in my television cabinet.

"Mind if I keep this?" he asked.

"What is it?"

"A Swiss stamp."

I flinched. "I don't know why that's there. You can have it."

He took a pair of tweezers and small paper bag out of his pocket, picked up the stamp, and dropped it in the bag.

I again noticed his tobacco-stained fingers.

"I'd like to ask your permission to do an in-depth search of your apartment."

"And if I don't agree?"

"Then I can take you down to headquarters for some additional questioning while I obtain a search warrant."

"No need for that," I said. "You can look to your heart's content."

He proceeded to go through every drawer and cabinet, looked under my bed, lifted up the mattress, and searched my closet. Given the tiny one-room hovel, it didn't take him long.

"You satisfied?" I asked when he finished.

He wrote something in his notebook and snapped it closed. "You and I will be speaking again."

"Whatever you want, Detective. By the way, I'd suggest giving up smoking. It's not healthy for you."

He glared at me. "I've tried. Back to the subject at hand, I have to ask you not to leave the islands until this is cleared up."

"Don't worry. I don't travel anymore."

"We'll be in touch." With that, he stalked out of my apartment.

I felt as if I'd been punched in the stomach. This was all happening too quickly: finding myself in a strange place, discovering a dead body, and being linked to the murder victim.

Taking a deep breath, I tried to get it all in perspective. I'd have to be careful with Detective Saito. He was convinced I was tied to the murder. And I'd have to learn more about this Tiegan fellow. I could try to contact my son, but first I'd see what I could find out on my own. Maybe my new eating buddy Meyer could lend some insight.

At lunch I returned to the same table where I'd eaten breakfast.

"Do you remember who I am?" Meyer asked me as we both watched Henry slurping his soup.

"Damn straight. You're the guy who can't see." I pointed to Henry. "And this crazed eater is your baseball almanac."

"Very good."

"You're beginning to sound like a doctor rather than one of the inmates," I said.

"Your medical case is interesting," Meyer said. "You seem to remember fine during the day. But overnight your short-term memory blanks out."

"How do you know that?"

"You couldn't remember meeting me yesterday."

"Still don't," I said. "But we talked at breakfast."

"Case proved."

"You've figured me out, Doc. I can still dredge things up from the distant past as well. I remember being a kid in San Mateo, going to college, getting married, raising a family, running my business in L.A., retiring. Enough about my strange memory. How long you been held here?"

"I moved in two years ago," Meyer said. "It was right after I had to give up driving."

"You come here on your own free will, or did you get locked up by some overzealous relative?"

"It was a little of each. I knew I couldn't take care of myself. My kids were afraid I'd burn my condo down when I tried to cook."

"So they sent you up the river."

"It's not that bad," Meyer said. "We visited half a dozen places, and I selected this one."

"What convinced you?"

"Kina Nani has an excellent staff. There's a nice view as long as I'm able to enjoy it. And finally, I can be entertained by people such as Henry."

"Right," I said. "Henry's a barrel of laughs."

"You'll learn to appreciate his talents.

32

Henry, who won the American League batting title in 1907?"

The spoon kept scooping without a pause. "Ty Cobb."

"What was his average?"

The spoon left his mouth. "Three-fifty."

Meyer smiled. "What more could you ask for? I have my own baseball statistician right here at the table."

I shook my head. "I can't even remember yesterday, and this klutz has a brain full of baseball facts. Ever stump him?"

"Not yet. But I keep trying. Henry, who won the 1945 All Star Game?"

"Trick question. No one. No All Star Game was played that year."

"Who won the Cy Young award in 1973?" Meyer asked.

"Tom Seaver and Jim Palmer."

Meyer took out a notepad and wrote on it.

I looked over. He had written some large misshapen letters.

"What's that for?" I asked.

"I'm going to check his answer in my sports reference book after lunch."

"I thought you couldn't see to read?"

"I can't," he said. "I have to use a magnifying glass."

"It must be the shits to lose your eyesight."

"It can't be worse than losing your memory."

"You got me there," I said. "Say, we had some excitement up on my floor this morning."

"I heard some sirens. That have anything to do with it?"

"Yeah. There was a dead body in the trash chute."

"What? Was it an accident or murder?"

"Apparently murder. Guy had a gash on his forehead. Someone must have stuffed his body in the trash chute."

"Who was the victim?"

"Man name of Tiegan."

"Marshall Tiegan," Meyer said. "I've met him."

"Strange situation. I don't remember ever seeing him, but the detective claims he was suing me."

"So are you a suspect?"

"I guess so," I said. "What do you know about Tiegan?"

Meyer scratched his head. "He wasn't a very pleasant person. He tended to gripe a lot."

"Sweet personality like Henry here?"

"I hope they give you the electric chair," Henry said without looking up.

I laughed in spite of the situation. "I'm

sure the detective shares your view, Henry."

"You should talk to a lawyer if you're a suspect," Meyer said.

"I hate scumbag lawyers even more than I hate swimming. Hell, even though I can't remember squat, I know I didn't have anything to do with the dead body."

"Your life could get pretty unpleasant if you're a suspect," Meyer said.

"I guess I'll just have to deal with it."

"There's one other idea." Meyer formed his fingers into a steeple. "I have a lot of contacts in the police department."

"Why's that?"

"I used to be, as you so quaintly put it, one of those scumbags." He gave me a wink. "I was a district attorney and also spent a stint as a municipal judge. I'll poke around a little."

I felt two inches tall. Nice going, Jacobson, I told myself. The guy who could assist you was a damn attorney, and you started it out by insulting lawyers. But he did seem willing to help.

Then I had a thought. "Wait a minute. I overheard that the trash chutes are locked between eleven P.M. and seven A.M. and that the murder occurred between one and five A.M. The murderer must have had a key."

"Bingo," Meyer said, giving me a big smile. "Now you have something to go on."

CHAPTER 3

Rather than waiting for the police to lock me up as their favorite suspect, I needed to get my butt in gear to learn more about this place.

I had one stop to make. By inquiring, I found the office of the facilities manager on the first floor. He was the short, chunky, part Hawaiian man I remembered seeing with the cleaning lady and Farns earlier in the morning. He was leaning back with his hands clasped behind his head and his feet resting on a scratched desk.

"I'm Paul Jacobson."

"Yeah. You da guy who found da body this morning."

"That's me. I was wondering. Who would have been on duty after midnight last night?"

"Only two people here. Jason Kam on da front desk and Moki Iwana on security."

"Would Moki have been on the sixth floor?"

"Yeah, maybe two times."

"What about Jason Kam?"

"He stay at da front desk fo' watch da lobby."

"Is Jason around now?" I asked.

"Nah. He be here tonight."

"I understand that the trash chutes were locked around eleven P.M. last night."

"Yeah. Moki made da rounds."

"Any chance he forgot to lock it?"

"Nah. He'z okay. Lock da chutes on all da floors by eleven and unlocked dem by seven in da morning."

"Where can I find Moki?"

"No work today. Nex' time night shift tomorrow."

I thought for a moment. "Who else has a key to the trash chutes?"

"Jus' Moki, Harold, and me."

"Who's Harold?"

"Second night watchman."

"And would your key be lying around for someone to use?"

He pointed to a peg board with keys on hooks behind his desk. "Jez hang it dere."

"But anyone could get the key, then."

"Nah. I leave dis office locked when I go 'way."

"So how do other people get in here when you're not around?"

"Easy. Everybody has key to dis office."

I left shaking my head. Only three copies of the trash chute key, but anyone with a key to the office could have taken one of them. Still, I'd need to talk to Moki when he was back on duty.

My next stop was at the front desk. A pleasant middle-aged woman wearing a purple and white orchid lei greeted me.

"Do visitors sign in?" I asked.

"Absolutely."

"I'd like to check the visitors' sign-in log from last night."

"Should still be there," she said, pointing to a clipboard.

I thumbed through several pages. Most of the visitors had signed in early afternoon and signed out by dinner time. There was one illegible name that signed in at 9 P.M. There was no sign-out time marked.

"Do you recognize this name?" I asked.

The woman squinted at the place I pointed. "No. Looks like an 'H' at the beginning, but I can't make out any other letters."

"Did you see someone come in?"

She shrugged. "I wasn't on duty then. You'd have to talk to Jason Kam."

"Could you run a copy of this page for me?"

"What for?"

"I'm trying to track down who visited last night. Didn't the police want to see this as well?"

She stared at me over the top of a pair of reading glasses. "No. You're the first to inquire."

"Make me a copy, but save the original. I'm sure the police will get to it eventually."

"Okay." She removed the page, stepped to the back of her office area, and inserted it in a copy machine.

With copy in hand, I headed back to my room, wondering if I could get any useful information from Jason Kam.

At dinner I was back filling out the three-some.

"I've been thinking about your memory problem," Meyer said.

"You going to help me find those lost brain cells?"

He chuckled. "Those are probably gone for good. But I have a suggestion for you. Every night you should write down what happened during the day. Then the next morning you can read it to know where you are and what happened the day before."

I hesitated in mid-bite.

"Let me get this straight," I said to Meyer. "You think this'll help me remember things?"

He shrugged. "It couldn't hurt."

"A diary like a teenage girl?"

Now he gave me a Cheshire cat smile, peeking out from his white beard. "It might do the trick. You'd need to remember to read it every morning."

"I'd have to write myself a note and leave it on the diary: 'Read this before you pee.' Then the only problem would be deciphering my own handwriting."

"You'll have to print neatly."

"You sound like my second grade teacher, Mrs. Ames," I said.

"See? You remember *her* better than what happened to you yesterday. How long have you been this way?"

"Who knows. I can't remember."

"So try thinking back. What's the last thing you remember?"

"Your dumbass question."

He laughed. "Okay. Before today, what's the most recent thing you remember?"

"I sure don't remember coming to this hell hole. Let's see. After I retired, Rhonda died, may she rest in peace. I lived in a condo in Honolulu. Played some golf. My granddaughter came to visit. She was six years old. That's about the last thing I recall."

"How old is she now?" Meyer asked.

"I have no clue."

"So all you have to do is find out how old your granddaughter is today. Then you'll know how long you've been having memory problems."

"What good will that do me?"

"Probably not much," he said. "But we'll know what we're up against. Aren't you curious about it?"

"I'm more curious where my memory cells went. But I'm also willing to find out how screwed up I am."

"Anyway, try keeping a journal," Meyer said. "By the way, I found out a little regarding the Tiegan case."

"So, are the police going to lock me up?"

"You are a suspect. With the connection between you and Tiegan, there is motive."

"I still don't remember him," I said.

"That's another good reason for you to keep a journal."

"It's a little late for that. As a casual observer, I'd say it doesn't look good for me. How do you know I didn't do it?"

"After years of dealing with criminals, I have a sense for this," Meyer said.

"Guillotine," Henry chimed in.

"No, in Hawaii it would be life imprisonment," Meyer said.

"That wouldn't be much longer for me," I said.

Later that night I found my address book and looked up the phone number of my son. I intended to talk to him to see what he might know about Tiegan and to find out how old my granddaughter was. My daughter-in-law Allison answered.

"How old is Jennifer?" I asked.

"You wake me up at midnight with that question?"

"Damn. I forgot the time zone difference. I'm sorry to disturb you, but as long as you're awake anyway, what's Jennifer's age?"

"She's eleven, Paul."

"That's amazing. I last remember my little granddaughter being six. Since then my mind has been piss poor."

"Please watch your language."

"Oh. My apologies. When did you notice my memory going in the crap . . . going bad?"

"You've had trouble remembering things for at least five years."

"I can't even recall what happened yesterday anymore."

"That's why Denny went over to relocate you to the new place."

"He's in the islands?"

"He moved you in, but had to go to Maui for a business meeting. He'll be back to see you tomorrow."

"I don't remember him being here. But I also don't remember coming to this joint."

"So how do you like your new home?" Allison asked.

"There's a problem. It's full of old people."

"Of course. It's a retirement home. Meet anyone yet?"

I thought of telling her I found a murder victim, but decided that would be unproductive. "I have two eating buddies. I like one of them, Meyer. He's the one who suggested I find out how old Jennifer is since I last remember her being six years old."

"We'll all be over to visit in less than a month, when Jennifer's done with school."

"That's good news. I look forward to seeing my favorite daughter-in-law and granddaughter. Thanks for putting up with my mistimed phone call. I still can't believe it. Jennifer's eleven years old!"

After I hung up, I sat there stunned. Where had five years gone? I needed to get a handle on this strange world of mine. I had the impression I'd been plunked down into someone else's life. As I reviewed the day, I thought about what Meyer had said. The events were still clear in my mind. Then I tried to remember the day before. I squeezed my eyes shut, clenched my fists, and tried to extract any memory I could find. One big blank. I considered the advice given me by a fraternity brother, "Live your life one day at a time." By default, that was exactly what I was doing. But it might be in prison if I didn't clear my name.

I started getting sleepy around nine-forty-five. Apparently, I wasn't much of a night owl. After rereading the same paragraph six times in a Tom Clancy novel, I washed my face, and took the elevator to the ground floor.

A bored-looking young man in a brown uniform sat at the reception desk. I looked at his scraggly black mustache and then into his sleepy eyes. It made me want to yawn. "You Jason Kam?"

His eyes focused, and he stared back. "That's me."

"Do you remember any visitors late last night?"

"Wouldn't have been any after ten P.M."

"How do you know that someone didn't drive up and sneak into the building?"

He smiled at me like a teacher regarding an idiot student. "The gate locks at ten."

"What gate?"

"The front gate automatically closes at ten P.M. No one can drive in without contacting me. There's a button and speaker by the gate."

"And no one called you last night?"

"Nope," he said.

"What about earlier than ten P.M.?"

His gaze flicked up toward the ceiling. "I don't remember anyone specifically after eight."

"There was at least one visitor that evening," I said. "Take a look at the log."

He narrowed his eyes at me. "Why are you so interested?"

"It happened on my floor. I don't like the idea of dead bodies on my floor."

Pretty lame, but he bought it.

He shuffled through the sheets on the clipboard, stopped, and then went through them again. With a puzzled expression he looked up at me. "That page is missing."

I clutched the counter. "It was here earlier today."

"Someone must have taken it," he said.

"I have a copy. I'll be back in a moment."

I headed toward the elevator with a knot

in my gut. Who could have removed the page? The police? Someone in Kina Nani management? Or had the murderer returned to get rid of the evidence?

CHAPTER 4

When I reached my room, I opened my secret hiding place, the underwear drawer. Rummaging through, I extracted a folded piece of paper imbedded near the bottom of the stack of shorts. Success.

Back at the front desk, I showed the page to Jason Kam. "Do you recognize this signature?" I asked.

He squinted at it. "Looks like an 'H' and some squiggles."

"I got that far. You must remember someone coming by."

"No," he said, shaking his head. "This person must have signed in when I was in the back room."

"Great. We have this mystery visitor that nobody can identify. What kind of security do you have in this place?"

"This is a retirement home, not a prison."

"You could have fooled me," I said.

■ ■ ■ ■

With no more useful information from Jason Kam, I retired to my room for the night. I sat at my desk, picked up a pen and pad of paper. I tapped the pen three times on the edge of the desk and began writing.

Where was I? This was my bed, my nightstand, and lamp, but I didn't remember the room.

In the faint light my eyes focused on a picture mounted on the far wall. Yes, that seascape. I remembered painting it in 1955. Rhonda and I were driving from L.A. to San Francisco on Highway One. Stopped in Cambria for a bite to eat, wandered down to Moonstone Beach, and watched the waves breaking on the rocks as the fog lifted at sunset. Took out my sketch pad and pastels and caught the moment. Back in our apartment a week later, I completed it in oils.

Okay, the painting was mine. What else looked familiar?

I turned on the light. There was a big note on top of a pile of paper on the nightstand. "Read this before you pee." My handwriting. I didn't remember writing it. Where the heck was I? I thought about throwing the paper away. Still, the note said to read it. What the hell?

I started reading.

What a surprise. It appeared my memory had been crapola for five years. I was in a place called Kina Nani. I ate my meals with two goofballs named Meyer and Henry. I was a suspect in a murder. It was like reading someone else's story. Did this really happen to me yesterday? I certainly didn't remember it. Yet, this was definitely my handwriting. I didn't lie to myself. Except for that one time with the blonde in Cleveland. But that had been sixty years ago.

I dressed and then a manic young woman came and stuffed a mountain of pills down my throat. Following the instructions I had read, I took the elevator to the second floor, where I saw dozens of old people shuffling along with their canes and walkers. Then I found the chow hall. I didn't recognize anyone. A nice young woman with dark, warm eyes steered me over to a table.

A man sitting there pointed to the empty chair. "Good morning, Paul. Have a seat."

"Do I know you?"

He laughed. "Sure do. I'm Meyer."

The name clicked. "I read about you."

50

His eyes twinkled under a baseball cap and above a snow-white beard. "Good for you. You wrote down what you did yesterday."

"I found this epistle in my handwriting. I don't remember anything about it, but it had the names Meyer and Henry in it."

"That's right. Henry's our other companion here."

I looked at the other guy, a little squat pissant. "Not much of a conversationalist is he?"

Henry ignored us and kept right on eating.

"We have an interesting problem here," Meyer said. "Yesterday, you and I had good conversations, but you don't remember anything about them."

I scratched my head. "Not a thing. But the journal referred to our talks. What's this about me being a suspect in a murder?"

He frowned. "That's right. You found a body yesterday, a victim you were linked to."

"This is the shits. I can't remember anything. How am I going to defend myself?"

"That's why I recommended that you get a lawyer."

"I hate lawyers."

"You told me that yesterday," Meyer said.

51

"I was a lawyer."

"Present company excepted."

He chuckled.

I could imagine a bowl full of jelly except he was skinny.

"One other thing," I said. "I read that I called and found out my granddaughter is now eleven years old."

"So your memory has been bad for five years," he said, shaking his head. "That's a long time not to remember things. And you lived on your own all that time?"

"I suppose so."

"How'd you do it?"

"Not so good, I guess. That's why I'm an inmate here."

"We're going to have to work on that attitude," Meyer said with a laugh. "I'll help you as much as I can by partially being your memory. You need to continue to write down everything that happens during the day in detail every night before you go to bed. You could even keep a computer journal."

"Hell no. I've never learned to use a computer and I'm not going to now."

"Then keep a handwritten diary and leave a note on top like you did last night to remind yourself to read it first thing in the morning," Meyer said. "Then at breakfast you and I will need to review the previous day."

"Damn it," I said. "Seems like a lot of trouble just because I can't remember which end I piss with."

Meyer flashed me his pearly whites. "I don't mind. I have nothing better to do, anyway."

He stood up and began pacing around.

"What are you doing?" I asked as he circled behind me.

"I can't sit in one place long."

"Crap. Get your butt back in your chair. I can't carry on a conversation with you waltzing all over the place."

He settled back down, recounted his version of what happened the day before and asked, "Sound familiar at all?"

I shook my head. "But seems to fit with what I read. That's about it."

"Are you on any medication?"

"I'm taking every color and shape of pill they can find. Does nothing for my brain cells that I can tell. I hate taking pills. That girl showed up this morning and stuffed three capsules down my throat."

Meyer popped up from the table.

"You're pacing again," I said to Meyer while he circled the table.

"I get restless sitting. I have to get up and

work off some nervous energy."

"You always been that way?"

"Yeah, in addition to going blind, I have attention deficit disorder."

"Well, pay attention," I said. "I have something important to tell you. From what I read, it sounds like my son will be visiting today."

"Good. I'd like to meet him."

"We'll have a regular old party. Henry, you can come too."

Henry had stuffed a last bite of sausage in his mouth. He chewed quickly, adjusted his metal-rimmed glasses, and then said, "I hope your son isn't another criminal and as ugly as you are."

"Actually, he looks a lot like a younger Meyer without a beard. Tall, not bald and squat like you, Henry."

Henry gave a dismissive wave of the hand.

Meyer said. "Would you like to take a walk with me?"

"Fine by me. That'll be an easier way to talk to you than when you're traipsing around here."

"Do you want to join us, Henry?" Meyer asked.

Henry looked up from his plate. "Nope. Going to work on my coin collection."

"What's with you, Henry?" I asked. "You

the strong silent type? Not up to socializing with your table buddies?"

"I don't associate with murderers, and my coin collection is more interesting than you," he said, wiping his mouth on the back of his wrist and leaving the table.

"He may not say much, but you know where you stand with Henry," Meyer said.

"Yeah," I said. "People are obviously at the bottom of his totem pole."

"You'll get used to him. Are you ready for that walk now?"

"Sure. Why don't you give me a tour of my estate?"

We descended the stairs and strolled out the front walkway.

"Was it hard for you to give up your independence and move here?" I asked Meyer.

"Yes and no. Having to hang up my car keys was the most difficult part. But I knew it was necessary when I couldn't see traffic lights and signs clearly. After I got to Kina Nani, I realized I had been having difficulty taking care of myself. Now there is a kind of freedom in going down at mealtime and not having to hassle with food packages I can't read. At first I thought Kraft was making the labels smaller. Then I learned it was me losing my eyesight."

I peered at him. "I don't know. It's kind of depressing being around all these old people."

He shrugged. "You get used to it. You can take a cab or walk somewhere when you need to get away. There are excursions. It's not like anyone is confining you here."

We wandered around the grounds and came to a shuffleboard court.

"I have just the solution for your hyperactivity," I said. "I'm going to challenge you to a game of shuffleboard."

"I haven't played in years."

"Go grab a stick," I said. "I'm going to whip your ass."

"Oh, yeah? You and who else?"

With the gauntlet thrown down, we engaged in a heated battle. I discovered I wasn't good at getting the puck in the scoring area, but could blast Meyer's disc out when he had one in position.

After several rounds, Meyer said, "First one to a hundred points wins."

"At the rate we're playing that could take the rest of the day."

"Paul, what else do we have to do?"

"You're right. I'd probably just get in trouble with the police anyway."

We started slowly and finally got the hang of shooting the puck down the cement court. Back and forth we went until Meyer scored on a shot, knocking one of my pucks into the grass and bringing his total to a hundred-and-three to my ninety-five.

He slapped me on the back. "Good try, but you weren't as good as the old master."

"Shit. We were both pretty pathetic."

"Uh oh," Meyer said. "I need to get to a restroom quick or I'll have an accident."

"Go ahead. I'll pick up the equipment."

He raced off toward the building while I reached over to retrieve the errant puck that had ended up in the grass. I noticed something shiny on the ground. Bending over, I extracted a key.

I inspected it and decided I'd be a good Samaritan and turn it in. I walked inside and stopped at the front desk.

The receptionist was at the back of the office, filing some papers, so I dropped the key on the counter.

"Here's something for the lost and found," I said to the back of her head.

"Thanks," she said without looking up.

I stopped to sip some water from the drinking fountain in the lobby, and Meyer came bounding out of the restroom. He gave me a whack on the back, causing the jet to spurt water on my chin.

"Besides getting whipped at shuffleboard,

what do you like doing for exercise?" he asked.

"Walking," I said, wiping away the remaining drops from my face. "And you?"

"I enjoy swimming and the water aerobics class."

I grimaced. "I hate swimming."

"You're something else, Paul. You hate swimming, lawyers, and pills."

"Hey, everyone has his preferences. I like reading."

"That's what I miss, curling up with a good book."

"Do you listen to books on tape?"

"I tried that, but with my poor eyesight I kept getting the tapes mixed up. I'd be listening to the beginning of a murder mystery, and suddenly it was solved. I didn't realize I had jumped from the first to the last tape."

"Why don't I read to you?"

He stopped and looked at me. "You joking?"

"No. I used to read out loud to Rhonda. I enjoy it, and we could share a good story together."

We took the wait-forever elevator up to the eighth floor and traipsed down the hallway to Meyer's apartment.

The first thing I noticed was that his place

was neater than mine. No clothes thrown on chairs, although some books had fallen over on his bookshelf. The blue flower-patterned couch looked almost new.

Right inside the living room stood the only unusual item. On top of a tall three-legged table with a white marble top, rested a red, blue, and green oriental vase. It didn't seem to fit in with the rest of the décor.

I was going to ask about the vase when Meyer signaled me over to the sliding glass door.

"What I like about this apartment is the view . . . or more correctly, what I remember about the view because everything is pretty fuzzy now. At sunrise on a clear day the mountains are a vivid orange. Now I still look for the color, although I can't make out the shapes of the peaks very well."

"But you remember what it looks like," I said. "I can see sunrise clearly, but it's a new experience for me every morning."

My attention returned to the multi-colored oriental vase. I reached my hand toward it.

"Careful," Meyer said. "Please don't touch that."

I pulled my hand back like I had been burned.

"Valuable heirloom?" I asked.

"It's Martha."

"What's Martha?"

"The vase contains the ashes of my wife Martha," Meyer said.

"Sorry, didn't mean to disturb her." I looked at it more carefully, glad that my wife Rhonda was buried and not in a container in my apartment. "A pretty vase, but is it such a good idea to keep the remains of your wife here?"

"It helps me remember her."

I thought back to Rhonda and all our happy times together. Even with my defective memory, I could still remember her crooked little smile and the glow in her eyes when she was excited about one of the accomplishments of our son Denny. I didn't need any ashes for that.

"Must be quite a chick magnet when you have a woman up to your apartment," I said.

Meyer laughed. "You have such a quaint way of stating things."

"That's me. One friggin' quaint guy."

I looked toward the bookshelf. "What would you like me to read to you?"

"This may sound strange, but why not *Alice in Wonderland?*"

"That's appropriate," I said. "I feel like I've gone down a rabbit hole. May give me insight into this nuthouse I'm in."

■ ■ ■ ■

When I returned to my apartment, the light on my phone was flashing, so I called the operator and received a message that my son Denny would be arriving for lunch.

I was looking forward to seeing him, but there was some underlying irritation I couldn't put my finger on. Anyway, we'd sit with Meyer and Henry. That would provide a good neutral territory to start off.

I had barely finished that thought when my doorbell rang. I opened the door. There was Denny, six foot even, neatly cut hair, mustache with a hint of gray. He looked older than I remembered. He had grown into a successful businessman, husband, and father. I liked seeing my only offspring. Yet, he was too intense. Probably my own fault.

"Hi, Dad."

He handed me a box of chocolate-covered macadamia nuts. We'd never been a family that hugs.

"Come on in to my new villa. It's good to see you."

"It's only been two days," he said.

"Yeah, well I forget things. How's that granddaughter of mine?"

"Jennifer is growing like a weed. She's

looking forward to coming to visit you this summer."

"I'd like to see her again," I said. "You still gainfully employed?"

He laughed. "Job's going great. Closed a deal on Maui yesterday; so in addition to getting you moved in, it has been a profitable trip." He looked at me carefully. "You look in good physical shape, Dad. Keep up your daily exercise."

"I plan to. I enjoy walking, and it keeps my legs strong."

Denny strolled through the kitchenette. "Does it feel like home yet?"

"No. It's like a whole new adventure every morning."

He raised his eyebrows. "You taking your medicine?"

"Sure. Doesn't seem to do any good."

He shuffled his feet. "I know you weren't anxious to move here, but it's best for you."

"Yeah. Yeah. I'll get used to it. Say, it's chow time. Let's head down to the mess hall. I want you to meet a couple of people."

At lunch Meyer and Denny hit it right off. They discussed business while Henry did his thing with the tuna sandwich and barley soup.

"You interested in baseball?" Meyer asked Denny.

"One of my favorite sports."

"We have our own almanac here in Henry. Ask him any baseball trivia question."

Denny scrutinized Henry.

Henry kept eating without looking up.

"Okay," Denny said. "Who won the 1949 American League pennant and who was the manager?"

"Easy," Henry said still without looking up. "Yankees. Casey Stengel."

"National League batting champion for 1939?"

"John Mize . . . 349."

"Not bad," Denny said.

"Henry and I have very similar memories," I added.

"Except yours leaks like a sieve," Henry said. He looked up at Denny. "Did you know your father's a criminal?"

"What?"

I jumped in. "It's only a little matter of a murder. I found the body."

Denny's eyes widened. "That's horrible. Must have been quite a shock to you."

"I guess. It happened yesterday, so I don't remember the particulars other than what I wrote down. From the notes I made last night, I know that the police questioned me.

The victim was someone who sued me."

"That Tiegan guy?" Denny asked.

"That's the one."

After lunch we returned to my apartment. Denny surveyed my living room and picked up one of the two novels lying on the end table. "Looks like you've settled in."

"Yeah. My home away from home."

"What do you mean by that, Dad?"

"Nothing. I'm getting used to this place."

The doorbell rang. A stranger who resembled a bulldog in a dark suit stood there. "Yes," I said. "What can I do for you?"

"I need to ask you some further questions," he said.

I grimaced. "And who are you?"

"We talked yesterday. I'm Detective Saito."

"I remember reading that name, but you don't look familiar."

"Your memory problem?"

"That's it."

"May I come in to speak with you?"

"Sure. My son's here."

"We can talk another time if it's more convenient," he said.

"That's all right. Denny can hear what you have to say."

Detective Saito walked inside.

"Denny, Detective Saito is here in regards

to the murder investigation I mentioned to you."

"I need to ask you some questions about Mr. Tiegan," Detective Saito said.

"Fire away," I said. "But I don't remember him."

Denny looked up. "I know something about Tiegan, but I don't know if I should discuss it with the police."

"Doesn't matter to me," I said. "I'm anxious to learn more with regards to this whole situation anyway."

Denny cleared his throat. "Marshall Tiegan sued my dad. I've seen the paperwork."

"Give me some details," Detective Saito said.

Denny wrinkled his brow and looked at me again.

I nodded my head.

Denny let out a breath. "It seems Dad and Tiegan were acquaintances from the condominium where they both used to live. Tiegan showed Dad his stamp collection and then went into his kitchen, leaving Dad scrutinizing the stamps. After Dad left the apartment, Tiegan discovered that some stamps were missing. He accused Dad of stealing them and filed a suit."

"How much did he say was missing?" I asked.

"Six thousand dollars' worth," Denny replied.

"Shit," I said. "I wouldn't take something like that. Stamps, I mean."

"You accused Tiegan of lying," Denny said.

"He must have lied. I don't steal."

"So a trial date was set for a month from now," Denny said.

I looked at Detective Saito. "This is all news to me. I can't remember any of it."

"Do you know what kind of stamps were in Mr. Tiegan's collection?" Saito asked.

"Since I don't remember, I can't help you there, Detective," I said. "Denny, do you know?"

"I don't recall," Denny said.

"It seems, Detective, that memories are kind of sparse around here," I said.

"That's all very interesting." Saito's gaze met mine. "It was a Swiss stamp collection. Bring back some recollections, Mr. Jacobson?"

At first I didn't know what he was getting at. Then I remembered something I had read in my journal.

"You found a Swiss stamp in my apartment yesterday," I said with a gulp.

Chapter 5

"Very good, Mr. Jacobson," Detective Saito said. "Your memory is coming back."

"No, but I read some notes this morning about what happened yesterday."

"So how did you and Tiegan both end up here?" the detective asked.

Denny said, "That's a surprise to me. I moved Dad in two days ago. I didn't realize that Tiegan lived here as well."

"What time did you leave that day?" Detective Saito asked Denny.

He thought for a moment. "It was right before dinnertime. Probably five-thirty. I had an eight P.M. flight to Maui."

Saito turned his gaze from Denny to me. "Mr. Jacobson, we found your fingerprints on the handle of the trash chute."

I shrugged. "Doesn't surprise me. Apparently, I was throwing away a bag of trash and opened the chute. That's when I saw the body."

"Could also have been prints from when you stuffed the body in the trash chute."

"Give me a break, Detective. I found the body. I didn't put it there."

"What else did you do the night of the murder?"

"Look, Detective, I'll help any way I can, but I really don't remember things from day to day."

"That's true," Denny said. "I can get a statement from Dad's doctor if that will help."

"What's the name of his doctor?" Detective Saito asked.

Denny gave him the information.

"Detective, you're wasting your time with me," I said. "If I were you, I'd look elsewhere. Someone has a key to the trash chute. See, I had no way to get into that locked trash chute during the night. But someone else did. For starters, the night watchman, Moki, had a set of keys. I'd pursue him."

"That's a fascinating theory. You keep bringing up keys. Any chance you made a duplicate copy of the trash chute key, Mr. Jacobson?"

"Why'd you think that?"

"Just curious."

"The answer is no," I said. "But go check

with the facilities manager or Moki."

"You keep coming back to Moki," Saito said. "You seem overly interested in him."

"He was there the night of the murder."

Saito scribbled some notes on his pad and then looked up at me. "We're closing in on you, Mr. Jacobson."

"I didn't do anything."

Detective Saito stared at me. "If you can't remember, how do you know you weren't involved?"

After Detective Saito left, trailing behind the aroma of stale cigarettes, I sat there pondering what I'd heard. This guy Saito seemed intent on getting me to confess to something. But I had nothing to confess. What if he arrested me? Not much I could do to prevent it. Then I'd have to get a damned lawyer. But still there wasn't anything useful they could drag out of me. Maybe they could hypnotize me. Would I remember any better under hypnosis? Probably not. What if I had done something, but couldn't remember it? Nah. I'd never been that kind of person. What if I'd undergone some kind of permanent change like those people who start swearing when their brains go on the fritz? Hell, I already swore. No change there. My brain was defective, but it hadn't gone that haywire. No, I'd have to figure out what was going on in my own half-assed way.

I gave Denny my journal. "Here, go through this. It'll give you an account of what's happened."

Denny read the material, then raised his eyes to peer at me. "Finding a body in the trash chute must have really shaken you."

"Not as much as being accused of murder."

Denny nodded his head. "And you and Tiegan both moved here."

"It does seem strange that he and I ended up on the same floor."

"That part is understandable," Denny said. "When I signed you up for Kina Nani, there was quite a wait. Then things were expedited because they converted the sixth floor from administrative offices to residence rooms. You and Tiegan must have both moved in as the new floor opened up."

"So what happens to the lawsuit with Tiegan dead?"

"Good question. I'm going to check." Denny pulled out his cell phone. "I have your lawyer and the other lawyer's phone numbers here." He punched buttons a number of times.

"This is Denny Jacobson. May I speak

with Frederick Kapana, please?" There was a pause. "And when will he be returning?" Another pause. "Okay. Thank you."

He lowered the phone. "Your lawyer's on vacation for a few days. I'll try the opposing lawyer. Guy's name is Harrison Young."

Instead of watching Denny do his finger-punching thing again, I went to the bathroom. When I returned, Denny was pacing the floor like Meyer and glowering.

"Not good news?" I asked.

"Harrison Young wasn't very cooperative."

"You mean he's a typical lawyer."

"Worse than that. He says he knows you're a suspect in Tiegan's death. He accused you of stealing the whole stamp collection this time. He promised to come after you on behalf of Tiegan's estate."

"Maybe we can get him together with Detective Saito so they can take turns tearing off my limbs."

"Very funny." Denny scowled. "We need to get your lawyer involved as soon as he gets back from vacation."

"I'm not ready for that. I'll see what I can uncover on my own first."

"This whole situation worries me, Dad."

"Thanks for the concern, but I didn't do anything. I'll get it cleared up."

"I wish there was something that could be

done to help your memory," Denny said.

"You and me both."

"When I last spoke to your doctor, he was puzzled by your situation."

"Me, too."

"He said short-term memory loss was typical for someone like you who had experienced minor strokes, but your symptoms are unusual."

"I always like to be different," I said.

"Apparently, the loss of function is activated when you go to sleep."

"That makes sense. I remember things fine during the day."

Denny cleared his throat. "On another subject, we need to discuss finances."

"You going to stake me to a poker game?"

"No. You know what I'm referring to. Paying for Kina Nani."

"Unfortunately, I don't remember," I said. "What's the situation?"

"When I sold your condo, I put the proceeds and your other savings into an annuity. Your social security and interest on the annuity pay for this place, but you don't have a lot to spare. After the annuity comes due in a year, you'll be able to take money out to afford a more expensive care facility if needed."

"Meaning I better watch my expenses and

not try to support any of the widows clunking around here."

"Meaning you're covered for now, as long as you have no major medical expenses."

"If I get sick, I promise to die."

"That's not what I'm saying, Dad."

"Well, what are you saying?"

He sighed. "You're not making this easy."

"I'm not making it anything. What's on your mind?"

"You can afford things right now if you don't get worse and have to go to a care home too soon."

"Worse? You mean if my mind really craps out?"

He frowned. "Something like that."

"I'll be economical and try not to let my brain turn to mush. And I do want to leave you a little inheritance."

"It's not that. . . ."

"I know, but I don't want to be a burden on you and your family," I said. "Let's see how things work out. You don't mind if I donate fifty-thousand dollars to the Kaneohe Orphans' Society?"

"What?"

"Just testing your sense of humor. I'll watch what I spend. Maybe they would cut my fees if I live on bread and water."

Denny grimaced. "It'll work out. As I said,

by next year you'll be in good shape for more expensive care, if required."

"That and the fact that I won't be around that much longer anyway."

"Don't think that way, Dad."

"Well, it's true. I'm getting up there in years. Any time now, *poof.*" I snapped my fingers.

Denny jumped. "You're still in good physical shape, Dad. Keep walking."

"That and staying away from murderers."

Denny helped me get my bills assembled. Then while he ran some errands, I wrote checks and licked envelopes. Searching around my apartment, I couldn't find any stamps, so I decided to take a little expedition.

At the elevator I asked an old, tottering, female inmate leaning on a walker where to find stamps. Shouting my query a second time so she could hear it, she directed me to the business office on the second floor.

After an elevator ride with nothing more eventful than the old broad dropping her walker on my foot, I got off and found the office.

"I need to buy some stamps," I informed the young woman who was loading paper into a copier.

"If you'll lift that metal box up on the counter, I'll be right with you," she said.

I stepped behind the counter, found a gleaming silver box, and hoisted it up.

When she finished her other task, she turned and her eyes lit up. "Hi there," she said.

A young man with a goatee and wearing a baseball cap waved. "Yo, Helen."

"What are you doing here?" she asked.

"Picking up my check."

He headed down the hall, and Helen said, "Bye, Moki."

This was the guy I needed to speak with! I rushed out of the office and looked around the corner, but he was gone. Oh, well. I'd try to hook up with him at night when he was on duty.

"Did you want stamps?" Helen asked, tapping her fingers on the counter.

I handed her a five-dollar bill, and she gave me stamps and change.

As long as I was out and about, I decided to interview anyone who worked at the front desk to see if I could find out what happened to the missing visitor registration page.

Neither of the two women at the front desk knew who had taken the missing page. Either that or their memories were as bad as mine.

"No wonder a murderer could easily commit a crime here," I said to Denny that night at a Thai restaurant. "The security sucks."

"Kina Nani isn't a prison," he said.

"Let's not go there."

"You don't look happy, Dad."

"I'm depressed about my damn memory, this Tiegan thing, and that I have to keep a journal and rely on Meyer if I want to know what I did the day before."

"At least you don't remember yesterday's problems."

"I'd put up with that if I could wake up and know where the hell I am."

"Can I order you a drink, Dad?"

"Yeah. Arsenic."

Back at Kina Nani, we said our good-byes. Denny was catching a flight to the mainland, so I wouldn't see him until his next visit, scheduled in less than a month.

"Let me know if I can help with the Tiegan situation," he said.

"I'll keep you appraised. If I end up in jail, check in with Meyer for details."

He grimaced. "That's not funny."

I shrugged. "At my age it doesn't matter much if I'm here or in prison."

"Don't start that again."

"All right," I said. "I'll behave."

I watched him climb into his car. We waved to each other, and he drove off.

Back up in my apartment, I found the message light flashing. I checked and found that Meyer wanted me to call him.

When he answered, he said, "I tried to reach you earlier pertaining to some disturbing news." There was a pause.

"I was out to dinner with my son. You sound concerned. What's this tragic news?"

"It concerns the murder," Meyer said, clearing his throat. "I talked to my mole again this afternoon. The police have some additional circumstantial evidence that doesn't bode well for you."

"Saito stopped by this afternoon and has been harassing me again."

"And he may be ready to arrest you soon," Meyer said.

"He hinted at that. They find a confession from me that I don't remember signing?"

"No," Meyer said. "But the next worst thing. The staff at Kina Nani had been asked to notify the police if any keys were found. Someone left a key at the front counter. The receptionist called the police who checked it out and guess what the key was?"

"Probably not the key to my heart," I said. "It was the trash chute key."

I slapped my nightstand. "It could have been dropped by the murderer!"

"Could be. But the police found your fingerprints on the key."

"Well shit," I said. Then I remembered what I'd done that morning. "I found a key after we played shuffleboard. It would have my fingerprints on it because I picked it up and left it at the front desk."

"Then the receptionist can tell the police what happened," Meyer said.

"The problem is that she wasn't paying attention at the time. No one saw me turn it in." I thought back to my earlier conversation with Saito. "This explains Saito's comment about keys."

"You're going to have to be careful, Paul."

"All right," I said.

After I hung up, my stomach churned as I sat there trying to figure out how to get out of all these entanglements. I needed to stay awake late enough to speak with Moki when he came on duty.

And Meyer really wanted to help me. Here I couldn't remember him from day to day, yet he was looking out after me. Would I do the same for someone who couldn't remember who the hell I was? Probably not. My mind circled back to friends I'd had. Rhonda had been my best friend. We'd do anything for each other. Except when we launched into one of our infrequent spats. But we always made up. I had had friends in the neighborhood, golfing buddies, acquaintances in the Chamber of Commerce. I was always willing to give someone a ride, or cover if they had a sick kid. But this guy Meyer seemed genuinely willing to help me with my crappy memory and this strange murder case. And how did I thank him? By forgetting who the hell he was when I woke up.

This other guy Henry was strange. I couldn't imagine anyone getting close to him. How had his wife put up with him? He'd be a real pain to be around more than at mealtimes. Still, I could consider him entertaining. As Meyer said, where else could you have your own talking baseball almanac? If only Henry weren't such a jerk.

Later, I wandered down to the front desk. "Where can I find Moki?"

Jason Kam was on duty. "You snooping again?" he said.

"Yeah, I need to speak with Moki."

"He's doing his rounds." Kam looked at his watch. "Probably half done. Usually starts at the top of the building and works his way down."

I decided to wait on the second floor in one of the chairs outside the dining room. If he was checking every floor he'd come right by there, and it would be more private than waiting in the lobby with Jason Kam overhearing our conversation.

A wicker chair with soft padded cushions accepted my tired body. I had to make sure I didn't doze off. I looked across the hallway at an oil painting of Rabbit Island. I couldn't remember yesterday, but I recalled hearing how Rabbit Island was used for target practice by the military during World War II and how after the war kids went over and found live ammunition. One had his hand blown off. Who knows if that really happened, but it served the purpose of keeping people away from the rocky island. Unless you went there to collect ammunition.

I heard a door squeak open and a young man in a brown uniform exited from the stairwell. He had a goatee and stood approximately five ten with narrow darting eyes. I recognized him as the man who had called to Helen in the business office earlier in the day.

"You Moki?" I asked.

"Yeah."

"I want to talk to you about the night of the murder."

His eyes focused on the center of my forehead. "What you want?"

I suddenly realized I didn't know what I wanted. Have him confess to the crime? Say he'd seen someone skulking through the hallway? Then I remembered what I had read.

"What time did you lock the trash chute on the sixth floor that night?"

He scratched his head. "Would have been ten-forty-five. I started at the top at ten-thirty and it took me half an hour to do all floors."

"Have you by any chance lost your key to the trash chute?"

"Why you asking these questions? You trying to play amateur cop?"

"I take it kind of personal when someone gets whacked and the police think I'm a suspect."

"You're *that* guy."

I did a double take. "What guy?"

His lips twitched. "Just heard that one of our residents might be a murderer."

"Don't give me that crap. Someone else did this. And I'm going to find out who."

A strange smile came over his face. "Say, I saw you in the business office earlier today."

"Yeah, and I heard Helen call out your name."

Now his look hardened. "The police will get the murderer. I don't need anyone wandering around causing trouble on my watch."

"It seems like there's already been some major trouble caused on your watch."

After that, Moki refused to answer any more questions and said he needed to continue his rounds. I thought of following him, but that wouldn't do me any good and would piss him off more than he already was. In my mind he was a prime suspect. He might have overheard that Marshall Tiegan had a valuable collection of stamps, and he did have keys to all the doors at Kina Nani. And the trash chute. Didn't give me a comfortable feeling knowing he could get into my place at any time.

CHAPTER 6

My head snapped up from my breakfast plate at the sound of chairs scraping. Two men I'd never seen before sat down.

"Good morning, Paul," the taller of the two said.

"Who the hell are you?" I asked.

"Uh oh," he replied. "You didn't read your journal this morning.

"What journal?"

He sighed. "Paul, you write in a journal that you keep on your nightstand. You obviously didn't read it this morning. It's your tool to deal with your short-term memory loss."

"That would explain why I don't know squat about where I am. Who's the stiff?" I pointed to the bald-headed runt who was up to his elbows in a bowl of oatmeal.

"That's Henry and I'm Meyer."

"Names don't register," I said.

"Paul, first thing you need to do when you

get back to your room is to read your journal."

"Yeah. Yeah. Whatever."

"There's some big excitement this morning," Meyer said. "Someone broke into the business office last night and stole some money."

"Probably one of the inmates collecting snack money," I said.

Meyer laughed. "You have quite a way of stating things, Paul."

"Yeah. I guess it's because I can't decide if I woke up in a nuthouse or a prison."

After breakfast I wandered out of the dining room and was accosted by a stocky man, a good three inches shorter than me.

"We need to talk, Mr. Jacobson," he said.

"Shit," I said. "Everyone knows my name. Who are you?"

He rolled his eyes and flicked open a wallet, revealing a police badge. "I'm Detective Saito."

"Do I know you?"

"Please have a seat," he said, motioning toward one of the lobby chairs.

I sat down, wondering why he was here, and he pulled another chair up in front of me so that he was facing me two feet away. His intense dark gaze bore in on the bridge of my nose.

"Now, Mr. Jacobson, would you care to tell me what you were doing last night?"

"Sleeping."

"Let's be a little more specific," he said.

"I went to bed and slept."

He scowled, and the corners of his mouth twitched like a dog ready to bare its teeth. "Cut the B.S. I want a full account of everything you did after dinner last night."

"That's going to be difficult. The only thing I remember is getting up this morning."

Detective Saito let his breath out. "I'm getting tired of this memory excuse."

I looked into his eyes. "What do you mean memory excuse? I don't even know who you are and you act like you know me."

"The Kina Nani business office was broken into last night," he said. "What do you know about it?"

"Only that a guy named Meyer mentioned it. He was at my breakfast table."

"Money was stolen from a cash box. . . ." Saito paused to look at me.

I shrugged. "So what's that have to do with me?"

"Your fingerprints were all over the box. Can you tell me how they got there?"

I flinched. "Why would my fingerprints be

on a cash box?" I tried to think back, but everything before waking up was a blank.

"I think you went into the office, broke into the money box, and stole the contents."

This didn't make any sense. I had always been honest, had run a decent business, and hadn't take advantage of people. The last time I stole anything that I could remember was a pack of gum from a store when I was six. My mother beat the crap out of me, and that was the end of my criminal spree.

Saito removed a notepad from his pocket and thumbed through several pages. "Mr. Jacobson, late last night you were seen sitting outside the business office right in this lounge area that we're in now. The night watchman reported having a heated argument with you. Was that before or after you stole the money?"

"Now you're irritating me," I said. "I didn't have anything to do with your burglary."

"It seems to me that you're a one-man crime wave in this place."

"What's that supposed to mean?"

"You've forgotten your other crime?"

"Other crime?" I repeated, wondering what he meant.

"Don't give me that innocent stare."

"I'm sorry, Detective. I have no recollection of even meeting you before, much less any reference to another crime."

"Maybe a trip to police headquarters will help shake up your memory. I have enough evidence to put you in jail right now."

My head jerked. "I don't think that would be productive. It won't change the fact that I remember zip from yesterday."

He regarded me again, his radar beam of a stare trying to penetrate my forehead. "I think we should go up to your apartment to check around for some missing cash."

"If you have a search warrant, I'd be happy to let you look around."

His eyes gave away that he didn't. "You think hard about what I've said, Mr. Jacobson. In the meantime you may need to find a new place to live."

"Now what are you implying?"

"You've been implicated in two crimes and have been reported to be harassing several employees. The retirement home director may not want you as a resident any longer."

"Doesn't bother me. I don't particularly want to be here anyway."

He jumped up. "We'll be talking again, Mr. Jacobson. Very soon."

"A real pleasure, Detective." I stood up and headed toward the elevator. While I waited with a herd of decrepit old people, someone tapped me on the shoulder.

I turned around to see a tall skinny man with slicked back dark hair, horned rimmed glasses, a pointed chin, and a long neck above a wrinkled brown suit.

"May I have a word with you, Mr. Jacobson?"

"Sure. You look too young to be part of this crowd. Who are you?"

"We've met before. I'm Alexander Farns. The director of Kina Nani."

I regarded him, my gaze drawn to a protruding Adam's apple that bobbed above a yellow tie. The aroma of newly applied, cheap aftershave lotion permeated the air.

"So you run this joint," I said.

He cleared his throat. "Yes. I'm responsible for the business oversight of Kina Nani."

"Can you do something about all the old people around here?"

His forehead wrinkled up like an accordion, and he cleared his throat again. "I was wondering if you might step into my office for a moment so I can have a word with you."

"Why not?" I replied.

I followed him down a short hallway to a cramped room with his name on the door.

He motioned me to sit down in a chair that looked like it was ready to collapse at any time.

Farns steepled his fingers. "As I was saying, in my role as director of Kina Nani, I need to look after the best interests of the majority of residents."

"In other words you need to keep the paying customers happy."

His gaze darted from side to side. I expected him to start wringing his hands.

"No . . . I mean, yes. It's just that . . . uh . . . we're concerned with reference to the recent events and your . . . uh . . . proximity to them."

"I can see your dilemma," I said. "I'm one of your cherished residents forking over my hard-earned cash, but if it gets down to brass tacks, you'd like to see me march off into the sunset so as not to disturb the other paying vegetables."

He shuffled from side to side. "That's not exactly how I'd phrase it, Mr. Jacobson. But I don't know if it is advisable for you to remain in residence here."

"Can't say as I'm all that fond of this place, but I don't cotton to getting the boot, Mr. Farns. I think I'll stick around to see what other excitement is in store."

He opened his mouth like a fish gulping

air on dry land.

I stood up. "Watch out for headless horsemen and pumpkins," I said. Then I turned my back on him and walked away.

Man, what a crazy place.

When I returned to my room, I located the journal Meyer had mentioned. There was a big hairy-ass note on top that I had missed before.

I read all the pages.

What a mess. No wonder Farns wanted to ship my butt out on the next flight. I'd got myself tangled up in a murder as well as this recently reported burglary. From circumstantial evidence, I looked guilty as hell. I'd picked up the money box yesterday, so that explained why my fingerprints were on it. Then I'd been in front of the business office on the second floor, arguing with Moki late at night, and the next morning the money's gone. Shit. I needed a good lawyer, but I hated lawyers. Maybe Meyer could help out.

No goons showed up to expel me and the horse I came in on, so I read a spy novel until I felt hungry. Then I headed back to the mess hall and found my two buddies at table eleven.

"Did you read your journal after breakfast?" Meyer asked me.

"Yeah. My brain cells are refreshed."

"You remember things fine during the day," Meyer said. "You should be grateful for that."

"Yeah. I'm one friggin' grateful guy." I paused for a moment. "And by the way, they're accusing me of the business office theft and threatening to kick me out of my mansion."

He dropped his fork onto his plate. "That's ridiculous. They can't do that."

"Seems I was in the wrong place at the wrong time again. This guy Farns wants me out. And a detective wants to put my ass in jail."

"Why don't you confess and get it over with?" Henry said.

I grabbed his shirt. "How'd you like a new set of teeth?"

Meyer put his hand on my arm. "Calm down, Paul. I'll talk to Farns. Worst case, he can't get rid of you without notification."

"That's encouraging," I said.

"The administration here has to follow a process to remove a resident," Meyer said.

"I apparently just moved in here, don't even know much about the place, and they're trying to kick my ass out."

"Good riddance," Henry said.

"Watch it, Henry," I said. "If I'm this vicious, thieving murderer, you might be next."

He choked on his BLT sandwich, so I whacked him on the back. This caused him to cough more.

"Before you go around insulting people, maybe you better learn how to swallow," I said.

He caught his breath, gave me a deer-in-the-headlights stare, and went back to munching on his sandwich.

"So much for serious dialogue with Henry," I said.

"He's not much of a conversationalist," Meyer said.

"That's an understatement. It's like speaking to a doorknob." I rubbed Henry's bald head and then turned toward Meyer. "So, counselor, pertaining to my case? Will I be sleeping in the streets?"

"Not to worry," Meyer said. "It's in good hands."

"You sound like all the shyster lawyers I've ever dealt with."

"Come on, Paul. We're not all sharks."

"Yeah. Some are barracudas and moray eels."

"I'm glad you think so highly of the legal profession," Meyer said.

"I can't stand lawyers. One set me up when I was in business, but you're different." I took a deep breath, figuring it was time to move on to something else. "What did you do for hobbies before getting locked up here?"

"There's one thing I used to do. Letters to the editor."

"What crazy kind of hobby is that?"

"I enjoyed taking shots at the incompetence of local government. There are so many stupid things our officials do. When something irritated me, I would write a letter to the editor of the local newspaper."

"Give me an example," I said.

"When I was still driving, there was a push to add speed bumps and traffic circles all over the section of lower Nuuanu were I lived. Proponents saw this as a way to slow traffic down. I pointed out that it kept cars on the street longer and increased pollution to say nothing of the additional expense to the city. Then they had the nerve to try to put these transportation prevention devices on the streets leading to Queens Hospital, the only hospital in our part of town. Fire trucks wouldn't even have been able to get through."

"There's a lot of emotion in your voice, Meyer."

He smiled. "I guess it goes back to my attorney days. I could get passionate when involved in a case."

"You still write these letters?"

His smile faded. "No. You may not remember, but my eyesight is degrading, due to macular degeneration. I can read with a magnifying glass, things like labels on bottles, but it doesn't work for writing letters or reading books. I've given that up. Now I'm learning Braille."

"That's quite an undertaking. Particularly at your age."

"Probably true," Meyer said. "A kid could pick it up easily. I have a nice young woman who works with me twice a week. Maybe a year from now I'll be able to read a book in Braille, but writing legibly is something I'll never be able to do again."

"You could dictate your letters to someone."

He shook his head. "That wouldn't be the same. It was the thrill of grabbing a pen and dashing off a diatribe."

"You could still write it out even if you couldn't read what you wrote," I said.

"But the letter had to get published in the newspaper. That was the whole point. I have a scrapbook full of my letters to the editor."

"What good is that if you can't read them

anymore?"

"I know they were published," Meyer said. "That's enough."

"Seems like strange logic, but no weirder than the way Henry acts."

Meyer had circled the table and slapped me on the back, causing me to almost choke on a mouthful of coffee. "Welcome to the wonderful world of Kina Nani."

"Yeah," I said. "I may be the only normal person here. Except I can't remember jack shit."

"Think of the positive side," Meyer said. "We each have our own unique quirks."

"That's so encouraging. I'll be able to learn about them over and over again, every day."

"See. You never have to get bored."

"No," I said. "Every day's a brand new adventure in the land of decrepit old fossils."

When I'd finished eating, I walked around the prison yard on my own, contemplating what Meyer had said about my memory. I needed to use the capabilities I had. Remembering during the day allowed me to collect clues to try to get Detective Saito off my back. I'd continue keeping an accurate journal. And I could remember practically word for word what I had read this morning. I still had a photographic memory! But every night someone pulled all the film out of the camera. Oh, well. As long as my memory didn't crap out during the day, I could get by.

I came to a stop, looked up, and assessed this new home of mine. Not exactly an intimate structure, with twelve stories, institutional construction, two wings off a central core. But I had to admit it was attractive in its own right with a huge monkey pod tree shading the dining area, which was enclosed by floor-to-ceiling glass windows.

And the winding driveway leading up to the building was lined with hibiscus and plumeria, the bright white, pink, yellow, and orange flowers acting as cheerleader pom-poms to welcome visitors. And a sweet aroma of jasmine wafted by on a gentle breeze that tickled my arms. Behind the building, a green jungle provided a rustic backdrop. In the trees around me I could hear the cawing of myna birds and in the bushes sparrows hopped, and the occasional red head of a cardinal flashed its greeting.

Maybe this place wasn't so bad, after all.

I should have known better than to get complacent.

CHAPTER 7

When I returned to my apartment, I found a note taped to my door. It read, "This is your official notification to vacate your room in thirty days."

I wadded the paper up and tossed it over the railing. I stormed inside, located a directory of resident phone numbers, and called Meyer. "I just received a love letter telling me to get ready to pack my bags."

"I'll get right on it."

"You do that, counselor, or I'm firing your ass," I said.

"You can't fire me. You're not even paying me."

"I know. I like to talk that way to lawyers. And by the way, thanks for offering to help."

There was a pause on the line. "Paul, you're not the crusty old curmudgeon you always pretend to be."

"Yeah. Yeah. I'm a big marshmallow. Don't let the word get out."

After I hung up, I spotted the card with Detective Saito's phone number on it. Why not? I decided to call him.

While waiting for an administrator to track down Saito, I watched an ant crawl up the wall. Poor dumb ant. I could have reached out and squished him. Kind of like what Farns and Saito were trying to do to me.

Finally, when I thought it must be getting close to dinner time, a deep male voice came on the line. "Yes, Mr. Jacobson."

"I discovered something about last night that I thought you should know."

"Memory coming back?"

"No, but I found some notes. Turns out I went to the business office to get some change. The gal there asked me to lift the cash box up on the counter. That's how my fingerprints got on it."

"How convenient."

"You don't have to take my word for it," I said. "Check with Helen in the office."

"I'll do that."

"And I was talking with the guard, Moki, late last night. He and I had a heated discussion, talking about the night of the murder. I'd check him out, Detective. He should be your prime suspect for both crimes."

"Trying to divert attention away from yourself?"

98

"I'm just giving you my opinion. You can do whatever you want." I slammed down the phone and then sat there stewing. This Detective Saito was convinced I was worse than a Colombian drug lord. Whatever I said, he twisted it around. And I knew he wasn't after anyone else but me, so I'd have to be careful.

Around this place people needed all kinds of external aids: walkers, oxygen tanks, hearing aids, teeth, and various bionic parts. One guy even had to carry a stomach bag around with him. Me, I had to have an external memory because the one I was given had crapped out. What a pisser.

With nothing better to do, I decided to write up what happened so far that day. I reached for my journal.

Where was I? In a strange room. Something wasn't right. I got up from bed, groggy. I was in Bermuda shorts and a tee shirt. I opened the curtains and looked outside. It was partially cloudy and I recognized the mountains. The shadows looked like it was later afternoon. I must have been taking a nap, but where the heck was I? I was in a building and I could see part of Kaneohe.

There was a knock on the door.

A young woman entered and smiled at

me. "Mr. Jacobson, time for your medicine."

"What medicine? Who are you?"

She opened a locked metal box on the counter by the sink.

"Your afternoon pills. I'm Melanie."

"What is this place?"

"You're at Kina Nani. This is your new home."

"Home? I don't remember moving here."

"You've only been here a few days." She handed me a glass of water and three pills.

"I have to swallow these horse pills?"

"Twice a day."

I grimaced and managed to get them down without choking to death. "When can a guy get some grub around this place?" I asked.

"Dinner starts in fifteen minutes."

"Where?"

"On the second floor."

After she left, I washed my face and changed my clothes. I still didn't get it. I was in some building I'd never seen before.

I moseyed down the corridor and found an old couple waiting by the two elevators. They were holding hands. The woman smiled at me. "Elevator's so slow at dinner time, Mr. Jacobson." she said.

I flinched. "You know me? Who are you?"

The woman said, "We're Helen and Albert

Nakata. We met you a couple of days ago when you were moving into the Reynolds's place. They had to go into a care home a week ago."

I had no clue what she was referring to. Then the elevator arrived.

Getting off on the second floor, I followed the lovey-dovey couple to the mess hall, a big room full of tables with old people filing in. I scratched my head as I watched the scene of mass chaos.

A comely young woman in a muumuu came over to me. "You're at table eleven, Mr. Jacobson."

I nodded and found a sign with "11" on it. This was getting spooky. People here seemed to know me, but I had no clue who they were. I pulled out one of the three chairs and sat down.

I was munching away at my Caesar salad when two men approached the table. The short bald one with glasses said, "You're in my chair."

I looked at his poorly shaved face. "Yeah. Who says so?"

The other man with white hair and a white beard jumped in. "Henry is very particular regarding where he sits."

"Well, I don't know who the blazes Henry is, and he can sit anywhere he wants, except in my lap."

"Uh oh," the white-haired man said. "Paul, you've forgotten everything again."

I slammed my fork down on the table. "This is starting to bug me. You know my name, but I don't know who you are."

He sighed. "I'm Meyer Ohana and this is Henry Palmer. We sit with you each meal. Your short-term memory is shot and you keep forgetting. What did you do this afternoon?"

"I don't remember," I said. "I woke up from a nap and I'm in this nut house where strange people know my name."

Meyer laughed. "That explains it. You went to sleep and did a reset, like when the power goes out, and the VCR clock starts flashing."

Henry piped in. "I want my chair."

I stood up ready to clock the asshole, but Meyer grabbed my arm.

"Easy," Meyer said. "Henry has problems. Just switch seats."

"You can have your goddamn chair," I said. "You can also have your half-eaten salad."

Henry and Meyer sat down. Henry switched salads and started masticating like we were going to run out of lettuce.

"I'm confused," I said to Meyer, who

seemed to have some handle on the situation. "I don't know where I am, who you are, or what's going on around here."

"Let me give you a recap," he said, then explained the last several days to me.

"So I belong here?"

"This is your new home."

"I must have died and gone to Hades."

He laughed. "It's not so bad. You'd get used to it if you could just remember. When you get back to your apartment, read the journal on your nightstand."

After dinner, I found what I wrote before taking a nap. I read it through carefully. I was a suspect in a murder. This was creepy.

The next morning I woke up in my usual confused state, but immediately caught sight of a note on my nightstand. My stomach growled, and I thought about stacks of pancakes, but I decided to read the stack of sheets, first. It all made sense in an absurd kind of way.

I went down to breakfast and found table eleven with two old men sitting at it.

I looked at the white-bearded guy whom I'd never seen before. "You must be Meyer."

"Very good," he said.

"My secret decoder ring described you."

He chuckled. "Now we're getting somewhere. Sit down. I thought I was going to have to give you a picture so you'd remember me."

"Let me get this straight," I said. "I've been here for a few days and we've become friends."

"I'm glad to hear that's how you wrote about me, Paul."

"And this must be Henry." I pointed to the bald-headed midget gobbling a waffle.

Henry kept shoveling. "Good morning, jerk," he said without looking up. "When are they going to arrest you?"

Meyer laughed. "Henry's taken a shine to you. He's usually not this friendly with people."

"I'd hate to be here when he's unfriendly," I said.

Meyer helped me catch up on my memory from the day before.

"Besides getting involved in murders, what's there to do in this joint for excitement?" I asked.

"We have recreation time at nine this morning," Meyer said.

"What do we recreate?"

"There's a balloon volleyball game scheduled. Are you any good?"

"Hell, I don't know. I played volleyball when I was a kid. It's been a while."

"You're probably better than most of the old folks around here," Meyer said.

"How can you play balloon volleyball? Thought you couldn't see well."

"My eyesight is still good enough to spot a slow-moving, large, red balloon," Meyer said. "You can be on my team."

At nine I showed up in the recreation room and scanned the group of a dozen old fossils standing alongside a net strung across the room. Meyer grabbed my arm. "You're over here."

He picked up an inflated balloon and swatted it over the net. A geezer on the other side watched it float to the ground.

"Come on, people," Meyer shouted, "hit the ball!"

"What ball?" one old woman in black leotards shouted back. "All I see is a balloon."

Meyer slapped the side of his pants and turned to me. "See what I have to put up with?"

We volleyed back and forth several times, and one of the women on our team stood motionless as the balloon struck her shoulder and sank to the floor.

"What's the matter with you?" Meyer shouted. "Why didn't you go for the ball?"

"I didn't see it," the woman said, pursing her lips.

"What kind of team is this?" Meyer asked in disgust.

"Consists of old, blind, crippled, incontinent vegetables," I said. "Don't get so upset."

"Where's your will to win, Paul?"

"Don't care one way or the other," I said with a shrug. "No one besides you seems to care, either."

"Where's the excitement?" Meyer shouted. "Where's the zest? Where's the desire?"

"Not in this room," I replied. "I don't think a cattle prod or a ton of Viagra would bring that back."

Afterward, Meyer and I watched a staff member take the net down.

"You really get into balloon volleyball," I said to Meyer.

His face was still red. "Yeah, it's my A.D.D. I can't stand to sit still." He paced back and forth and pounded his right fist into his left hand. "I can't get these people to care about the game."

"You're lucky they show up. Attendance is a victory at this age."

He sighed. "I guess you're right. I need

some more exercise. You want to walk over to the shopping center?"

"Sure. Have that much left in this old body."

As we strolled over, I asked, "What's with the A.D.D.?"

"I was always hyperactive as a kid. In the District Attorney's office I drove people nuts with my questions. It wasn't until I was in my sixties that I was diagnosed with attention deficit disorder."

"You are different from most of the people around this infirmary, Meyer. You act like you're alive."

He laughed and slapped me on the back, almost knocking me over. "I'll keep going until the old ticker gives out. I only have two speeds: full speed ahead and stopped."

At the Long's Drug Store I bought some throat lozenges and a candy bar. Always good to have an energy snack in case the guards forgot the food.

On the way back Meyer said, "Besides Denny, do you have any other kids?"

"No. Just him. Shot blanks after that. And Denny has only one kid, Jennifer. Wish I could remember what she looks like."

Meyer chuckled. "You'll be able to artificially remember some things now with our new system. Between writing in your journal and me to harass you, you'll be a regular Einstein."

"More like the absent-minded professor. I still don't remember you from yesterday."

"Henry and I could play games with you," Meyer said. "We could pretend to be each other. That would really mess with your mind."

"Wouldn't matter. The next day I'd have forgotten anyway."

Back in my apartment, I started contemplating how I was going to clear my name with all the crime going on around my new home. My thoughts returned to the stamp collection. Obviously, this was the key to the murder. Someone had taken the stamps, probably the murderer. May have been the same person who broke into the cash box in the business office.

How did you track down a stolen stamp collection? First, you needed to know what was in the collection. I wondered if anything associated with the lawsuit over the stamps would shed any light on this. I opened the brown metal box in which I kept my valuable papers. There was a manila folder with TIEGAN penciled on the tab.

Leafing through the pages in the folder, I

found nothing helpful. The only thing I located was the name of my lawyer, Frederick Kapana, and a phone number. Great. Even though I hated lawyers, I decided to call.

After speaking with a receptionist and an administrative assistant, I was put on hold. I sat there drumming my fingers on the nightstand. Finally, a booming voice came on the line.

"What can I do for you, Mr. Jacobson?"

"I'm calling regarding the lawsuit with Marshall Tiegan over the stamp collection."

"I received word that Mr. Tiegan died."

"How does that affect the suit?" I asked.

"All depends on what the executor of his estate decides. We'll have to see."

"But the reason I called, do you have anything that describes the stamps?"

"Hold on a moment."

I listened to seventies elevator music and imagined being in a prison where this was the constant background. Maybe Kina Nani wasn't so bad after all.

"All right." The loud voice came back on the line. "Here it is." I had to hold the phone away from my ear. "I found a list of all the stamps with the missing ones circled."

"Can you send me a copy?"

"Sure. You'll have it tomorrow. I have your new address."

"How'd you get that?"

"Your son called when you moved into the retirement home. He also notified the opposing lawyer, Harrison Young. Speaking of whom, I had a call from him. He says he's considering filing new litigation. Claims you stole the whole stamp collection this time."

I shuddered, remembering from what I had read that Denny had called Harrison Young. "Yeah, the guy seems out to get me."

"I'll let you know when anything happens officially."

"Great," I said. "I can hardly wait."

As I hung up the phone, I wondered whether I should have discussed being a suspect in Tiegan's murder. That's what Denny and Meyer wanted me to do. No, I didn't want a lawyer mucking with my life any more than I had to. I'd keep working this on my own for the time being.

That taken care of, I went down to the second floor for lunch.

Meyer and Henry were both working on their salads when I arrived. As I sat, Meyer was asking Henry, "Where do you buy coins for your collection?"

"Catalogs and coin stores," Henry replied.

Meyer raised his eyes to glance at me. "Henry's recounting the life of a coin collector."

"Do these stores handle stamps as well as coins?" I asked.

"Most of them," Henry said.

"How many deal with stamps on Oahu?"

Henry paused for a moment and closed his eyes. "One in Kaneohe, one in Kailua, and two in Honolulu."

"You're a genius," I said.

"I know," he replied.

After lunch I accompanied Henry to his apartment. He lived on the fourth floor in the opposite wing in a single room suite like mine.

"You must have a good housekeeper," I said, noticing the immaculate interior.

"I don't like clutter."

While he opened a desk drawer, I saw a plaque resting on his bookshelf. It was a mathematics award from Princeton.

"This is impressive," I said. "When did you win this?"

"When I was working on my Ph.D."

"Where did you go after you got your degree?"

"I taught at the University of Oregon."

"Did you enjoy teaching?"

"Not much. I liked the research."

I could picture Henry struggling with bored students.

Then I saw a photograph of a woman on Henry's dresser. Plain-looking woman with short hair, but a pleasant smile.

"Was that your wife?" I asked.

"Yeah. Grace died of a heart attack four years ago."

"You must miss her."

He didn't answer, just nodded his head.

For a moment I thought I saw tears in his eyes, but then he turned back to the desk drawer. He removed a neatly labeled folder and extracted a typed sheet of paper.

"You can make a copy of this," he said. "Has store names, addresses, and phone numbers."

I thanked Henry and left his apartment, wondering if maybe he wasn't such a jerk after all.

I headed to the Kina Nani business office, where I sweet-talked the secretary into making a copy of Henry's store list for me. Back in my apartment, I checked the phone book and found two other stores listed under "stamp collectors," which I added to Henry's list.

Later that day, a woman padded up to me.

She had vivid blue eyes, a fetching pug nose, and a curled silver coiffure that looked like she'd been to the beauty salon. She beamed a pleasant smile, highlighting her full red lips around even white teeth. "You're Paul Jacobson," she said.

"That's me."

"I'm Marion Aumiller. Meyer Ohana suggested I talk to you. I'm putting on a little party tomorrow evening to welcome new people to Kina Nani." She had a twinkle in her eyes.

I looked at her more carefully. She stood almost five-foot-six, trim figure, and noticeable breasts pushing out the top of her orange blouse. Not bad for an old broad.

She put her hand on my arm. "I would like it if you could join us."

"Sure. What're the specifics?"

"Seven P.M. in the rec room," she said.

"I'll be there. Save the last dance for me."

She smiled again and shuffled away, displaying a pleasant, rounded posterior filling out her black slacks.

Damn, I thought to myself. That would be an appealing woman to get to know.

CHAPTER 8

The next morning I remembered to read my journal. What a life! Things happened, I forgot them, and then I had to peruse my written account to make up for a lousy memory.

If I kept this up, I could spend the whole day reviewing what I'd done in the past. Then I wouldn't have to do anything new, just stuff my face with meals three times a day. I wondered if I'd been writing down exactly what happened. What if I invented things? No, I wasn't that kind of person. If I had gone to the trouble of keeping a journal, the damn thing would be accurate. It also seemed I could verify things with this guy named Meyer. I wondered if I'd recognize him at all today. I tried to imagine what he looked like. The only hint I had was what I had written. He had white hair and a white beard and looked a little like an aged version of my son Denny.

At breakfast I found my table and stared at the white-bearded guy. "You don't look anything like Denny," I said.

"Good observation," he said. "He's better looking and forty years younger."

"I read my journal and tried to think what you looked like. The writing says I know you, but I can't remember ever seeing you before."

"It's like a little game for us, Paul. Every morning you start over and by the end of the day we're old buddies. By the way, I hear you have a girlfriend."

"What's that supposed to mean?"

"Marion Aumiller stopped by a little while ago, all atwitter that you're coming to her party tonight."

"I read that name," I said. "What's she look like?"

Meyer pointed across the room. "She sits over there. I can't see her clearly with my bad eyesight, but she has on a dark blue muumuu."

I squinted in that direction and a woman waved to me. Never seen her before.

"You should get a little action there, Paul."

I dropped my fork. "You implying what I think you are?"

Meyer leaned close to me. "There's one thing about retirement homes. Look around this room."

I scanned the dining hall.

"What do you see?" he asked.

"A bunch of old people."

"But what else?"

I looked again. Then it hit me. "Except for this table and a few others with both men and women, most of the tables have only women."

"Bingo. See, women wear us down and outlive us. You, Henry, and I are the exceptions. Our wives died first. Typically, it's the other way around. The three of us are prime meat for these women. If you're still up for a little old-age sex, it's readily available."

"Haven't had sex since before Rhonda died," I blurted.

"Then maybe you better avail yourself of the one benefit of a retirement home."

I glanced around the room once more. A hand raised from the blue muumuu and waved at me again.

"Don't know if I remember what to do," I said.

"It's like breathing. It'll come back to you. Just make sure there's some Vaseline around."

I sighed and returned to my pancakes.

After breakfast Meyer and I took a walk.

"You have many visitors?" I asked.

"No." Meyer said with a grimace. "I seem to have outlived my close friends. I don't have much family on Oahu anymore. My roots are typical of the islands. My ancestors include a Hawaiian fisherman, a Portuguese sailor, a Scottish businessman, and an Irish rogue. A regular goulash of backgrounds. But somehow along the way, my side of the family went off on its own, so there were no big gatherings of distant cousins. My kids visit once in awhile, but they have pretty busy lives."

"They live close by?"

"My son's in Chicago. He's a stockbroker and wrapped up in his work. He comes here with his two kids once a year. My daughter is married to a contractor in Hilo. She visits every couple of months and often brings one or more of her three teenagers. I expect to see her in a week or so."

"So you ever get off this rock, or have you been here forever?"

"I was a local boy who went to Kamehameha School — made possible by my one-sixteenth Hawaiian heritage. Then I went to Occidental in Southern California as a history major, of all things. I did a stint in the navy on a destroyer escorting supply ships in the European theater. After VJ Day, I used the GI Bill of Rights to go to law school at Boalt Hall in Berkeley, and then practiced law in a small town in northern California before returning to the islands, back to my roots."

"We must be approximately the same age," I said. "And we were undergraduates in the L.A. area at the same time. I was at UCLA right before the war. And I was in the European theater. With the army in England, preparing for the Normandy invasion."

"See? We're practically brothers." Meyer whacked me on the back, and I had to catch my step so I wouldn't fall over.

We passed a large banyan tree, with its aerial roots dropping toward the ground. Two young boys dangled from a branch.

Meyer looked up at the gigantic tree and he sighed. "Did you ever go to the amusement park in Long Beach when you were in college?"

"Yeah. That old rickety roller coaster that went out over the pier. Looking down at the ocean from up there scared the piss out of me. I tried to be brave to impress Rhonda."

"That roller coaster was something. Martha and I used to go there when we were dating. I met her when I was a senior at Occidental. But we didn't get married until after the war."

"She waited for you?"

"I guess she didn't get any better offers along the way."

I thought back to Rhonda and me courting, driving around in my beat-up yellow roadster which rattled like a collection of tin cans dragging on the pavement. We chugged up to Big Bear, along the coast to Santa Barbara or down to San Diego. Then an apartment and home in Long Beach. Now replaced with this retirement home. It was really the shits.

Meyer and I stopped in front of a hedge of yellow and pink hibiscus.

"I used to garden," he said. "How about you?"

"Gardening wasn't my favorite thing. Played golf, did some painting. Haven't done either in recent years, as far as I know."

"How's your investigation going?" Meyer asked.

"Kind of crappy. I reread everything I've discovered. Don't know how I can accomplish anything when I have to start over every morning."

"So what does your journal tell you?"

"Night before last I talked to a suspicious night watchman named Moki Iwana. Trouble is, I wouldn't recognize him if he spit in my face."

"What caught your attention about him?"

"He had access, was here the night of the murder, and has keys. Keys. . . ." I needed to do something about that.

When we returned to the building, I stopped by the facility manager's office. I knocked on his open door, and he waved me inside.

"Can I get a new lock with my own key?" I asked.

He shook his head. "No can do. We need get in all da rooms fo' cleaning and fo' any emergency."

"Doesn't say much for privacy."

"Dis a retirement home, not a private residence. Besides, my boss say you moving out next month."

"So they tell me."

I spent the rest of the morning feeling sorry for myself, wallowing alternately in the two feelings of anger and dread.

What a pisser having this crapola memory of mine. It was like misplacing a sock in a drawer. I was rummaging around trying to find something. I'd empty the drawer. No sock. Must have lost it in the washing machine.

How could I remember my childhood so clearly and not be able to remember yesterday? Not anything. Like it never happened. It was no different than if I'd gone into a coma for five years. Here I was with absolutely no connection to anything that happened to me recently.

If I read yesterday's newspaper, it would still be news to me. And it would be news tomorrow and the day after.

How did that make me feel? There was a big void in my gut to match the one in my cranium. It made me want to cry, kick the wall, scream, throw a glass against the wall.

It wasn't fair. I was in great health, otherwise. I could be a useful senior citizen if I didn't have this one little glitch in my system. Kind of like an airplane getting ready to take off. All gleaming silver. Great meals ready to be served to the passengers. Everyone buckled safely in. Flight attendants had made all their announcements. Pilot put his hand on the throttle. One problem. No engines.

Whenever I saw people around this joint, I wondered if they knew me. I could have made a great friend yesterday and wouldn't recognize him from a hole in the wall. Most people carried memories around that got triggered by sight, sound, or smell. With me, nothing. Did I know that guy? Did he know me? When I sat down at breakfast this morning, Meyer was a brand-new acquaintance. Then I talked to him, and he had all this information about me. It was spooky. Like my evil twin had been here for days and I'd just shown up. What did my twin do or say? Did he get in trouble? What was his connection to this murder? I had no clue.

I told myself to shake it off. I had something to do.

I went down to check for mail and found a Fed Ex envelope waiting for me. I ripped it open to find four pages. The first page was titled "Switzerland" and had a list of numbers and letters: 1L1, 1L2 . . . 2L1 . . . 3L1 . . . 1, 2, 3. . . .

What was all this nonsense? I turned the page. More numbers. All the remaining pages had almost consecutive numbers. After looking at all the pages, I reviewed the document. 5, 13, 14, 32, 32A, and 91 were circled.

As much as I hated to, I called my lawyer. An obsequious female voice told me to hold. I twiddled a pencil in my fingers as I waited. Finally, a loud male voice came on the line. "Mr. Jacobson. What can I do for you?"

"I received four pages of numbers that you sent. What is this crap?"

He chuckled. "That's the list of Mr. Tiegan's stamps."

"But it's just a bunch of letters and numbers."

"Those are the Scott catalogue numbers that identify each of the stamps in his collection. Based on the quality of each stamp, a value can be placed on it."

"And the circled numbers represent the ones that Tiegan claims I stole?"

"That's right. That's what the suit claims."

"Would a stamp store recognize these numbers?"

"Any reputable dealer would be familiar with them."

After hanging up I went downstairs to make copies, this time leaving a five-dollar bill for the office administrator. Then I called a taxi.

The first stop was Tanabe Stamp and Coin in Kaneohe. I gave the driver ten dollars as an incentive to wait for me.

"I'd like to speak to the owner," I said.

"That's me," the short man with thick glasses answered from behind the counter.

"I'm trying to purchase this list of stamps." I handed him the sheets of paper.

He clicked his tongue. "Pretty complete list of Swiss stamps."

"How much would it cost?"

He scanned through the list again and

punched some numbers on a calculator. "It would depend on if you want primarily unused or used stamps."

"Give me a range."

"Probably two hundred thousand dollars for used and five hundred thousand for unused."

I whistled. "Just for little hunks of paper?"

He frowned. "You obviously aren't a collector."

"No. I'm buying for a friend."

He dropped the sheets onto the counter and pushed them back to me.

I nudged the pages back in his direction. "I'd like you to hold on to this list. If you can hook me up with anyone selling a collection like this, I'll pay you a ten-percent commission. My name and phone number are written on the first page."

He looked at the top sheet again. "Okay. But it will be more realistic that someone is selling only part of this list."

"Fine. Call me if someone approaches you."

I spent the rest of the day speaking with owners of other stamp stores and making the taxi driver rich. By late afternoon we were sitting in rush hour traffic, heading back through the Pali Tunnel toward the windward side of the island.

Since a portion of Denny's inheritance was now going to this taxi driver, the man was happily humming.

"Any more stops?" he asked.

I imagined dollar signs dancing in his eyes. "No. Back to Kina Nani."

"Any time you want to do this again, give me a call." He handed me a card with the name Ray Puhai and a phone number.

"I don't expect to go through all this again, but I'll keep you in mind."

"Thanks, braddah."

At dinner, I described my sojourn to Meyer and Henry.

"You should turn this all over to the police," Meyer said.

"I'm a suspect. If I give them the list, Saito will twist it around as a motive for having killed Tiegan. Besides, I think some of these shop owners will be more inclined to call me rather than the police if a customer shows up selling Swiss stamps."

"You'll probably get shot before they hang you," Henry said.

"Thanks for the encouraging thought," I said.

"You going to leave that dinner roll?" Henry asked.

"Go ahead," I said. "I'm not that hungry."

Henry grabbed the roll off my plate and happily munched away.

After dinner, I searched through my closet and found a tie that looked like it was only ten years old. I splashed on a little after-shave lotion. Now I was armed and dangerous.

I planned my arrival for exactly 7:10. When I got there, the room was full of old people. I guessed that when you're sitting around a retirement home with nothing to do and there's an event, you get there right when it starts.

A woman in a wheelchair sat next to a phonograph and periodically changed records. The music was big bands and Perry Como from the early '50s. All pre–rock and roll. When "Smoke Get in Your Eyes" played, several couples limped out to a corner of the room and shuffled around leaning on each other. I could smell the aroma of burnt popcorn.

A woman whom I recognized as the one who waved to me at breakfast raced over as fast as her old legs could carry her. She wore a pink dress, showcasing a trim figure. She obviously had taken care of her old body.

"Paul, I'm so glad you came."

"I wouldn't miss this for the world." I gave

her a hug.

"Oh, my," she said and returned the hug. She stepped back and grabbed my hand. "You need to meet some people."

Everyone was new to me except for Meyer. Henry had apparently declined in favor of his coin collection.

I was introduced to four men and a mob of about twenty women. Several of the women eyed me from head to toe. Marion grabbed my arm and propelled me to the next group. I felt like I'd been claimed at a slave auction.

After another series of introductions, Marion grabbed my arm again. "Come on, let's dance."

I tried to remember the last time I had been on a dance floor. My fiftieth wedding anniversary. I was an adequate dancer back then.

Marion steered me to an open spot and we began dancing. I could feel her warmth even with the trade winds cooling the room. She thrust herself close against me, and we put our cheeks together. She knew her stuff, and we glided around the floor, as much as two old fogies can glide.

After the dance Meyer came up to us.

"You two cut a mean rug," he said.

"Comes from having a good dance partner," I replied.

Marion beamed and hugged my arm. "I have to leave for a minute. There's another new resident I need to greet."

She trotted off.

Meyer punched me on the arm. "I see a promising relationship starting, buddy."

"Hope I'm up to it," I said.

I drank too much fruit punch and had to visit the restroom twice. As the crowd dwindled, I found myself with Marion and two other ladies cleaning up the paper cups and bowls of half-eaten popcorn.

"Nice party," I said as she turned off the lights to the rec room. "Want to go sit outside?"

"That would be perfect," Marion said and gave my arm a squeeze.

I wondered if that arm was going to get worn out between her squeezes and Meyer's punches.

We strolled through the garden area and sat on a bench in a gazebo that overlooked a hillside of well-manicured grass, sparkling in the moonlight. I put my arm around Marion and she snuggled close against me.

"How long have you been at Kina Nani?" I asked her.

"Three years. I lived alone for awhile after my husband died, but got tired of cooking for myself."

"Any family in the islands?"

"No. Two daughters on the mainland."

She snuggled closer against me.

"It's nice being here with you, Paul."

"The pleasure is all mine." I probably hadn't been on a date since my wife died. Not that I could have remembered it anyway.

She ran her finger down my cheek. "Well, it's time we both had a little companionship. I met a man here a year ago. I thought of getting involved, but put it off. Just when I finally decided to get intimate with him, he had a heart attack and died."

"Well, I won't do that to you," I said and hugged her.

We shared our backgrounds, and I was only shaken from my reverie when my back became stiff from sitting on the hard bench. I looked at my watch and couldn't believe we had been out here for two hours.

"How would you like to join me for a restaurant meal tomorrow night?" I said.

"That would be a nice change."

"Good. I'll make a reservation and get us a cab. Say six o'clock?"

"Thank you, Paul."

"Marion, this has been a wonderful evening." I reached over and gave her a kiss.

She kissed me back.

I couldn't believe this was happening to me. At my age a woman acted interested in me. I hoped I wouldn't blow it.

We came up for air, and I looked at Marion in the dim light. She smiled.

She was quite a woman. Putting up with an old fart like me. Should I leave things at this level? I hadn't been in this situation for half a century. What to do? For now, just see what would happen.

We walked back to the building with arms around each other. I accompanied her to her door on the twelfth floor, and we parted with another kiss. I felt like a teenager on his first date, as I practically skipped back toward the elevator.

CHAPTER 9

The next morning my journal reminded me that I still had the problem of clearing my name; I was still a murder suspect. I reviewed what I knew. An employee of Kina Nani could have committed the murder. Two employees were on duty when it happened: Jason Kam at the front desk and Moki Iwana on patrol. Of the two, Moki was the prime suspect. Or it could have been an acquaintance or relative of Marshall Tiegan, even Tiegan's lawyer. Someone who knew of my involvement in the lawsuit and set me up. Motive: get Tiegan's stamp collection. And how did a Swiss stamp end up in my apartment?

With that question unanswered I headed down to the dining hall where Meyer needed to point Marion out to me.

"I saw a notice of an event you might want to attend this afternoon," Meyer said.

"What's that?"

"There's going to be a memorial service for Marshall Tiegan."

I thought for a moment. "Might be a good way to meet his family. Determine if there was some relative anxious to get him out of the way."

That afternoon I selected my most somber dark slacks and a white short-sleeved shirt. I met Meyer in front of the building and we clambered into a shuttle van that had KINA NANI spelled out in bright blue letters. Once we were tucked in, I looked around at the other detainees, half a dozen women.

"These some of Tiegan's girlfriends?" I asked.

Meyer chuckled. "No. I call this group the 'Mourner's Club.' They diligently show up for every memorial service. It's their hobby."

"Beats killing people," I said.

When we disembarked at St. Matthew's Lutheran Church on Kamehameha Highway, the old broads raced across the parking lot ahead of us.

"Look like they're trying to get the best seats in the theater," I said.

"Either that or they want to eat all the food first," Meyer said.

Inside, a minister stood greeting the throng, which turned out to be ten other people besides the Kina Nani contingent. A tape deck played Gregorian chants in the background as the minister mounted the steps and stood for a moment between two large bird-of-paradise flower arrangements, with his hands folded. Then he reached over and flicked off the tape player, cleared his throat, and showed us a most sincere wrinkled forehead. "Thank you for coming. We are here to remember our beloved friend, Marshall Tiegan."

Meyer leaned over and whispered in my ear. "Those are two words that have probably never been used to describe him before."

"After the service there will be a reception out on the patio." The minister then launched into an elegant eulogy for the dear departed. I started thinking how nice an air-conditioned room would be. One woman yawned. Another blew her nose. I felt the urge to take a nap but didn't want to face the consequences of waking up with my memory reset.

After hearing that Tiegan should be sitting on the right hand of the pope, if Lutherans had a pope, the minister ran out of gas and introduced Barry Tiegan, the deceased's nephew.

Barry dropped a sheet of paper on the

lectern and adjusted his glasses. "Uncle Marshall was a fine man. I remember him visiting our house in Walnut Creek when I was a boy."

"I bet that was the last time Barry saw him," I whispered to Meyer.

After a few unimaginative comments, Barry sat down, the minister said the Lord's Prayer, and we adjourned for the food.

I moseyed out to the patio to fetch a snack and mingle with the other mourners.

The minister was clasping people's hands in both of his like he was trying to wring water from a stone. I sidled up to Barry Tiegan as he munched on a Safeway sugar cookie.

"I'm sorry about your uncle," I said. "Sounded like the minister knew him well."

Barry gave a derisive laugh. "Uncle Marshall hadn't been to a church in forty years, much less this one. The retirement home director recommended this place, and it was available. I gave the minister some background and the rest was his own spiel."

"Were you and your uncle close?"

Barry's eyes focused on mine, as if I had awakened him from some deep thought. "He wasn't close to any of the family. His wife died a number of years ago, and they never had any children. Uncle Marshall was pretty much of a loner. I talked to him on the phone once a year, but that was it."

"It was nice of you to come all the way over here for his memorial service."

Barry shrugged. "I'm between jobs right now in L.A., so I guess I was the logical family representative."

"No other relatives in Hawaii?"

"No. Just my two sisters and me, all in California."

"Did your uncle have any enemies that you were aware of?"

Barry squinted at me in the bright sunlight. "I wouldn't say enemies. But he didn't have any friends."

"The loner bit," I added helpfully.

"Yeah."

"If you're the closest family, he must be leaving something to you in his will."

Barry wrinkled up his nose like he smelled a skunk. "It *all* gets split between my sisters and me. I spoke with his lawyer and the *all* isn't much. Apparently, there was a stamp collection, but it was stolen when Uncle Marshall was mur . . . you know, when he died."

"Speaking of your uncle's lawyer," I said, "does he happen to be here?"

Barry looked around. "No. He had a trial today and said he couldn't make it." Barry leaned toward me. "I didn't get your name."

"I'm Paul Jacobson."

Barry's head jerked like I had slapped him. "My uncle's lawyer mentioned your name to me. He says you're the one who stole the stamp collection."

Now, I flinched. "Wait a minute. This lawyer is spreading lies. I did nothing of the kind."

"The only thing of value and you took it." Barry glared at me.

"I think you'd better find a more honest lawyer."

A vein on the side of Barry's forehead began to pulse. I didn't know if he was going to have a heart attack or punch me.

A man off to my right cleared his throat, and both Barry and I jumped. The man wasn't dressed for a hot Hawaiian day, sporting a dark suit. I noticed nicotine stains on his fingers, his short stocky stature — "You're either the undertaker," I said, "or Detective Saito."

"Very good, Mr. Jacobson. You do remember me."

"No, but I read about you this morning, so it was an educated guess."

"It seems like you're having a little altercation," Saito said.

Barry leaned forward. "If you're a detective, you should arrest this man. He stole my uncle's stamp collection."

"How interesting," Saito said and leered at me.

"I'm being set up," I protested. "Some scumbag lawyer is spreading lies and innuendos."

"Or he's got you pegged, Mr. Jacobson."

"Lock this old man up," Barry said. Then he stalked away.

"You're not making many friends, Mr. Jacobson."

I thought of what I'd heard. "Someone's going to an awful lot of trouble to make me look bad. Doesn't that seem strange to you, Detective?"

"I haven't heard any claims yet that couldn't be true. And I've been curious. Were you ever in Marshall Tiegan's apartment?"

"I don't remember being there, but I don't remember not being there either. It's all a blank."

"How convenient."

"Look, Detective. You have your job to do, and I want to help you find the murderer, but you and I are up against a big obstacle here. My memory is mush."

"I'll do what I can to help jog it."

"I'm sure you will, Detective. Since we

seem to be seeing each other regularly, why don't you tell me something about yourself?"

He stared at me.

"You must have some hobbies or outside interests," I said.

"I collect butterflies."

"Butterflies?"

"Yes. I catch them and mount them in glass cases."

"Kind of like catching criminals," I said.

"Exactly." He gave me his million yen smile.

"You'll have to show me your collection sometime, Detective."

"When I bring you in, I'll be happy to show you some samples I keep in my office. Pins right through the wings."

Having made a reservation at an Italian restaurant and lined up a cab, I rang Marion's doorbell promptly at six P.M.

The cab ride, dinner, and return trip flew by with a comfortable intimacy. It was amazing that two old goats could get along so well.

"Want to stop by my apartment?" Marion asked as we entered the Kina Nani lobby.

"Sure."

We took the elevator to the twelfth floor.

She unlocked her door, and we walked into an apartment similar to mine, but much neater. Colorful watercolor paintings of flowers and Hawaiian mountains decorated the walls. I walked over to the sliding door and looked out over the city below. "Nice view from the high rent district."

She laughed. "I had to wait six months to get this place on the top floor. Only disadvantage is the longer elevator ride, but at meal time I get on before it fills up. Can I offer you a drink?"

"What do you have?"

"Whatever you want." She opened her cabinet, revealing a fully stocked bar.

"Bourbon and water," I said.

She put on some music. Soft instrumentals from Broadway plays. We settled in on her couch.

One thing led to another, and we were mashing lips together.

I felt an arousal in my groin.

We came up for air.

"I don't usually do this," she said, "but there's no guarantee how much time is left. . . ."

"Yeah," I said. "At our age, it's a victory just to wake up each morning."

"I don't want you to think I'm forward, Paul."

"I'm delighted that we're here together."

I reached over and kissed her again. We re-engaged in a close embrace.

I took a breath, and Marion's head bobbed up.

"I want to make sure this is what you want to do," I said.

She ran her hand through my hair. "Our children probably wouldn't approve of this, but so what." She giggled.

I was amazed and astounded that I was here with this wonderful woman. I had to be fair to her before things went any farther. "There's something you need to know about me," I said.

Her eyes widened. "You're not married or a murderer?"

I thought of the second alternative, but decided I'd avoid bringing up the investigation.

"No," I said with a laugh. "Nothing like that. I have a memory problem."

"Meyer mentioned something to me. But we're all a little absent-minded at our age."

"It's not forgetting some things. I forget everything."

"What are you saying?"

"Every morning, when I wake up, I can't remember anything from the day before. Apparently, I've been to all kinds of specialists, and there doesn't seem to be any medication that helps. I won't remember you tomorrow morning."

Marion wrinkled her forehead. Then she set her lips and her eyes flared. "You mean you didn't remember the party and our conversation in the gazebo last night?"

"That's right. I had to jot down notes about what happened and a reminder to make a dinner reservation. This isn't something I'm proud of. I try not to call attention to it, but I thought you ought to know."

She looked at me again, and her smile returned. "Well, if that's the biggest problem with you, Paul, I guess I can handle it. I have one thing to help you."

She walked over to her dresser and brought back a picture of herself. "Here's something for you to keep in your apartment to help you remember who I am."

I laughed. "Thanks for being so understanding."

She sat back on the couch. I cupped her chin and kissed her again. She leaned against me, and I held her close to my body.

We re-engaged, and I marveled at her soft lips. Was this what she wanted? Was this what I wanted? Hell. Who knew?

As long as she wasn't offended by me, why not? But what if I couldn't perform? No telling what condition the old equipment was in. Hadn't had any practice lately. What if something went wrong?

Then she stood up, took my hand, and led me toward her bed. She doused the lights, and next I knew, our clothes were coming off. Took a little while given all the arthritic fingers. When she pulled the covers down, I sniffed a scent of lilacs.

My heart was thumping, and I didn't know if it was excitement, fear, or I was having a heart attack. I took a couple of deep breaths. My ticker kept on going, so I started fondling her breasts. Not bad for an old broad.

She sighed.

This was getting interesting.

She rubbed up against me.

Prospects looked promising.

I ran my hand down her stomach.

She spread her legs apart.

I took another deep breath. Now was the moment of truth. Then it happened. For some reason my penis decided to go on strike. Where it had been engorged one moment, the next it shrank to the size of a slimy worm. It wouldn't come back. Where was Viagra when I needed it?

Marion reached down and started fondling the worm. Nothing happened. I tried thinking of all the half-naked female movie stars I could remember. The worm wriggled, but didn't grow.

I thought of caves and warm beaches. Finally, the worm received the message and revived.

Not wanting to take any chances, I sent it toward the cave. Unfortunately, the cave opening was kind of dry. I pushed. She pushed. She held the cave door open. I plunged in.

We were doing it. I thrust back and forth. She thrust forth and back.

We revved up some good friction. This went on for awhile, and I was gasping for breath. Would I collapse, complete, or have that heart attack first?

Finally, I shot my wad and lay there exhausted.

Marion stroked the back of my head. I kept panting for several minutes. I was too tired to move.

She seemed content for me to lie there on top of her. My back hurt. I hoped I hadn't thrown it out.

I could imagine an attendant coming to separate us because I couldn't move. Eventually, I rolled off and lay next to her, still breathing heavily. In my youth I would have been back at it, but now I couldn't conceive of doing that again for a month.

I almost dozed off, but then realized that if I went to sleep I wouldn't remember anything. If I woke up here in the morning with my usual blitzed memory, I'd have no clue where I was or what was going on.

Marion was now snoring, so I climbed out of bed, grabbed my clothes, threw them on, picked up her picture, and sneaked out the door to return to my apartment. I hoped I wouldn't run into any late night murderers roaming the halls.

CHAPTER 10

I woke up and stretched. I knew where I was! I remembered having sex the night before with Marion. This was weird. I looked at Marion's picture on my dresser. I didn't even need that as a reminder. After getting dressed I went down to breakfast and knew where to sit.

"I know who the hell you are, and I didn't even have to read my journal," I said to Meyer.

He raised his eyebrows. "This is the first time that's happened."

"Yup. Memory just like it's supposed to work."

"Why do you suppose that is?"

I stopped cold as if he had slapped me. "I don't know. Maybe something I ate. Or. . . ."

He grinned at me. "I bet you got a little action last night and it shook that clogged brain of yours loose."

"Damn. You may be right."

"So, Paul, the whole thing is simple. You just have to have sex every night and your memory will be fine. Your brain is obviously hardwired to your prick."

"I was accused of that as a teenager. But now. . . ."

"You need to get your juices flowing and your brain won't reset when you go to sleep."

"But I don't think I'll be up to that again for weeks."

"Then you'll be back to forgetting." Meyer squinted in the direction of a table where two women sat. "I can't tell for sure, but I don't think Marion is here yet. She's usually one of the first down for breakfast."

"Hope I didn't kill her," I said.

"Don't get carried away. She's probably too embarrassed to show up."

I ate and watched Henry shovel in his eggs and bacon. "It's even good to recognize you, Henry, although you still don't carry on much of a conversation when you're stuffing your mouth."

"Maybe you'll get the clap," Henry said without looking up.

"Well, aren't you the loquacious one?" I said. "You've been eavesdropping on my conversation with Meyer."

He grunted and continued to chew his cud.

As I was getting ready to leave, Marion arrived at her table and waved to me.

"That's a relief," I said. "She survived."

Meyer laughed. "Remember. You need a repeat performance if you want your memory to work. Just don't marry her. You'd break up our trio here and probably wouldn't get it anymore."

For the first time I noticed that Marion sat with two other women.

"She has two friends," I said to Meyer. "I should hook them up with you and Henry. Henry, you got time between your coin collection and baseball statistics to entertain a woman?"

"Been there, done that," he said.

"Henry made the rounds when he first arrived here," Meyer said. "He was quite the stud."

"Did they want someone who was short enough to kiss them on their navels?" I asked.

"It didn't matter about his lack of stature," Meyer said. "He was one of the few available bachelors. But he insulted a number of the women afterwards. They stay away from him now."

"Hard to imagine," I said. "Henry has

such a sweet personality."

After dinner that night, I asked Marion to take a walk with me.

"Do you remember who I am?" she asked.

"I could never forget you," I said. "Thanks for putting up with my defective memory. I have your picture right in the middle of my dresser."

Marion invited me up to her place for a repeat performance.

I squeezed her hand. "I'd love to, but my old body needs some time to rejuvenate."

She pouted. "Rain check then?"

"You bet. Give me a few days."

We parted with a hug, and I headed back to my apartment.

The next morning at breakfast, Meyer said, "How's your memory?"

"I can remember you from yesterday, but it's all pretty hazy."

"Looks like the effect of your cure wears off over time."

"That's the shits. I'll have to go back to using my journal and having you remind me."

"Have you signed up for the picnic today?" Meyer asked.

"What picnic?"

"Once a month there's an excursion. Today's the day for a trip to Lanikai Beach."

"I'm not much for the ocean," I said.

"Not many people go swimming. You can walk on the beach and eat sandwiches."

"I can handle that."

"So all you have to do is sign the list on the counter across from the elevator on this floor," he said. "We meet in front of the building at eleven for the bus."

After breakfast I found the sign-up list, added my name as the nineteenth victim, and then headed up to my apartment for an exciting morning of watching the wallpaper.

At ten-to-eleven I took the elevator down to the first floor, exited the building, and found Meyer pacing back and forth by the curb, near a group of old biddies seated on benches.

He looked at his watch. "About time you arrived."

"Relax," I said. "Plenty of time to spare. Henry joining our little expedition?"

"No. He's working on his coin collection."

"Henry the party animal. Missing all the excitement." I stared at a woman napping with her mouth wide open and drool flowing down her chin.

The bus arrived, and everyone shuffled, limped, and staggered aboard. I dropped into the seat next to Meyer.

"I'm surprised this many people are willing to expose themselves to skin cancer," I said.

He grinned. "If the sun hasn't gotten them by now, it probably won't. Besides, this is pretty much the same group that shows up for all the events . . . the active residents."

I glanced around at the occupants of the bus. "Hate to see the inactive ones."

"Everybody happy today?" the bus driver shouted.

From around the bus came a mixed chorus of "yes."

"Quick trip," he continued. "We'll park by a right-of-way. You'll have a short walk down the path to the beach. Our picnic today is ham, turkey, and beef sandwiches, chips, cookies, and lemonade."

"I don't know if my poor heart can stand all the excitement," I said to Meyer.

"You have to get in the swing of things around here, Paul. There are lots of activities for those who want them. But everything's optional."

"Like living?"

"We're going to have to keep working on that attitude of yours."

"My attitude is one of my best attributes."

The crowd was mainly women with a few

150

married couples. As the two unattached men, we offered to help the driver carry the food down to the beach.

Meyer and I made two trips, hauling lunch supplies. After completing our civic duty, we strolled down the beach.

"You don't seem that happy at Kina Nani," Meyer said.

"Gee. And I thought I was hiding my feelings better. Just because I'm stuck with a bunch of old farts, present company excepted, accused of theft and murder, and have a brain that holds memories like a bag with a hole in it, what more could I ask for?"

"There's Marion."

I came to a stop. "That's true. She's quite a gal. But a day from now I probably won't remember her from a pin cushion."

"Unless your memory gets jogged."

"Yeah. But I can't count on that very often."

"You could always just accept your situation."

I squinted at him. "Like you accept going blind?"

"Touché."

"I have more fun complaining and being a general pain in the ass," I said.

"Maybe when we get your named cleared, you'll feel better."

"I like the way you said 'we.' "

"Of course, Paul. I'm here to help you any way I can."

"This from an ex-lawyer?"

"And regarding your attitude toward lawyers, we're not all slime bags."

"Well, you're the first one I've met who's a human being."

Meyer chuckled. "You just don't know many lawyers. There are all kinds."

"Yeah, but I still prefer the dead kind."

We came to the east end of the beach where the sand gave way to rocks and sandbags.

"This used to be a wider and longer beach," Meyer said. "There's been a lot of erosion. If this continues, in a few more years there won't be any sand left."

"I can identify with that. Kind of like my memory."

We sat down on a remaining spit of sand and watched two kayaks paddling toward the Mokulua Islands a mile offshore.

"There was a time when I would have swum out to those islands," Meyer said, as he threw a pebble into the water.

"Are you nuts? There was a time when I would have stayed right here. Still is."

"You're not a big fan of the ocean," he said.

"I like sitting on the beach and watching a scantily clad bikini bunny or a good sunset, but get me in the ocean and I get the shakes. Give me dry land where my feet can rest on something solid, and there aren't any lawyers swimming around with me."

We resumed walking. I kicked a rock as we headed back toward the picnic.

"I have to track down whomever stole Tiegan's stamp collection," I said. "I don't believe our benevolent police are searching for anyone else, especially since I'm their prime suspect."

"At least they haven't arrested you yet."

"Small consolation. I expect Detective Saito is waiting for one more piece of evidence to fall in place before he hauls me to the clink. I'd have to trade one cell for another."

"Don't be so negative. At Kina Nani you have a room to yourself."

"Yeah," I said. "And I get to eat with a hundred of my closest friends."

"You do have one friend."

I put my hand on Meyer's shoulder. "And I'm grateful for that."

After an exhilarating lunch of roast beef peppered with grains of sand, I watched a couple of wrinkled old broads dip their toes in the water. Then when the excitement reached too high a level for me, I strolled back to the bus.

I sat by myself contemplating my predicament. Getting old was a constant battle between worry and boredom. Would my memory get worse? Would I start forgetting during the day? Could I get Detective Saito off my back? Maybe being a murder suspect added a little spice to my life. No. It gave me one more worry. Once I figured out who stole those stamps and I got Saito on the right track, I could settle down to the real excitement in my life. Things like watching Henry eat.

What about Marion? She was a good person and didn't deserve to be burdened with someone who had a defective memory. What kind of relationship could it be if I didn't even remember who she was every morning? Unless we'd had sex the night before.

Meyer climbed up the stairs to the bus and plopped down next to me.

"Are you getting anti-social?" he asked.

"Needed a little time to myself."

"I thought you already had enough of that."

"That may be so, but I needed to think things through," I said.

"Did you reach any conclusions?"

I decided to keep my thoughts to myself. "Only that I need to get Detective Saito focused on the murderer rather than me."

"That's a noble cause, but so far there's nothing to clear you," Meyer said.

"Crap. Guilty until proven innocent."

"Fortunately, the system doesn't work that way," Meyer said.

"Maybe not, but that's how Saito thinks."

Meyer shrugged. "We'll find something. Hang in there."

"Sure. I don't have any friggin' choice anyway."

At dinner Meyer said, "I've been checking up on the murder case."

"How am I doing?"

"Not so good. There was blood found on Tiegan's rug. The police are doing a DNA match to verify that it's Tiegan's."

"No big deal. Someone obviously whacked Tiegan over the head in his apartment."

"But blood was also found on one of the bottles in the bag you were throwing away."

Now he had my attention. "So the police are checking to see if that matches Tiegan's DNA as well," I said.

"Exactly. A Heineken bottle in your trash may have been the murder weapon."

"But I don't even drink beer."

"My source says there were Heineken bottles found in Tiegan's refrigerator," Meyer said.

"And fingerprints?"

"The police discovered no fingerprints on the suspected murder weapon. But in the same bag with the Heineken bottle, they found Pepsi cans with your fingerprints."

I shrugged. "I drink Pepsi. Probably have some unopened cans in my refrigerator."

"If the blood matches Tiegan's, the evidence will point to you hitting him over the head in his apartment and then trying to dispose of both the body and the bottle."

"So I'm a competent enough criminal to wipe the fingerprints off the bottle, but not competent enough to dispose of the murder weapon?"

"That's it."

"Shit. If I were that stupid, I'd deserve the electric chair."

"The rack would be better," Henry said.

"Thanks Henry. I love you, too." I turned toward Meyer. "So how was I supposed to have disposed of Tiegan?"

"They think you dragged the body down the hallway and crammed it in the garbage chute."

"So there must have been some blood found on the hallway carpet."

"No. Strangely, they didn't find any."

I thought back to my journal. "The morning I found the body, there was a woman cleaning the corridor carpet."

"That must be it," Meyer said. "She wiped up any trace of blood."

"I bet the blood on the bottle and on Tiegan's rug match his," I said. "The only problem is that I didn't do it. Someone else bashed Tiegan, disposed of his body, wiped off the bottle, and somehow hid it in my apartment."

"Seems more far-fetched than you having done it," Henry said.

I ignored Henry and kept on with my train of thought. "Unless someone had a master key and could get into Tiegan's apartment and mine. Like a night watchman."

"That's possible," Meyer said. "The murderer could be an employee of Kina Nani or someone who stole the keys and copied them."

"From reading my notes, there were two employees here the night of the murder — the desk clerk and the night watchman. There was a visitor with illegible handwriting that no one can remember. And any resident."

"Like you," Henry said.

"Henry, if they arrest me, you'll have to

get used to a new table mate," I said.

"No great loss," he said.

"You better be careful, Henry," I said. "If I'm this vicious murderer, I might poison your food."

He actually looked up at me, his eyes widening. He pulled his plate closer and guarded his food like a mother lion protecting her cubs.

"Now you've scared him," Meyer said.

"Good."

CHAPTER 11

"You need to get back with Marion," Meyer said to me the next morning.

"Which one is Marion?" I asked, remembering squat about the last few days.

He pointed in her direction.

I squinted and looked across the room. Same woman as in the picture on my dresser. Not a bad-looking old broad, but I didn't remember seeing her before.

"My journal indicates that she and I were . . . uh, intimate."

"It seems to be the only thing that helps your memory," Meyer said.

"Then I guess I'll have to make a sacrifice for the cause."

"That's the spirit," Meyer said and slapped me on the back.

Henry didn't look up but said from his oatmeal, "Male whore."

I didn't know whether to hit Henry or laugh. I went with the latter.

After breakfast, as Meyer and I were leaving the dining room, a short, stocky man accosted me. "Mr. Jacobson," he said, "we need to talk."

"And who are you?"

He frowned. "I'm Detective Saito."

"I've read about you. You're investigating the murder and burglary. May I see your identification?"

He held out his badge. I saw cigarette stains on his fingers.

"I have to check these things since I don't remember day-to-day."

"That's what you've told me. Now, I need to ask you to accompany me to police headquarters."

I turned to Meyer. "What does my lawyer advise on this?"

"It's up to you, Paul."

I turned back to face Saito. "Since you're such a nice guy, Detective, I guess I'll join you. It means having to give up watching the mold grow in my bathroom, but why not?"

He led me to the curb and opened the back door of a white Ford with a blue stripe along the side. Once inside, I found myself locked in. At least he didn't cuff me.

The car pulled into the police department parking lot on the corner of Waikalea and

Kamehameha Highway, near the library. I looked across the street and saw a sign for the Reverend Benjamin Parker Elementary School. Nobody messed with those kids.

I was ushered into a white stucco institutional building with a brown roof. It was full of police and glum people sitting in chairs, not even a box of doughnuts in sight.

Detective Saito turned me over to a stern-looking woman who reminded me of the nurse from my elementary school days. Either that or Nurse Ratched. She nudged me into a small room with two chairs on each side of a scarred wooden table. I picked the chair facing a one-way mirror, waved, and sat down.

Five minutes later, Detective Saito appeared.

"Let's start with the night of Marshall Tiegan's murder. What do you remember?"

"Nothing."

"And why is that?"

"Because my short-term memory is as sharp as the knife on this table."

"There's no knife on this table," Detective Saito said with a scowl.

"Exactly. No knife, no memory."

"Enough of the games, Mr. Jacobson. This is serious. Tell me everything you can in connection with the night of Mr. Tiegan's murder."

"I'll repeat for your friends behind the mirror. I . . . don't . . . remember . . . anything. Now I'll tell you what I've been told and what I've learned. Would you like to hear that?"

"Yes."

"Okay," I said. "My son moved me into the Kina Nani retirement home that day. I woke up the next morning confused, with no memory of the day before and not knowing where I was. What I've learned is that a guard named Moki claims he locked the garbage chute around ten forty-five P.M. and unlocked it at seven A.M. Apparently, between one and five, Tiegan was hit over the head and stuffed in the garbage chute. I assume you've spent a lot of time with Moki because he should be your prime suspect."

Detective Saito glowered. "What happened the next morning?"

"Again, I don't remember. But I'll be happy to tell you what I've read in the journal I keep."

"Go ahead."

"What I've written indicates I was going to the garbage chute to dispose of a bag of trash when I discovered the body wedged inside. I called 9-1-1 to report it."

"Why were you throwing away the trash?"

"I suppose to clean up my kitchenette," I said.

"Or to get rid of evidence?"

"If you think I committed the murder, I'd be pretty incompetent to try and get rid of evidence the same way as the body."

"I've checked with your doctor," Saito said. "You do have a memory problem. I think you forgot the evidence and discovered it the next day. Then you panicked and tried to throw it away."

"Right. I must have been real panicked to leave the bag next to the trash chute for your cop buddies to find."

"I think you were hoping that we'd overlook it."

"In your scenario why'd I call 9-1-1 to report the body?"

"To try to draw suspicion away from yourself."

"Let me get this straight," I said. "You think I committed a murder, left evidence the next day near the body, and then reported finding the body?"

"You ready to admit it?"

I laughed. "You must be crazier than you think I am."

"Care to give me a statement, Mr. Jacobson?"

"Fine. Here's your statement and listen

carefully. I . . . didn't . . . do . . . it."

"We could hold you here, until you reconsider," he said.

"Do whatever you need to do, but keep looking for Tiegan's real murderer."

Detective Saito grimaced, jumped up from his chair, and stomped out of the room, leaving me alone with the hidden eyes behind the one-way mirror. I waved to the mirror again and closed my eyes to rest. I just wasn't going to fall asleep.

He must have let me stay like that for half an hour. Then he re-entered the room.

"Anything more to say, Mr. Jacobson?"

"Yes. I think you better find whoever stole Tiegan's stamp collection."

He smiled. "Like someone who has been visiting stamp and coin stores all over the island?"

Shit. He'd been following me. I should have paid better attention.

"Find the stamp collection and you've got your man," I said.

"We will, Mr. Jacobson. We will."

"Are you going to lock me up or send me back to my paradise home?"

He watched me for a moment. "I'm going to let you go, for now. But remember. I've got my eyes on you. We can pick you up any time."

■ ■ ■ ■

When I returned to the big house, lunch was under way. As I sat down, Meyer said, "I have some news."

"I hope better than what I've been through this morning," I said.

"It's not good. According to my sources, the blood on Tiegan's carpet and on the bottle both match Tiegan's."

"So that explains Detective Saito's renewed interest in me. He's convinced that I killed Tiegan. With the murder weapon in my bag of trash, it's a natural conclusion."

"How did the bottle get into your apartment?" Meyer asked.

"That's the stay-out-of-jail question. The murderer had access to the trash chute and my apartment. The one person who had keys to both that night was Moki the night watchman. But I don't think Saito is pursuing Moki, given his hard-on for me."

"If he arrests you before the end of lunch, can I have your cookies?" Henry asked.

"Sure," I said. "Remember, Henry. You could be next."

He started chewing his carrots at double time.

"There's a reward for anyone giving

evidence leading to the arrest of the murderer," Meyer said.

"There you go, Henry," I said. "An incentive."

"How much?" Henry asked.

"Five thousand dollars," Meyer replied. "It's being put up by Kina Nani. There's a note in the elevator."

"That would give you some coin money, Henry," I said. "Find out who got into my apartment and you'll get the reward."

"Or prove you did it," Henry said with a smile.

"Have at it," I said. "You're welcome to scour my apartment for evidence."

"Might do that," Henry said.

"Just you, me, a bottle of Heineken, and a trash chute," I said, baring my teeth.

Now he looked worried and went back to eating his mystery meat.

"I have an idea to take your mind off of all this," Meyer said to me. "There's a water aerobics class this afternoon. I thought you might want to join it."

"I hate swimming," I said.

"This is easy. We float and stretch. Meet me at the pool at four o'clock."

"Any skinny-dipping women in the class?"

"No, it's all very proper," Meyer said.

"Damn."

■ ■ ■ ■

After lunch I asked where I could find the retirement home doctor and was directed to Dr. Fry's office on the third floor.

"I have an emergency," I said to the receptionist. "Is the doctor in?"

"What's the nature of your problem?"

"It's a personal matter."

She cleared a strand of hair from her forehead and wrinkled her nose. "He should be able to see you in fifteen minutes."

"I'll wait."

After reading an article about shark attacks on the east coast in a year-old *Newsweek,* I heard my name called and the receptionist pointed toward an empty examination room.

Shortly, a doctor-looking kid in white lab coat joined me. Dr. Fry was in his thirties. I didn't know why he was practicing with old people, since he probably had no clue about the problems of aging.

"I understand you have a personal problem," he said.

"Doc, I'm in a pinch. I need some Viagra."

He clicked his tongue, took out a pad, and scribbled a prescription.

Later, I found my old baggy swim trunks, changed, and then sauntered down to the pool, leaving my robe and slippers on a deck chair. A light breeze rippled through the trees as I approached the pool. A young woman with a blond ponytail stood by the edge. She encouraged Meyer and his harem of four old ladies to tread water.

I stuck my toe in the water. Pretty warm.

"You need to put a belt on," the drill sergeant shouted.

"Yes, sir . . . ma'am," I replied.

I noticed Meyer and his women were all floating high in the water. I grabbed one of the blue foam belts lying by the side of the pool and wrapped it around my middle.

I ventured into the lukewarm water up to my waist. The aroma of chlorine caused my nostrils to twitch.

"Come out here!" Meyer shouted.

"I don't float so well," I said. "I'm kind of like a rock."

"The flotation belt will take care of that."

I looked at him halfway across the Pacific. I hated this. Why did I decide to get in the pool? The thought of being in over my head gave me the heebie-jeebies.

"Are you joining us or not?" Meyer shouted again.

"Hold your water," I said. "I'm getting there."

I kicked off, ready to do my usual ballast trick, but to my surprise, the belt held me up. Then I floated out into the deep end toward the rest of the shark meat.

"Hey, I'm not sinking," I said. I pushed the water with my hands and flopped forward like a lame seagull.

"Everybody, this is Paul," Meyer said.

I waved but got water in my mouth and started coughing.

The drill sergeant adjusted her dark glasses and began shouting, "Okay let's get going. Kick, one, two, three . . . put your arms above your heads. Move them in a circular motion . . . keep kicking . . . stretch those arms . . . now drop them into the water."

I followed her directions, always three seconds behind the rest of the group. Oh, well. I was a little water-challenged.

After I had been fully water-aerobicized, I floated into the shallow end of the pool and was prepared to mount the stairs to escape to dry land when Meyer caught me by the shoulder.

"Paul, there's one other thing you should try."

"You mean drying off?"

"No," he said. "As long as you've gotten this far, let me show you something that's a really good workout for your old body."

"My old body is water-logged and ready to get back to the safety of solid ground. Look at my hands. They're blanched prunes."

Meyer laughed. "Here. Grab one of these kick boards."

He handed me a hunk of blue foam from a stack on the side of the pool. "Between the flotation belt around your waist and holding onto this board, you can kick and do laps in the pool."

"If I were nuts enough to want to do laps."

"Come on, Paul. Don't be so negative. I'll show you how easy it is."

He kicked down the pool and back while I watched.

After he stood up, he gave me a push and I floundered out into the deep end. At first it felt uncomfortable holding onto the board and kicking, but once I discovered I wasn't going to drown, I moved my legs in synch and was surprised to discover that I was traveling along at a steady clip. When I approached the deep end of the pool, I made a slow lazy turn and headed back toward Meyer.

After several laps, I almost forgot I was in the water. The old legs kept flapping and I didn't sink. I must have completed a dozen laps before I cruised into the shallow end and tossed the board up on the side of the pool.

Meyer clapped me on the back. "See? You'll turn into a regular fish if you keep it up."

I detached the flotation belt and dropped it onto the cement. "It's this thing around my waist. Otherwise, I'd be like a boat anchor."

I sat on the edge of the pool and watched Meyer swim several laps unassisted by any belt or board.

"Show-off," I said when he climbed out of the pool.

"It just takes practice," he said.

We sat in chairs in the sun to dry off.

"So you actually enjoy floating around with the other inmates?" I asked.

"It's a good way to stretch the old muscles and to meet chicks."

"Not exactly swimsuit models any of them." I looked over at two old biddies sitting on the other side of the pool.

"After all your complaining about getting

in the water you did fine."

"Better than a poke in the eye," I said.

"Why are you so negative about swimming?"

"I've always hated going in pools. I sink. I start paddling and it's like weights are attached to my legs. Rather than staying on the surface, my feet dive like a submarine."

"Nothing that can't be overcome by a little practice."

I shook my head. "I took swimming lessons as a kid. All the other kids in the class turned into fish. I turned into a clam and settled to the bottom of the pool."

"Come on, Paul, you're exaggerating."

"No. Unfortunately, I'm not. I remember it as clear as a day in the desert. All the kids splashing around and me floundering. Instructor thought I was doing it on purpose. When I almost drowned, she realized I wasn't faking."

"Why not float on your back?"

"Other people float, I capsize. I don't like being in the water, other than a shower or Jacuzzi."

"Speaking of which, the hot tub's empty now. Are you ready for a soak?"

"Fine by me."

We plunked our bodies down in the warm water.

"Ah, that's good," Meyer said with a sigh.

"I can handle this," I said. "Shallow and nothing swimming around."

That night I took Marion out to dinner at a nearby Chinese restaurant. We feasted on sweet-and-sour shrimp, moshu pork, and lemon chicken, complemented with a bottle of Bordeaux. When she went to the powder room, I gulped down a pill. We headed back to her place and took up where we left off.

When she saw my drug-induced erection, she said, "Oh, my."

Before I knew it, we were humping like teenagers. The wonders of modern medicine.

The next morning I ached all over but could remember everything from the night before. How much more of this could my body take?

I staggered down to breakfast.

"Hey, Don Juan," Meyer greeted me.

I dropped into a chair.

"I don't know if I've died and gone to heaven or just died," I said.

Later that morning, Meyer convinced me to do laps again with the kick board. To my surprise, I lasted for twenty laps.

Afterwards, we sat in the sun.

"Marion is good for you," Meyer said. "The evidence is conclusive now. You're two for two on having sex and then remembering things the next day."

"Yeah. This is a hell of a state. I'm old and lose my memory. Then I'm too old to have sex often, and sex is the one thing that brings back my memory."

"You have to view sex as medicine."

"I don't know if Marion's going to appreciate that. 'Here, I'm ready for my next dose.'"

"From what I can tell, she'll go along with it for a while."

"But will I be able to keep up?"

"You'll have to figure out what works for the two of you. If she gives up on you, you'll just have to whack off periodically."

I turned toward him. "I'm not going to start that again. I gave it up when I was a teenager."

Meyer shrugged. "Maybe your doctor would have some suggestions."

"Good old Doc Fry. My purveyor of Viagra. I don't know if he's good for much else."

"Go talk to him," Meyer said. "It can't hurt."

I put on my robe, and as we walked from

the pool into the lobby, to my surprise I saw Detective Saito there talking to a woman in a wheelchair.

"I did it, Officer," she said in a voice that sounded like she had gravel in her throat. "You can arrest me now for the murder."

Meyer stepped forward and spoke to Detective Saito. "That's Mrs. Quinn, Detective. Whenever something happens around here, she confesses to it. The staff thought some silverware had been stolen two months ago. Mrs. Quinn confessed to taking it, then it was found in the back of the storeroom."

"And I expect to receive the reward for turning myself in," Mrs. Quinn said, ignoring Meyer.

"She's as guilty as I am," I said.

Saito glared at me.

"Mrs. Quinn, why don't you get up and show the detective how you committed the crime," Meyer said.

"Oh, that's not possible. I haven't been able to get out of my wheelchair for two years."

"I know for sure I'm in a nut house now," I said.

"Just accept it as entertainment," Meyer replied.

I offered to read to him, and we took the

poky little elevator upstairs, and I resumed reading *Alice in Wonderland.*

"This place is like the Mad Hatter's tea party," I said. "I can picture Henry as the dormouse."

We were interrupted by a buzzing noise. I opened the door and found a studious young woman, who stood there with books under her arm.

"Oh, it's Doris," Meyer said.

"Your date?" I asked.

"No," he said with a chuckle. "She's here for my Braille lesson. I forgot she was coming today."

"I'll butt out," I said. "We can read some more another time. You learn to feel those bumps in a book."

Later that day I went to Dr. Fry's office. His receptionist asked the nature of my appointment.

"Just a matter of needing the doctor's advice," I said.

She looked at me like I was a floating turd and scribbled a note on her pad.

Thirty minutes later I was ushered into the examination room and sat on a gurney covered with a white cloth. I've always wondered why doctor's offices and mortuaries looked so much alike.

After the nurse poked a thermometer in my mouth and took my pulse and blood pressure, the kid walked in.

"Weren't you here yesterday?" Dr. Fry asked.

"You prescribed Viagra for me. I have this problem. . . ."

"Not strong enough?"

"No, that stuff worked fine," I said. "It's my memory."

He wrinkled his forehead.

"It's like this," I explained. "As you know, my short-term memory is crapola. After sleeping, I can't remember anything from the day before."

"That's not unusual," he replied. "With some forms of dementia you can lose your short-term memory while still retaining good use of your long-term memory."

"Yeah, I remember things fine from five years ago and before," I said. "With the short-term memory loss, I may have stumbled upon a temporary cure. If I have sex, I seem to remember things okay from the day before. My problem is, Doc, how do I build up my sexual endurance so I can perform more often and remember?"

"If I had an answer to that, I'd be a billionaire," he said.

"Any hope for an old poop like me?"

He shook his head. "Other than the right balance of exercise, a healthy diet, and a little assistance from Viagra, not much else I can suggest."

I left with what I expected. Nothing. Not even an offer to be assisted by a nurse's escort service.

"Dr. Fry was as useless as hair on your butt," I said to Meyer at dinner.

"Kind of like you," Henry interjected.

I was tempted to squirt catsup on his bald head but contained myself. Ignoring him, I said to Meyer, "I don't have any new solution to my memory problem."

"Guess it's all up to Marion then," Meyer said.

"It's not that easy. The sex only seems to help my memory for a day or so. Then I'm back to remembering squat until I can replenish my ammo."

Chapter 12

I woke up in a strange sterile room. The aroma of rubbing alcohol permeated the place. A white curtain pulled around my bed ran along an overhead track. I heard some voices. My head throbbed. Where the hell was I?

I tried to get up, but my back was stiff. I fell back in bed, having decided to just rest.

As I closed my eyes, I heard snatches of phrases: "Head trauma . . . no broken bones . . . dehydrated. . . ."

Sounded like a medical TV show. I opened my eyes again. I examined my surroundings. A paper cup and a push button device rested on a gray table beside my bed. There was an IV stuck in my arm. I was in a hospital.

But where?

The curtain parted, and a young man in a white coat greeted me. "How are you feeling, Mr. Jacobson?"

"Head hurts. Where am I?"

"Castle Hospital."

"What happened to me?"

"That's what we're trying to find out. What do you remember?"

"Nothing."

He frowned. "All we know is a Good Samaritan called 9-1-1 after finding you unconscious in a ditch in Kaneohe."

I tried to squeeze some recollection out of my aching head. Nothing.

"In your wallet we found an expired driver's license with an address in Honolulu and a newer ID card with the address of Kina Nani on it."

"What's that?" I asked.

"It's the retirement home where you must live. We've called them, and they're trying to find someone who might know what you were doing."

I looked at him, my mind a blank. "I have no clue what's going on here."

"Get some rest."

He sauntered away, and I closed my eyes since I had nothing better to do.

Before I could even have a dream of a scantily clad nurse, my phone rang. I picked it up to hear Denny's distinctive voice. "Dad, what happened?"

"I don't know. I'm in a hospital, but can't

remember why. They said I fell in a ditch."

"What were you doing in a ditch?"

"Lying there unconscious, apparently," I said.

"But how did you get there?"

"Good question. My soggy brain doesn't have any answers, and it seems no one was with me."

"Do you want me to fly out?" he asked.

"No need for that. I'll be fine, once my head stops aching."

He said he'd call again later.

After awhile a nurse came in and told me I had a visitor.

A man I'd never seen before walked in and said, "Paul, what have you gotten yourself into?"

"Who are you?"

"I'm Meyer. We're friends at Kina Nani."

"Never seen you before," I said.

He clucked his tongue. "I was afraid this would happen. You've been keeping a journal. I brought it with me so you could review what you've written." He handed me a stack of paper. "Read this, and then we'll talk."

I hunkered down and skimmed the first page. "Looks like my handwriting." Then I thumbed through a few more pages.

"Seems I've been put out to pasture in a

retirement home," I said.

"That sums it up."

"They say I was found in a ditch. Any idea how I ended up there?"

"I had breakfast with you this morning," he said. "You had forgotten everything again, but had read your journal. You've been putting a note by your bed to reread what you'd written every morning when you wake up. At breakfast the only thing you said was that you needed to get some cough drops. You must have been walking to the store."

"Why would I want cough drops? My only problem is my headache."

"I'll leave your journal here with you, and here's your note to read it when you wake up. They say you'll be here overnight for observation, so you'll have forgotten everything when you next wake up."

I started scanning through the manuscript. Then something caught my attention. "You know anything about this woman named Marion?"

"Yes," Meyer said. "She's your girlfriend."

"I'll be damned. I feel like I plopped down in the middle of a *Twilight Zone* episode."

"Get some rest. When you get back to Kina Nani we'll discuss your 'cure.' "

My head wasn't throbbing as much, so I

read the rest of my manuscript and found out I was a suspect in a murder investigation.

This was all too weird.

My son called and asked again if he should come to Hawaii to help me.

"I always like to see you, Denny, but I'm bouncing back. You don't need to make a special trip."

"Jennifer finishes the school year on Friday, and we're all going to be visiting you in two weeks."

"Just go with the planned trip. Nothing required before then."

I was too confused now anyway. I needed some time to get my life in order and digest what I'd read in my journal. Getting old wasn't all it was cracked up to be.

The young kid disguised as a doctor came in again.

"When can I blow this joint?" I asked.

He looked at his clipboard. "Probably tomorrow. All the tests so far are negative. How are you feeling?"

"Little headache, stiff, but ready to bust out."

He smiled. "I'd like to run one more test. There is some evidence of minor strokes."

"That's old stuff. I can't remember shit and have been that way for . . . well, I read it's been five years."

Doogie ran his test, I stared at the institutional white walls for awhile, and finally a nurse informed me that I had another visitor.

"This is getting to be like Grand Central Station," I said.

The nurse smiled. "I guess you're a popular guy."

"I'll probably have no clue who this visitor is, either."

And I was right. A bouncy old broad in a flowered dress rushed into my room. "Paul, I was worried." She dashed over to the bed and planted a big, juicy kiss on my cheek.

I didn't know who this woman was. Could she be the one described in my journal?

"Everyone is talking about you at Kina Nani. Did you get assaulted?"

"I don't know what happened. I woke up in the hospital, and they told me I was found in a ditch."

"Did you get robbed?"

"No. My wallet's in the drawer over there."

"I need you," she said with a come-hither look in her eyes.

This had to be the one in my journal.

"Marion?" I said with a quaver in my voice.

"Don't act so surprised. Of course."

That was a relief. Now I knew I had the right person. I'd never seen her before, even though we'd apparently been fooling around together.

"I should be able to leave the hospital tomorrow," I said.

"I hope you're not on restricted activities," she said with a wink.

This was getting interesting. I played along. "Not where you're concerned."

She blushed and squeezed my hand.

I considered telling her what I had read about her helping me remember. No. I decided to keep that information to myself.

"I think I'll arrange a little party to celebrate your return tomorrow night," she said.

"Why not wait until it's certain that they'll release me? The doctor's going to review the results of one more test."

She pouted. "They shouldn't keep you here. You look ready to go."

"I'm with you on that. I hate hospitals. Noisy and always poking things in you."

"As soon as I know you're coming home, I'll plan something," she said.

"I don't need a big party. You and I could have our own private little rendezvous."

"Oh, my," she said and her cheeks glowed again.

Imagine my amazement. I did have a girlfriend. This was like being back in high school.

She gave me a kiss and said she was off to run some errands.

I waved good-bye and lay back to consider the possibilities.

Later I asked for a pen and some paper and added to my journal. Then I placed the note Meyer left on top of the papers.

The next morning I woke up and saw the note. I read the journal with astonishment. I was some kind of old, sex maniac, murder suspect freak.

When a nurse came in, I asked her when I could go on parole. She checked the clipboard at the bottom of my bed and told me the doctor had approved my release. She said she'd call Kina Nani to have a van come get me.

"You'll need to keep a bandage on your head for a few days," she informed me. "Pretty nasty gash where your head hit the ground."

I dressed, watched the walls a little, and then a cheerful woman in a floor-length yellow muumuu came strolling into the room.

"Mr. Jacobson, time to go."

"Do I know you?" I asked.

"Sure. I'm Melanie from Kina Nani. I've come to pick you up."

I looked at her face again. Never seen her before. She had a nice smile, though. "If you're kidnapping me, I'm ready. It'll add some excitement to my life."

"You've already had some excitement," she said. "You were found in a ditch."

"I like to go ditch diving. Nothing unusual."

She wrinkled her brows. "Next time you better use our swimming pool."

On the van ride back, an empty feeling seized me. It wasn't hunger. I contemplated the subject of being old. I was still mobile, I could see as well as anyone, my hearing still worked, my teeth were all my own, no heart, lung, liver or kidney problems. It was my damned memory. Without that inconvenience I'd have been the poster boy for the AARP. They could run ads describing me as the example of vigorous health in the waning years. Look at Paul. Still active sexually (apparently), a girlfriend, guys to talk to at meals, walking around and falling in ditches. Even keeping the police hopping. What more could you ask for, unless it would be to remember what happened yesterday?

I had to get on top of this situation, clear my name, and get on with my life.

When we reached our destination, I asked Melanie what apartment I lived in.

"Six-fifteen, Mr. Jacobson."

"Okay. And thanks for the ride." I reached in my wallet to give her a tip.

"I can't accept money," she said with a winning smile.

Too bad I already had a girlfriend.

There was a note taped to my door. Said to call Meyer. After I put my stack of journal pages on the nightstand by the bed, I dialed the number on the note.

"Welcome back to paradise," he said.

"It's good to escape one nuthouse for another," I replied. "I'm starving. When can a guy get some food around this place?"

"I'll meet you at table eleven in the dining room in thirty minutes."

"From what I read, you're the old guy with a white beard."

"I'm old like all of the people here, Paul. We'll catch up on your field trip over lunch."

I resisted the urge to take a nap, remembering from my journal what that might do to me.

When I arrived at lunch, there were two men at table eleven.

The guy with white hair and white beard waved me to the empty chair. I watched the bald-headed guy chomping a cheeseburger.

I recalled the other name I read. "I've missed you too, Henry," I said to the top of his head.

"You should keep sleeping in ditches," he said without looking up.

"This is like coming home for the summer from college," I said. "I used to get the same warm reception from my folks."

Meyer laughed. "Marion and I are glad you're back. Deep down, Henry is too."

"That right, Henry? You still love me?" I leaned over and kissed the top of his bald head.

He almost choked on his cheeseburger.

"I'll take that as a yes," I said.

"I've been researching your excursion," Meyer said.

"Yeah?"

"I checked and learned that you were found a quarter of a mile from Kina Nani on the corner of Namoku and Kaneohe Bay Drive."

"So I was taking a hike."

"Apparently. There's no sidewalk there, and you must have been walking on the grass alongside the road. There's an embankment and you slipped and fell into the ditch. Then a passing motorist stopped and called 9-1-1."

"I'd like to thank that person," I said.

"He never left a name and drove off when the ambulance arrived."

"Any idea where I was going on my little jaunt?"

"That's the part I can't figure out," Meyer said. "At breakfast yesterday morning you had mentioned needing to get some cough drops. You might have been going to the store."

"That sounds logical."

"But there's a van that goes over to the shopping center every morning at nine. You knew you could catch a ride."

"Maybe I wanted the exercise," I said.

"Come on. You and I have taken walks around the grounds and to the store, but I've never seen you go walking that route."

I tried to remember what might have happened to me. No use. "I guess you're right. I can't figure out what I was doing."

"And the final thing. You were found in the opposite direction from the shopping center."

"Maybe I was trying to escape this prison camp."

"You were headed toward the bay," he said. "That makes no sense, unless you wanted to take a swim."

"I hate swimming."

"So that leaves us with no logical explanation of what you were doing or where you were going."

"We'll never know since I can't remember jack," I said. "We'll leave it in the category of other unsolved mysteries, like why there are mosquitoes and why the jelly side of the toast always falls face down."

"Speaking of face down, you must have hit the ground pretty hard to get a gash on your forehead."

"Wait a minute," I said. "I just remembered something I read. That murder victim was bashed on the forehead. You don't suppose. . . ."

Just then three old broads approached our table. The one who wasn't bad looking squeezed my shoulder.

"I'm glad you're back," she said.

I looked up at her. Didn't remember her, but it must have been Marion.

"Carolyn, Alice, and I were wondering if you three gentlemen would like to join us for the theater Sunday after next. Kina Nani has a bus going to the Blaisdell Center for a performance of *Beauty and the Beast.*"

I looked at Meyer. He nodded. Henry actually stopped eating, catsup dripping from the corner of his mouth. First time I'd seen something catch his attention.

"What do you think, Henry?" I asked.

"Yes," he said.

"Looks like we have a triple date," I said to Marion, "provided Henry isn't playing the part of the beast that day."

"Good." She squeezed my shoulder again. This kept up, I'd have some bruises.

After they left, we discussed plans.

"Which one do you want to pair up with?" I asked Henry.

"Alice," he said. "She has nice legs."

"You sly dog," I said. "You *were* paying attention."

"Not much escapes Henry," Meyer said. "You may think he's not watching, but he catches everything that's going on."

"Like the fact that your fly's open, Jacobson," Henry said.

I look down. "Shit. You're right." I surreptitiously zipped it up. "How'd you notice that?"

"Henry's good on details," Meyer said.

"I hope he doesn't gross out Alice at the theater," I said.

"I'm sure he'll be on his best behavior, provided the play is good," Meyer said. "He isn't tolerant of poor performances."

"If they've sent a cast all the way from the

mainland, I'm sure it's good," I replied.

Henry pulled himself out of his chair, threw his napkin on the table, and waddled away.

I leaned toward Meyer. "Before the ladies arrived, I thought over what happened to my forehead. It's the same type of wound the murder victim received."

"You don't suppose. . . ."

"Let's go check it out."

We walked to the corner where Meyer said I was found.

"Gully off to the side," I said. "Just grass. Nothing hard that I could have hit my head on." Then I noticed it. A Heineken bottle with dried blood on it.

CHAPTER 13

"The same person who killed Tiegan and set me up, hit me with a Heineken bottle," I said to Meyer as we walked back to Kina Nani.

"He must have been trying to kill you, as well."

"Good thing I have a hard head, otherwise you and Henry would have a table to yourselves."

I thought back over all that I had read in my journal. "And it would have to be someone who knew of the litigation between Tiegan and me. The killer didn't just drop the murder weapon in my room. He knew I had a motive. People who knew that include Barry Tiegan, Tiegan's lawyer, my lawyer, and Denny."

"But why would the murderer want to get you out of the way after he went to all the trouble to set you up for the murder?"

"He wouldn't, unless my snooping was

getting close. He must know that I was talking to people about Swiss stamps."

Just as we reached our building, I looked over at Meyer and saw a wet spot on the front of his pants.

"Uh oh," I said. "We better get up to your apartment right away."

Meyer's right hand grazed the front of his pants, and a look of pure panic swept over his face. Then he shot ahead of me at double time.

Once back at his place, he went into his bathroom to clean up and change his clothes.

While I waited for him, I picked up a scrapbook that lay on his coffee table and opened it. I leafed through letters to the editor, neatly clipped and mounted in clear plastic sleeves. I picked one at random:

Dear Editor,
In the upcoming election, I hope that all citizens pay close attention to the record of the incompetents seeking re-election to the city council. These are the people who over the last four years have resisted approving a new shopping center for our town. They have cited the need to protect the small town atmosphere and reduce traffic and congestion. All noble

causes. But they overlooked one important point. We need to have a tax base to pay for the basic services necessary to maintain our quality of life. The police force, social services, parks and recreation need funding. Our illustrious city council has suddenly realized that we have a tax revenue deficit. Duh! If all the citizens go elsewhere to shop, the tax dollars are flowing out of our city. Members of the city council seem surprised. It doesn't take a rocket scientist to figure out that not spending money locally equals no tax revenue. I urge you to vote the rascals out. Let's elect a new city council that understands the basics of economics and can apply a modicum of common sense to financing our local government.

It was signed "Meyer Ohana."

When Meyer returned, I pointed to the scrapbook. "Looks like you vent to the newspapers."

"Absolutely. I mentioned this before, but you may not remember. Whenever I encountered stupidity, I wrote a letter to the editor. It could have been a full-time job with all the incompetence around."

"You should take on the folks who run

this prison," I said.

"Nah. Half the fun is seeing the letters in print. I liked taking on issues that the newspapers were interested in."

"Was this part of being a lawyer?"

"I'm sure it was attributed to a combination of my attention deficit disorder and my legal background," he said. "I always enjoyed a good argument."

"You don't strike me as that way now."

Meyer wrinkled his brow. "I'm sure I've mellowed with age. I'm not as feisty as I used to be."

"Back to the matter at hand," I said. "Has this little problem of yours happened before?"

"It's only been this bad in the last week. Don't tell anyone."

"It's not about saying anything. People can see the results."

He hung his head. "If this continues, I'll have to go to a care home. I don't want that."

"Just use those old fogy diapers."

"I may have to resort to using them, although I hate to admit it."

"Better than having wet pants."

Meyer grabbed my shoulder. "Please don't mention this to anyone. I'm not ready to go to a care home."

"What's the big deal? It just means there's someone to help you."

"I've been to visit the care home facility here. Have you seen it?"

"Not that I remember," I said.

"It has six small sterile rooms. You're cooped up all day with five other people who can't care for themselves. I couldn't take that."

"Doesn't seem that much different than being stuck here with Henry and me."

"This is different," he said. "It was bad enough to give up my condo to come here, but I'm independent. I can set my own schedule and do what I want."

"Like eating at defined times and wetting your pants?"

"You obviously don't appreciate the situation."

"I know that if my brain gives out any more, I'll be sent out to pasture," I said.

"I'm taking you down to the care home facility right now. You need to see what the problem is."

"Fine by me. First I'm going to call the police to have them check the Heineken bottle in the ditch."

I returned to my apartment and found Detective Saito's card. After a five-minute wait I was connected with him.

"This is Paul Jacobson. I'm back from the hospital after getting bashed on my noggin."

"Yes, Mr. Jacobson."

"I checked the site where I was found unconscious and discovered a Heineken bottle with some blood on it."

"And why would that be important?"

"Because Tiegan was hit with a Heineken bottle, as well."

"And how would you know that, Mr. Jacobson?"

CHAPTER 14

I met Meyer in the lobby, and we walked down the road to a set of bungalows.

"Whenever I speak with Detective Saito, I seem to say something that makes me appear guilty," I said.

"What now?"

I explained about the bottle.

"And since he doesn't know that I told you about the bottle, he can only conclude that you murdered Tiegan," Meyer said.

"Yeah. I'm going to be locked up, and someone tried to knock me off like Tiegan. It'll be hard to clear myself if I'm in jail."

Meyer led me inside one of the larger buildings. There was a common area with a dining table and a kitchen off to the side. A woman sat in a chair knitting, a man and woman watched TV from a couch, and another woman slept in a wheelchair. Walkers lined the wall.

"Looks like a pretty lively place," I said.

"This is as good as it gets," Meyer replied.

We walked toward one of the bedrooms.

I peeked inside. Just enough space for a bed and dresser.

"They even have to share a bathroom," he said.

"So this is our future," I said.

"That's it. You can see why I'm not in any rush to come here."

"Well, remember to pee in the toilet and not in your pants. Then there won't be any problem."

His face sagged. "It just happens. I can't control it anymore."

"Then you better go with Depends so you won't embarrass yourself."

We headed back up the hill. I tried to imagine living in one of those little rooms. I understood Meyer's concern. I didn't want to get stuck there either. Where I lived now was no picnic.

I returned to my apartment. Depressed and contemplating my future, I sat down and reread what I'd written in my journal. Since I couldn't remember any of the stuff, it was enlightening to review what I'd been doing lately. There I was, running solo, completely disengaged from my memory. At least I didn't have to worry about anything I'd done. What a picture. Living carefree from day to day, no regrets, no concerns, *no friggin' memory.*

I needed to activate my memory device. I called Marion.

"Any plans this evening?" I asked her.

"Well, I had thought of going to Las Vegas, but I suppose I could change it."

"Good. Let's you and me get together after dinner."

"Your place or mine?"

I looked around at the clothes strewn on chairs and an unread stack of books on the floor. "I'll be by at eight."

I caught the afternoon van to the shopping center and bought a bouquet of posies.

That evening after struggling to swallow one of my magic erection pills and checking the retirement home roster for Marion's apartment number, I arrived at her door and presented the flowers.

Her eyes lit up. "Thank you, Paul."

"Beautiful flowers for a beautiful woman."

She lowered her gaze. We were both good at this.

The flowers found a new home in a white vase on her dresser. Cole Porter music played, and we each downed a bourbon and water while we chatted on the couch.

"You look like an Arab sheik with that

bandage on your head," Marion said.

"Yes, my dear. I have returned from the dangers of the desert."

She giggled. "Will you have it off by the day of our theater trip?"

"I think so. That outing should be an interesting event." I thought of Meyer's problem and how Henry acted. "Do your friends know what they're getting into?"

"Actually, Alice suggested it. She thinks Henry's cute."

"That bald miscreant?"

"Some women find bald men sexy."

"Maybe so, but Henry's a little strange. Is she prepared for how he acts?"

"At our age you can't be picky, present company excepted."

"Present company excepted." I raised my glass. "And Carolyn and Meyer?"

"They should be fine. Meyer's a gentleman and Carolyn wants some companionship."

We talked a little more and then started grabbing and pawing each other like randy teenagers. Hands squeezed, tugged, groped, and eventually we removed each other's clothes. I'd have carried her to the bed except I'd have thrown my back out. We adjourned from the couch. Under the covers we caressed each other, but my right foot snagged in the sheet. In trying to extricate it, my calf cramped and turned into a knot, hard as a baseball. I jumped out of bed, stomping my foot to get rid of the cramp.

"What's wrong?" Marion pulled the sheet up to cover herself while I danced around naked in front of her.

"Just a native mating dance I learned a number of years ago."

I was in pain and the knot wouldn't go away.

Marion massaged my calf, but that tickled and I jerked my leg, bumping my ankle into the nightstand. Now I had pain in two places. Meanwhile, the Viagra kicked in and my penis went into a high salute.

I was alternately limping and hopping and my engorged penis continued to point toward the ceiling.

I finally got rid of the cramp enough that I could return to bed.

Marion guided me inside and we went at it like newlyweds. Just at the moment of release, my calf cramped up again and I let out a yell.

I lay there spent, in pain.

Marion said, "My goodness!"

What I had to go through to aid my memory.

CHAPTER 15

The next morning I remembered everything, but my ankle was swollen double its
normal size. I tried to get up from bed, but
couldn't walk. I called health services and
they sent an attendant with a wheelchair.

My ankle was wrapped, and the attendant
wheeled me down to breakfast.

Meyer squinted at me. "What happened
to you?"

"Too much sex," I replied and drank some
orange juice.

"If you're like that, I'd hate to think what
your partner looks like," Meyer said.

"She's died and gone to heaven," I said.

Henry actually looked up from his
scrambled eggs and made eye contact with
me. "One more phase and it's over."

"What's that supposed to mean?"

"First, the memory. Then the legs. Then
poof." Henry snapped his fingers.

"My condition is temporary. You're not

getting rid of me that easily. Besides, I have to stick around to see how things go during your theater date with the leggy Alice."

Henry smiled and returned to his sausage.

"You may be human after all," I said to the top of Henry's head.

After breakfast Meyer offered to wheel me back to my apartment.

"So what really happened?" he asked.

"I got wrapped up in what I was doing."

"Maybe this cure has too many side effects."

"That's for sure," I said. "I'm awfully old for this young stud business. How are things with your . . . little problem?"

"It's better. I'm trying to drink less liquid and remember to visit the bathroom more often."

We chatted a few more minutes. Then he left me with the TV remote in my hand and my foot propped up on a stool.

I was rediscovering why I hated soap operas when my doorbell rang.

"Come in," I shouted. "It's unlocked."

A stocky man in a dark suit entered.

"Are you an undertaker?" I asked. "Have I already died?"

"Very funny, Mr. Jacobson. We need to have one of our chats."

"I guess it is funny, because I don't remember meeting you."

He sighed like he was dealing with a retard and held out his badge.

"Oh, you're Detective Saito. My journal mentioned you. It's good to put a face with the name."

"I know what you claimed happened to your head, but what about your foot?"

"I bet you wouldn't believe me if I said it happened from too much sex."

He shook his head. "Describe your accident alongside the road."

"As you must know by now, I can't remember fiddle fart from day to day. But I write some things down. What I last read indicates I was found unconscious in a ditch. I don't know why or how I ended up there. Afterward, my friend Meyer and I returned to the scene and found a Heineken bottle with blood on it. That's why I called you."

"Interesting little stunt, Mr. Jacobson."

"What do you mean by that?"

"To distract us in the murder investigation, you tried to produce a diversion."

"Yeah, right," I said. "Like I popped myself on the forehead with a bottle."

"Maybe this friend of yours, Meyer, helped you."

"Go talk to him," I said.

"I will."

"Did you find the Heineken bottle in the ditch?"

"I did. Very convenient. So why were you hit over the head?"

"I think the real murderer found out I was snooping around and sent me a message."

"And what would you like to share with me relating to this snooping of yours?" Saito asked.

"Several basic facts. Someone managed to get into the trash chute and my apartment. That someone needed keys. The night watchman Moki has keys. Go arrest him."

"We've talked to him, Mr. Jacobson. But he had no motive for the murder and you did."

"Sure he did," I said. "To steal Tiegan's stamp collection. Go find the stamps."

"You visited stamp stores all over the island. I bet you're trying to find a buyer. I think you have the stamps, Mr. Jacobson."

"Where? Under my pillow?"

"You've hidden them somewhere," he said.

"That's something I certainly don't remember."

"You seem to have a selective memory, Mr. Jacobson." He tapped my leg. "But I don't think you'll be going anywhere for awhile."

After he left, I sat there thinking. My good buddy, Detective Saito. His mother probably loved him, but other than that what could I say? He reminded me of a bulldog that chain-smoked. Wouldn't want to get close to a bulldog. You'd get your fingers bitten off. I wished he'd go harass someone else. It was probably good that I didn't remember who he was each time he appeared. I had that one item of satisfaction with him. He'd irritate me even more if I could remember him each time we met. He wasn't exactly intimidating, but I didn't feel comfortable around him. He listened to me as if he were trying to find something to use against me.

An hour later my phone rang.

"Kina Nani home for the mentally and physically challenged," I said.

"It's Meyer."

"To what do I owe this pleasure?"

"I just finished talking with Detective Saito," he said.

"And how is my favorite member of the benevolent society of police?"

"He questioned me about our trip to your ditch."

"Yeah," I said. "We had that conversation this morning, as well."

"He thinks you staged it."

"Did he speculate that you were involved?"

"Yes," Meyer said, "but I set the record straight."

"Good. He still won't believe either of us, but I guess that's what he's paid to think."

Next morning I graduated to a walker, and within another day I hobbled around solo again and had even removed the bandage from the ditch incident. By then, my memory was back to its usual defective state.

Meyer made me visit the pool each day, claiming that paddling with the foam board was good physical therapy. My ankle continued to improve, and I was getting in good shape kicking like a maniac in the pool.

At breakfast Meyer said, "Today's the big day."

"I read in my journal that we're going to the theater," I said.

"This afternoon we're meeting in front of the building where a bus will pick us up."

"How are you doing with your little problem?"

"I'm not having any coffee or juice before we go to the theater. That should keep me from embarrassing myself today."

"Can you fill in any details other than what I read about this murder investigation?"

"You're still a suspect, but the police haven't been bugging you lately."

"I should be grateful for small favors," I said. "I guess I'll get rested up for the big event."

"Don't take a nap. You'll reset again."

"Okay. I'll read a book, instead."

At one o'clock we assembled in front of Kina Nani. I wore a tie and a sports coat. A group of women sat on benches by the curb. One woman jumped up when she saw me and ambled over. She grabbed my arm.

"I'm glad to see you," she said.

"Me too," I said, assuming this was the right woman. I looked at her closely. Didn't recognize her at all.

Meyer arrived. He paced back and forth, and then said, "Where's Henry?"

Someone suggested he call Henry's apartment, so Meyer raced back to the lobby. When he returned he said, "Henry's on his way. Where's the bus?"

"You're pretty hyper," I said to him.

He stopped his pacing and looked at me. Then he smiled. "Yeah. I guess you're right."

"Take a deep breath," I said.

Moments later Henry and the bus arrived. The crowd of mostly old women limped and shuffled toward the bus. Besides Meyer, Henry, and me, there were only two other men in the crowd.

My companion, still attached to my arm, and I found seats together.

"I love the theater," she said.

"What do you know about the show?"

"Are you kidding, Paul? Everyone knows the story of *Beauty and the Beast*."

"Never seen it."

"I saw it on the mainland once. In Boston."

"Isn't it a kids' show?"

"You wait and see. It has colorful costumes and great music."

She snuggled up against me, and I felt her warmth in the over-air-conditioned bus.

When we arrived in Honolulu, Meyer went into overdrive, herding everyone toward the building.

We accepted our programs from an usher and then took our seats. Meyer and Carolyn sat next to Marion and me, with Henry and Alice in front of us.

I leaned over and whispered in Henry's ear, "I have my eye on you. Keep your hands to yourself."

He responded by putting his hand on Alice's thigh. She flinched a little.

The lights dimmed, the orchestra played, and Marion put her head on my shoulder.

As the play progressed, I wondered whether Meyer was going to have an accident or not. I looked over at him. He was fidgeting, but his eyes were focused on the stage.

There were no problems and during the intermission, we were milling around the lobby, when Meyer came dashing up to me.

"I caught a glimpse of a man who looked like Barry Tiegan, the nephew of the murder victim," Meyer said.

I pictured my journal page. Barry lived in L.A. Why the hell would he be here?

Unless . . . he was following me.

Maybe he still believed I'd killed his uncle and stashed the stamps.

Or maybe Barry was the murderer.

Could he be the one who'd bopped me over the head with a beer bottle?

Before I could voice my suspicions to Meyer, we returned to our seats and the lights dimmed.

In the second act, as Lumiere and

Cogsworth encouraged the Beast to dance with Beauty, I heard a loud whack in front of me. Henry raised his hand to his cheek. Alice stood up and pushed her way past people to reach the aisle.

Marion saw what was going on and also stood up to leave. At that moment I smelled an acrid aroma. I leaned over toward Meyer and whispered, "Time to go."

He had been absorbed in the show, but immediately jumped up and pushed past people in our row. Voices behind us murmured, "Sit down."

I found Meyer in the bathroom. He was crying.

"I can't control it," he said.

"Did you clean yourself up?" I asked.

"Yes. But I had to wipe off my pants with a paper towel, and there's a big wet spot."

"Hand them to me and I'll dry them under the hand dryer."

He held his trousers up over the top of the stall.

While drying the pants, another man came into the restroom. He looked at me askance.

"Dry cleaning service," I said.

He turned away from me and headed toward a urinal.

Once the pants were dry, I pushed them

over the top of the stall and returned to the lobby.

Alice was waving her hands and shouting, "That jerk!"

"Calm down," Marion said.

"Anything I can do, ladies?" I asked as I approached them.

Eyes flashing, Alice looked at me. "Creep!" she shouted, and stomped off to the powder room.

"What happened?" I asked.

"Your friend Henry tried to feel her up."

"Henry's not my friend. He just happens to sit at my table. This whole thing wasn't my idea anyway."

"You're all jerks," Marion said with a sputter. She turned away from me and dashed toward the ladies' room.

I stood there, speechless. I was not going to get any assistance with my memory tonight.

Meyer returned, tugging at his trousers.

"Pants a little wrinkled, but you pass inspection," I said.

"How am I going to face Carolyn?"

"You're in fine shape, but Henry's a pariah, and I'm guilty by association."

When Marion and Alice returned from the ladies' room, Marion pointed at me. "You go sit next to Henry."

"Yes, ma'am," I replied and saluted.

She glowered, grabbed Alice's arm, and they headed to their seats. Meyer and I followed.

When I sat down next to Henry, I whispered to him, "I'm your new date. Don't get fresh or I'll clock you."

He moved his hand toward me, thought better of it, and put his hand back in his lap.

I watched the Beast transform into a prince. I wondered if Henry could transform into a human being.

As we left the theater, Marion, Alice, and Carolyn chattered away. Henry said nothing, Meyer looked glum, and I tagged along.

I tried to strike up a conversation with Marion. "You were right. That was quite a performance. No kids' show."

She looked at me like I was a bug ready to be squashed and went back to her conversation with her trio.

I put my arm around Henry's shoulder. "You've really made us all popular."

He shrugged my arm away. "You're all a bunch of twats."

"You're a sweetie, Henry." I turned toward Meyer. "How you doing?"

"I guess I didn't embarrass myself too much."

"Yeah. Henry provided good diversionary cover. And that's the only positive thing anyone can say about Henry right now."

I got stuck sitting next to Henry on the bus.

"Do you have any idea what the effect is when you do something stupid?" I asked him.

"Do you know what an idiot you are, Paul?"

"Let's keep this focused on you for the moment. At least I can control my hands."

"She was asking for it."

"Right. Alice asked you to goose her in the middle of the theater."

"No. In the crotch." He chuckled and looked out the window.

I spotted an empty seat at the back of the bus and moved there.

When the bus arrived back at Kina Nani, I waited for everyone to get off, and then I went to my room by myself, resisting the temptation to stuff Henry down the trash chute.

CHAPTER 16

The next morning, I came down to breakfast and followed the directions I had left for myself to find table eleven. I looked at the white-bearded guy and the bald-headed one. "You're Meyer and Henry," I said.

Meyer grinned. "You're getting good at this, Paul."

"I followed the note on my nightstand. Still don't recognize you."

"Have a seat and relax, especially after yesterday's fiasco."

"What fiasco?"

"You must have described it in your journal."

"My instructions this morning said to read the journal, but to skip yesterday's entry."

Meyer chuckled. "That's a good remedy. You didn't want to remember what happened."

■ ■ ■ ■

After breakfast a woman came up to me and put her hand on my arm. I gathered from what I had read that this was Marion.

"Paul, I think I overreacted a little yesterday. You were right. I shouldn't have blamed you for Henry's action."

Since I didn't remember, I was magnanimous. "No problem. Apology accepted."

She squeezed my arm.

I considered some of the things from my journal. "How'd you like to go out for dinner tonight?"

Her eyes lit up. "I'd love that."

"Meet you in the lobby at seven."

I decided to take a walk. A little exercise would help the old body.

I strolled out the gate, along neighboring streets, and returned to the lobby of my palatial manor half an hour later.

A short, stocky man in a suit stood inside the front door.

"You look in pretty good shape, Mr. Jacobson," he said.

"Yeah. Not too shabby for an old fossil. Do I know you?"

He crinkled his mouth into a half smile.

"Here we go again. I'm Detective Saito."

"Oh. The Columbo of the Kaneohe police department."

"Seems to me that you certainly seem fit enough to have carried a body down the hallway and deposited it in a trash chute."

"No," I said. "I'm not into body lifting. But I was fit enough to have been sound asleep in my apartment when that happened."

"I stopped by to find out if you were ready to confess to the murder."

"From what I've read, you're spending an awful lot of time visiting me. Don't you have a large caseload with other people to harass?"

"It's just that I enjoy our conversations so much, Mr. Jacobson."

"I'm glad someone's getting pleasure from them. Doesn't do much for me."

"Once you confess to the murder, it will save us all a great deal of time and effort."

"You've already had one person confess. That didn't solve the crime. A confession from me would be worth just as much. Go get Moki to confess."

"This routine is getting old, Mr. Jacobson."

"But not as old as I am."

After Saito left, I took the elevator up to

my apartment. I had images of hanging by my arms in a dank dungeon. Obviously, he wasn't going to give up thinking I was the murderer. Still, he didn't seem to have enough evidence to arrest me or I'd already be in jail. I'd have to try and solve this murder myself, since it didn't look as if the police were going to do anything but bug me.

Inspired by Saito breathing down my neck, I called all the stamp stores to inquire if anyone had come in trying to sell Swiss stamps. I connected with all of them except one of the stores in Honolulu, which had a recorded message. No one had any news for me.

That afternoon I checked the phone book, found an Italian restaurant in Kailua, called to make a reservation, and arranged for a cab.

As I sat down to contemplate the possibilities of the evening ahead, the phone rang. It was my son Denny.

"Just wanted to remind you that we'll be there to take you out to dinner tomorrow night."

"I had forgotten."

"We spoke two days ago," he said in a clipped tone.

"Unless I write something down, it goes in one brain cell and out the other. I'll jot down a reminder as soon as we get off the phone. Where are you staying?"

"At the Princess Kaiulani in Waikiki. Jennifer's anxious to learn how to surf."

"My little granddaughter will be here?"

"She's not so little anymore," Denny said. "Eleven going on twenty. Our flight arrives around two P.M. With getting the luggage, picking up the rental car, checking into the hotel, and all, we'll be over around six."

"I'll be waiting."

"Don't eat dinner. We could be delayed, but we'll take you to Buzz's for a good steak."

"I'd like that," I said. "Better than the dog food I had for lunch today."

There was a pause on the line. "It's not that bad. I've eaten there."

"Yeah. It's passable. But not much variety. I'll be ready for a nice dripping steak."

"Good," he said. "See you tomorrow."

I immediately wrote myself a note and put it on my nightstand next to my journal. That provided another reason to give my memory a jolt.

Marion and I had a pleasant dinner together.

"That was quite a play we saw yesterday," she said.

Not remembering anything, I answered, "Sure was." I changed the subject. "My family's coming to visit tomorrow. You'll have to meet them while they're here."

She gave me a coy smile.

Score one for the Gipper.

Later, sated on young cow and red wine, we scrambled up to her apartment, grappled a little, and ended up in her bed. I performed pretty well for an old guy and didn't suffer a heart attack. It seemed like we were back to where we were before whatever happened the day before.

When she fell asleep, I dressed and slipped back to my apartment. I read what was in the journal from the day before. This guy Henry was really a jerk. From what I understood, I'd wake up tomorrow remembering everything from today. That would be useful since I'd be seeing my family.

Next morning I jumped out of bed. I was alert, remembered the day before, and knew my family was coming to visit! Since they were all I had, I looked forward to seeing them. My son Denny in his quiet efficient way. Allison, a good supportive spouse, always treated me well. A down-to-earth person. And Jennifer. I wondered what my granddaughter was like now. I remembered a little six-year-old, zooming all over the place like a car with an oversized engine and no steering. I had read that she was eleven now. Denny was a pretty active kid at that age. Kept knocking things over in the living room all the time.

I needed to get a present for Jennifer. I could catch the van to the shopping center later in the morning.

At breakfast I wasted no time. "Meyer, what would be a good present for an eleven-year-old girl?"

"You recognized me right off," he said.

"Memory's as clear as a polished window pane this morning."

"Guess you and Marion made up."

"Something like that. Any suggestions for a gift?"

"Girls that age are past dolls," Meyer said. "She's too young for a car." He scratched his head. "I don't know."

"Henry," I said. "Any ideas?"

"Boogie board," he said.

"Not bad," I replied. "She wants to learn to surf while she's here."

So I had one idea for a present for Jennifer. After breakfast I wandered over to Marion's table and bowed to the trio of women.

"Good morning, ladies."

Marion smiled at me. "Hello, Paul."

"I have a question that I thought you might be able to help me with," I said. "My eleven-year-old granddaughter is coming to visit, and I'm trying to decide on a present for her."

"Clothes," Carolyn said. "Get her a Hawaiian outfit."

"What are her interests?" Marion asked.

"She wants to learn to surf, and Henry suggested a boogie board."

"That creep," Alice said.

"He's not just a creep," I replied. "He's a jerk. But it's the best idea I've heard so far."

"He should be locked up." Alice stood up from the table and threw her napkin down. She stomped off.

I sat down in her place. "Other ideas?"

Carolyn and Marion discussed clothes for a few minutes. Finally, Marion snapped her fingers. "I know the perfect gift. Does she like stuffed animals?"

"I think so," I said.

"There's a line of Hawaiian collectibles like Beanie Babies. If you want, I can go with you to the store this morning. Point them out to you."

"That would be great," I said. "I hate to shop."

"Whereas we love to shop. Right, Carolyn?"

Carolyn nodded.

Marion and I agreed to meet in front of the building to catch the nine o'clock van to the shopping center.

At the store, Marion showed me a rack of stuffed animals. Each had a Hawaiian name and an attached passport encased in plastic. I scrutinized a white albatross with a lei around its neck, a multi-colored patchwork fish, and a green sea turtle.

"This will be perfect," I said.

"If she likes these, you can give her others from the set for future presents."

"I'll have to remember which ones I've given her."

"Keep a list," Marion said.

We picked out a mongoose, myna bird, and porpoise. "That's a good representation," I said. "Land, air, and sea."

"I'll help you wrap them when we get back," Marion said. "I have some gift paper and ribbon in my apartment."

Marion took good care of me and back at her place I soon had a professionally wrapped present for Jennifer.

Later, after I returned to my apartment, I

was looking for a clean tee shirt in a dresser drawer when I came across a picture of a young girl. On the back was printed the name JENNIFER. I'll be darned. That was what my granddaughter looked like. She had a vague resemblance to a six-year-old I remembered. I placed Jennifer's picture next to Marion's. My two favorite girls.

I realized my place was a mess. With visitors coming, I needed to apply a little spit and polish. I threw all my wrinkled clothes that were piled on two chairs into a basket, hid my Viagra in the medicine cabinet, and put half a dozen unread books back on the bookshelf. As I was making the bed, I noticed a piece of paper between the mattress and the night stand. Leaving it there wouldn't pass muster, so I picked it up and squinted at a phone number in my handwriting with three firm underlines. What was it? Dropping it on the nightstand, I finished cleaning up.

With everything as neat as the hair on Henry's bald head, I declared the cleaning session over.

The scrap of paper beckoned to me with an implied message that something was important.

What the hell? I dialed the number.

"Sampson's Stamp and Coin," a man said.

It was one of the stamp stores I had called, the one where I had heard a recorded message.

"Is this the store owner?" I asked.

"Yeah. This is Mel Sampson."

"My name is Paul Jacobson. I spoke with you a few weeks ago concerning a collection of Swiss stamps."

"Right. And I called you back."

"You did?"

"A man came in wanting to find a buyer for a collection of Swiss stamps," he said.

My old ticker beat like when I humped Marion.

"I told him I wasn't prepared to buy at this time, but might know someone interested," Sampson said. "I gave your name to him. He first looked angry and then indicated he'd contact you."

I felt a tightening in my stomach.

"Later I started thinking I should give you a heads-up. That's when I called you."

"My memory's not too hot," I said. "Can you repeat what you told me when you called?"

"Not much. I mentioned the man coming into my shop. Then you said your doorbell was ringing and you'd call me back. I didn't hear from you until just now."

"Do you remember what day that was?"

There was silence on the phone and the sound of paper rustling in the background.

"Must have been two weeks ago. It was the day the shop was busy. I think a Tuesday."

I knew exactly what day that was.

"Did you get the man's name?" I asked.

"No. He didn't identify himself."

"What did he look like?"

"Tall haole guy. Short black hair and a scar on his cheek, like he'd gotten into a fight."

After I hung up I started thinking. If it wasn't Moki, who was this guy trying to sell Swiss stamps?

CHAPTER 17

I had one thing to check out. I reread my journal and verified the date I'd been found in the ditch. Then I went down to the receptionist and asked to look at the sign-in log for that date. I scanned the names. Only two visitors that morning. Both women. Another dead end, so I returned to my apartment.

Later, I remembered not to go down to dinner and was reading a book when my phone rang. Denny said, "We're on our way. Be ready in thirty minutes."

"My appetite is ready for fresh meat," I said.

They arrived as predicted. Denny shook my hand, but my daughter-in-law Allison and granddaughter Jennifer both gave me hugs. "Welcome to my palace," I said.

"Grandpa, you have a great view!" Jennifer raced over to the sliding glass door to look out. She then scampered around my small room. "You have my picture! And another one." She picked up the photograph of Marion. "Who's this?"

No secrets from this girl. "That's a friend of mine named Marion."

"Cool," Jennifer said.

"We better get going so we don't miss our reservation," Denny said.

I remembered to grab the shopping bag with Jennifer's present inside.

After we ordered steaks, I pulled the wrapped present out of the bag.

"A little something for you, Jennifer."

Her eyes lit up and she tore off the wrapping paper to find the three stuffed animals. "Cool. Look at the mongoose, Mom." She lined up all three in front of her on the table. "They have Hawaiian names. Apike Wikiwike, speedy mongoose; Niniu, a porpoise, and Ohi Ohi, a myna bird."

"Each has its own passport," I pointed out. "Like an international traveler."

She picked the animals up and danced them around the table in front of her.

Allison leaned over and whispered in my ear. "A great present. You've made a hit."

After the raw cow arrived, Denny cleared his throat. "How's your memory, Dad?"

"Who are you?" I asked.

He scowled. "Very funny."

"Most mornings I don't remember anything from the day before. Other than that, I'm Mister Memory Man."

Jennifer, who I thought wasn't paying attention, suddenly looked at me and frowned. "Grandpa. Isn't there anything that helps your memory?"

I laughed. "Once in a while I remember. But most days it's a blank when I wake up."

"There are some days that I'd like to forget," Jennifer said. "Like when Patty and I fought. But most mornings I like to think back about the day before." She paused. "How do you know what you're going to do each day?"

"That's the problem. Every night I have to write down what's happened and leave a reminder note to myself ."

"That's silly," Jennifer said. "It's like being two people. I have a surfboard lesson tomorrow. If I were you, I'd have to leave a note to remind myself to go surfing."

"If you were me, you wouldn't go near a surfboard. I hate the ocean."

"Grandpa, how can someone hate the ocean?"

"I don't like getting in it. I sink, and there are things in it I don't want to get to know."

"Jennifer's a good swimmer," Allison

interjected. "She'll be on a summer swim team when we get home."

"Freestyle is my best stroke. Our relay team is going after a club record this summer." Jennifer paused again. "Grandpa, if you can't remember every day when you wake up, how will you remember me?"

I laughed. "I can't forget you. Besides, I have your picture on my dresser to remind me. You'll have to send me a new picture once a year so I can see how you look." I turned to Denny. "Something I just thought of. You and Allison should have a nice dinner together while you're here. Why don't you let Jennifer come visit me tomorrow evening, and you two can have some time to yourselves?"

"And I can meet Grandpa's friends," Jennifer said.

Denny and Allison looked at each other.

Denny said, "Sure, why not?"

Allison nodded.

We made plans for them to drop Jennifer off before dinner the next day.

"Then I can hear all about your surfing lesson," I said, "and you can have some of my gourmet food."

Denny wrinkled his brow and gave me a look, but I ignored it.

Allison reached in her purse and handed

me a small manila envelope. "We have a present for you."

I opened the envelope and found half a dozen letters. "What are these?"

"I sorted through a box of old pictures and memorabilia Denny packed up when you moved out of your condo," Allison said. "I found these letters your dad wrote. I thought you might enjoy reading them."

"Didn't know anything like that was still kicking around. Jennifer and I can read them tomorrow night."

"I like reading, Grandpa. I'm in the middle of *One Flew Over the Cuckoo's Nest.*"

"Isn't that a little grown up for you?"

She leveled a stare at me. "Grandpa, I'm going into the sixth grade next year."

"I thought you'd be reading something like *Black Beauty.*"

She rolled her eyes. "That's a kid's book. I enjoy adult fiction."

"And she reads constantly," Allison said. "She'd rather read than watch TV."

"I like to imagine what characters look like when I read," Jennifer said.

"With me, I try to imagine what I've already read," I said.

"You should read short stories instead," Jennifer said.

I looked at her. This girl was sharp.

"You've got something there. I'm struggling through this one novel. I don't read much of it because I spend too much time going back to see what's happened."

"I'd recommend O. Henry," Jennifer said.

Out of the mouth of babes.

"Maybe you and I can make a trip to a bookstore while you're here," I said.

"I love bookstores," Jennifer said. "There's so much to choose from. But I also order books online. Do you use a computer, Grandpa?"

"No. I'm awfully old to learn."

"I could teach you."

"I bet you could."

"I'm going back to the salad bar to get some more of those baby tomatoes," Jennifer said.

She jumped up and skipped off.

"What a ball of fire," I said. "If you could bottle that enthusiasm, you could sell it all over the place I'm stuck in."

After dinner Jennifer said, "Let's stop at a bookstore."

"There used to be one in Kailua right along the way we're going," I said.

"I thought you couldn't remember things," Denny said.

"This is a place I went to probably ten

years ago. I remember stuff from then fine. It's yesterday that's disappeared."

We parked and as we walked toward the store, I spotted a pod from a eucalyptus tree embedded in a pile of slender leaves on the sidewalk.

"You ever spin a top?" I asked Jennifer.

"What's a top?"

"It's a toy your dad used to play with. At different times of year kids used tops, yo-yos, and marbles."

"What about video games?"

"Didn't exist. Here's how a top works." I put the stem of the pod between my thumb and middle finger and flicked it. The pod spun on the sidewalk.

"Cool," Jennifer said. "Let me try it."

After a few failed attempts, the pod spun.

"Take that home to astound your friends with," I said.

"They'd be more impressed with a new video game," Jennifer said.

Inside the store she helped me pick out a collection of O. Henry stories and an anthology of murder mystery short stories. I was actually looking forward to reading now, knowing what the problem had been. Wouldn't even matter if I reread the same story. I'd enjoy it as new.

■ ■ ■ ■

The next morning, after I read my instructions to myself and reviewed my journal, I went down to the dining room and made plans for dinner. I lined up a guest table and invited Meyer, Henry, and Marion to join me.

"You can wow my granddaughter with baseball trivia," I said to Henry.

"I hope she's smarter than you are."

"Oh, she is. She'll run circles around you, Henry."

"We'll see." He actually smiled.

That evening my doorbell rang. After I opened it, Jennifer galloped into my apartment.

Denny and Allison waved good-bye and took off.

Jennifer was still bouncing around my place when the doorbell rang again. I opened it, thinking Denny and Allison had forgotten something.

"Mr. Jacobson, it's time for your medicine."

"You're Melanie," I said.

"Of course. Are you starting to remember me?"

"From this morning anyway."

Melanie saw Jennifer. "Oh, I didn't know you had company."

"Yeah, I better not bother with the horse pills while my granddaughter's here."

Melanie wagged her finger at me and smiled. "You can't get off that easy." She moved inside and unlocked my medicine box.

I should have thrown that thing off my balcony.

Jennifer skipped over and watched as Melanie handed three huge pills to me with a glass of water.

"Do you like your job?" Jennifer asked.

Melanie smiled and shrugged. "It's good training. I'm taking classes to become a registered nurse."

"I'm going to be a doctor," Jennifer said.

While they bantered back and forth, I managed to swallow the three pills without choking. After Melanie left I said, "Well, what did you think of Nurse Ratched?"

Jennifer clucked her tongue. "Oh, Grandpa. She's not anything like Nurse Ratched. Melanie's pretty and nice."

She circled the place one more time as if to let me know she approved of my digs and then said, "I'm hungry. When do we eat?"

I looked at my watch. "I think they start

serving dinner at six. We can go downstairs now, if you like. My friends should be joining us soon."

"Cool. Let's go."

Near the elevators, Jennifer poked her head into a common room.

"Computers! Come see, Grandpa."

I followed her inside the room. She sat down and started pounding on a keyboard.

"You should get an Internet account," she said. "Then we could send email to each other."

"What's wrong with good old regular mail? You know, letters."

"Oh, Grandpa. That's so old-fashioned. I have email friends all over the world. It's so easy and you don't have to wait days or weeks. Come see this picture."

I looked at the screen.

"Here's Nurse Ratched from the movie. She doesn't look anything like Melanie."

"You found a picture that quickly?"

"Sure."

I remembered something I read in my journal that morning. "Why don't you see if you can find some obscure baseball fact."

"How come?"

"It'll be something fun we can do at dinner," I said.

"Okey, dokey." She tapped away at the

keyboard, paused, looked at the screen, and then tapped again.

"Here's one. The Brooklyn Dodgers went on a tour of Japan in 1956."

"We'll try that one," I said.

As we waited for the elevator, Jennifer said, "Grandpa, why don't you learn to use a computer? You have a room full of them right here on your floor."

"At my age it's hard to learn new things. I grew up before computers."

"You're never too old to learn something new. I'm just now learning to ride a surfboard. You can do it if you really want to." She set her lips and stared at me.

"I guess I really don't want to," I said.

She shook her head. "Grandpa, I don't know what I'm going to do with you."

"I guess you're stuck with me the way I am."

When we entered the dining hall, Marion was already at the table waiting for us. I introduced my two girls to each other.

Jennifer's eyes lit up. "I saw your picture on Grandpa's dresser."

Marion smiled at me. "So you really did keep it."

"Of course," I said. I turned toward Jennifer. "Marion helped me pick out the Hawaiian stuffed animals for you."

"Those were great! I especially like the mongoose. Did you know mongooses were brought to Hawaii to catch rats?"

"You have more facts than Henry," I said. "Speaking of Henry, here he comes."

Henry waddled over and sat down. Meyer joined us moments later.

Meyer and Jennifer hit it right off. They started discussing surfing while Henry slurped his soup.

"Jennifer, you might want to ask Henry some baseball facts," I said.

"Okay," she said. "What team went on a tour to what country in what year in the 1950s?"

Henry looked up from his soup, liquid dripping from his mouth. He wrinkled his brow. He clenched his teeth. Finally, he squeezed his hands into tight balls. "It would have to be the Yankees, Dodgers, or Giants. It could be to the Caribbean or the Orient. Let me think."

You could almost hear the gears turning and see smoke coming out of his head. "Yankees to Cuba in 1954?"

"Nope," Jennifer said. "Dodgers to Japan in 1956."

Henry sagged in his chair.

"That's okay, Henry," I said. "We still respect you, even if you've been stumped by an eleven-year-old."

"First time this ever happened," Meyer said. He stood up and started pacing around the table.

Henry glared at us, then returned to his soup.

"There's a concert tonight at seven, lasts an hour," Marion said to me. "You and Jennifer want to come?"

"What kind of concert?" I asked.

"The Punahou School choir is singing."

I looked at Jennifer. She thought for a moment. "Why don't you go with your friends, Grandpa. I'll wait upstairs. I've brought my book to read."

After dinner I helped Jennifer settle into the easy chair in my apartment and adjusted the light for her.

"Why was your friend Meyer walking back and forth behind his chair?" she asked.

"Not much escapes you, does it?"

"I notice things. What was he doing, Grandpa?"

"He has an attention deficit disorder. He gets hyper at times and starts pacing."

"Oh. I had a kid like that in my class last year. Couldn't sit still."

"That sounds like the same thing. Now,

you're sure you don't mind being up here alone?"

"I'll be fine. I have to read more about the real Nurse Ratched."

At the concert, I sat next to Marion and held her hand. The kids in the choir sang a medley of Hawaiian songs and then ended with a round of pop tunes.

"Jennifer would have enjoyed hearing this," Marion said afterward.

"She seemed intent on reading her book, but I need to get right back."

I decided to sneak up on Jennifer. I opened the door to my apartment and tiptoed in. She was sitting in the middle of the rug, not reading her book, but reading my journal.

"What are you doing?" I shouted.

She flinched. "Grandpa, this is so interesting, what you've been writing."

"That's my private journal."

"It's all right. I'm not going to tell anyone. I keep a journal, but I like yours better."

"We need to talk," I said.

"Sure." Rising from the rug, she stacked the sheets of paper and sat on the couch. "How was the concert?"

"Don't change the subject. There are things in my journal that you shouldn't be reading."

"You mean being a murder suspect? I know you didn't do it."

"I'm glad for the vote of confidence," I said.

"But I know who did."

"Are you some kind of super detective?"

"No, I just read what you wrote," Jennifer said. "You also know who it is."

"Yeah, but go ahead and tell me anyway."

"See, someone hit Mr. Tiegan with a bottle and stole his stamp collection. Then he went to the stamp store to try to sell it. It's the man with a scar on his cheek."

"How do you suppose he got into my apartment to discard the bottle, then into the trash chute to get rid of Tiegan?"

"Easy. He copied the keys."

It all clicked. "You're a genius," I said. "That must be it. He stole Moki's keys. All along I thought Moki was involved."

"So all you have to do is find the man with the scar on his cheek."

"That should be easy. I can walk around Oahu until I find him."

She clucked her tongue. "No, Grandpa. You need to set a trap."

"I think I inadvertently already did that. Ended up in a ditch."

"You have to try again. Something to flush him out." She thought for a moment. "Besides the stamp stores, you should get more word out that you want to buy a Swiss stamp collection."

"We'll discuss that later. Now, about reading my journal, young lady. I also wrote some pretty intimate details that weren't for other eyes."

"Oh, the sex with Marion? That's okay. I know all about sex."

"You do?"

"We had a sex-ed class in school this last year," Jennifer said. "Mom and Dad won't discuss it, but the teacher answered all my questions."

"I need to explain about Marion and me. . . ."

"Are you going to marry her?"

"We're pretty old for that," I said. "I'd be hard to live with. No memory and all."

She pursed her lips. "You and Marion could live together without getting married."

"What kind of comment is that?"

"You should do what makes you happy. For me, I've decided not to have sex until I'm twenty-one."

"You could wait until you're married or in your eighties."

"Oh, Grandpa. You say the funniest things."

"I thought I was being serious."

"Kids my age are curious about sex. Still doesn't mean that I'm going to rush into it or that I'll wait forever."

"Just wait until you're really in love with someone."

She smiled at me. "That's exactly what I've decided. I'm not planning to be in love until I'm twenty-one."

"You can't always predict those things."

"But I have so many things to do in the next ten years. Once I graduate from college, then it will be different."

"Have you planned your life that far ahead?"

She laughed. "You sound like my mom. She's always telling me to lighten up. Parents are never satisfied. If I were a troublemaker, they'd be upset. Since I know what I want to do, they worry I'll grow up too serious."

"I'm still not pleased that you read my journal."

"It can be our secret, Grandpa. There's one other thing I read while I was waiting."

"Uh oh. What's that?"

"The letters from your dad that my mom gave to you. Have you read them yet?"

"I don't think I have. I don't remember for sure."

"There's one in particular you should see." Jennifer walked over to my dresser and selected a letter. "I'll read it to you."

She settled onto the couch, unfolded the letter and started reading: " 'Dear Marge —' "

"That was my mom's name. Your great-grandmother."

Jennifer nodded and continued. " 'I hope to wrap up this trip in another two weeks. Then I can get back home to you and Paul. I've closed three good-sized deals so we'll be able to buy that new ice box. One disconcerting thing happened today. I went to see Mr. Andrews at Granger to get him to reorder. His secretary told me I had already been to see him the day before. I checked my order book and sure enough, I had an order written down from the day before. I still don't remember going there. I must have been on the road too long and my memory is getting mushy. Give Paul a hug from me, and I have one saved for you. Love, Bart.' "

My skin felt clammy as it sank in.

"Your dad had memory problems too," Jennifer said.

"I never realized that. He died of a stroke when I was nineteen, but I never paid much attention to what was going on. I was in my own world, and my dad was gone a lot."

"You inherited your bad memory, Grandpa."

"So that's what's in store for me," I said. "A stroke. At least I've lived longer than he did. He died when he was in his late fifties."

"Did you miss him?"

"Of course. It's always hard when your father dies."

"Since you don't remember things, do you remember how you feel?"

"That's a strange question."

"Just wondering."

The doorbell rang, and it was Denny and Allison.

"Did you two have a good evening together?" Denny asked.

Jennifer grabbed her book and headed for the door. "Yes. I learned a lot about Grandpa." She turned toward me, gave me a wink, and skipped out the door.

After they left, I sat there, running my hand over my journal. My mind rumbled around with thoughts pertaining to the energy of youth and how I was going through what my father must have also experienced. I wondered what was in store for me. Then I pondered the question Jennifer had asked me. Did I remember what I felt yesterday?

Chapter 18

The next morning I woke up as confused as could be. Where the hell was I? Then I saw a note on the nightstand: "Read this and try to think how you felt yesterday."

What a dumb note.

I considered chucking the pile of paper, thought better of it, and finally sat down to digest what was written there.

Damn. My granddaughter had visited me, and I remembered zip.

I had written all this crap to make up for a defective memory. I didn't know whether to laugh or slit my wrists. Instead, I tried to answer the comment in the note. How did I feel?

I felt like the guy who woke up and discovered he was a cockroach. One moment in a blissful dream and the next in a world I didn't recognize. Nothing stuck from the day before. No event, no people, no specific feelings. Then a wave of sadness broke over me. My granddaughter and I had spent time together, and it was like reading about someone else's life. My feelings? Sadness. Regret. Reaching out for something that wasn't there. A mirage. A chimera.

My brain was stuffed full of old memories. Five years old and going to a park with my mom. Learning to drive a Model T in Long Beach. Getting married. Missing Rhonda. But yesterday? A blank. A void. Nada.

Fear gripped my gut. *Cut it out, you old fool. You have a brain that's on strike. Some people lose their legs, others their lungs. You got dealt mush in your cranium.*

And on top of it all, I was the prime suspect in a murder investigation. Jennifer had given me an idea, and I needed to do something. Immediately.

I dressed and followed the directions from the journal: down to the second floor, table eleven.

The bald-headed and white-bearded guys mentioned in the journal sat at the table.

"Your granddaughter is a dynamo," the white-haired guy said.

"Yeah, apparently so, from what I read."

"Keep writing in your journal," he said.

"I don't know what good it's doing. I don't recognize you. You're like a character in some novel I read."

"The name's Meyer," he said, holding out his hand.

We shook.

"Say, Meyer, I have a favor to ask you."

He looked at me. "What's that?"

"My granddaughter triggered a great idea for flushing out the murderer. I'm going to place an ad in the newspaper. I need a phone number for anyone answering the ad to call."

"Why not use your own number?"

"Concluding from what I read this morning, the murderer already has my phone number and might recognize it."

"What do you want me to do if he calls?"

"Set up a meeting at Star Stamp and Coin in Kailua. The pretext will be that you want to consider buying his collection and want an independent appraisal first."

"I guess I can handle that."

Henry looked up from his scrambled eggs. "Don't you get tired of this memory problem every morning?"

I stared at him. "That's an excellent question. To me at this moment, it's all new. But reading my journal, I've been through this every day. You experience it over and over. For me, it's new territory."

Henry grunted and returned to his food. I pondered his question. I'm sure if I remembered, I would get tired of this routine, but since I didn't remember. . . .

No sense going there.

But what had I done to deserve this? Why me? I looked around the room. Everyone here had some aspect of old age to deal with. Mine was memory.

Back in my apartment, I called the *Honolulu Advertiser* to place an ad.

"This is pretty unusual to advertise to purchase a stamp collection," the woman on the line said.

"Well, can you do it or not?"

"We can handle it," she replied in a clipped tone.

Later that morning Denny, Allison, and Jennifer showed up.

"We're taking you to Sea Life Park, Grandpa."

"As long as you don't make me swim with the fishes," I said.

"Oh, Grandpa. We're going to watch the fishes. And porpoises and seals."

After a pleasant drive along the coast, we arrived, paid our fee, and were soon walking down a ramp and looking through thick glass at a tank full of sea life.

"Look at all those fish, Grandpa," Jennifer said, pointing toward a school of mullet sailing by the window.

"As long as they're on the other side of the glass," I said.

"Wouldn't you like to be inside the tank using a face mask?"

"No way," I said. "This is close enough for me."

Over lunch Denny brought up the subject of a care home. "While we're in the islands, we should take you to see some care homes, just to be prepared if you need one."

"Why would I need a care home? I'm just getting used to this place. Not that I can remember it day to day."

"That's the point. With your memory, you may at some time need additional assistance."

"Hogwash. I'm getting along fine."

Jennifer jumped in. "I think Grandpa should stay where he is, with his friends."

"Enough, young lady," Denny said. "This is a conversation between your grandfather and me."

"I would listen to your daughter. She's pretty smart." I gave her a wink.

After we finished our hamburgers, we went to a sea lion show. I watched the lumbering beasts retrieve rings, balance basketballs, and eat fish. Reminded me of Henry eating breakfast.

These animals could learn new tricks, whereas I couldn't remember what I had learned the day before.

In any case, Denny didn't bring up the subject of a care home again.

"I have another surfboard lesson bright and early tomorrow," Jennifer said. "Eight o'clock."

"We thought we'd explore part of the island after that," Denny said. "You want to join us, Dad?"

"Sure. Where're you headed?"

"I want to visit one of the famous surfing spots," Jennifer said. "We're going to Makaha."

"Haven't been there in years, that I can remember anyway," I said. "I'm game."

"Expedition time," Jennifer said as she bounced into my apartment the next day. "Mom and Dad are waiting in the car."

"Are you kidnapping me?"

She rolled her eyes. "Oh, Grandpa, remember? We're going to Makaha today. To see the surfers."

"Just as long as I don't have to go in the ocean."

She stomped her foot, put her hands on her hips, and gave me a disgusted look. "We're watching from the shore. I wish I could go surfing there, but the waves are awfully big for me. I'm still learning on the small ones."

We drove on H-3 through the tunnel, intersected H-1 near the Honolulu stadium, passed Pearl Harbor, and sped through Nanakuli and Waianae.

As we approached Makaha Beach, we saw a long line of cars parked alongside the road.

Denny pulled in.

We walked half a mile to the beach, Jennifer holding my hand.

"Do you like hiking, Grandpa?"

"Yeah. As long as it's not all uphill. I try to get out every day for an hour or so of walking. Keeps my old wheels moving."

"That's good. My health teacher told me that people should exercise every day."

"That and not eating too much," I said, patting my stomach. "I've kept myself pretty trim for an old grandpa. You don't have to worry. With the energy you expend, you burn off any fat before it can form."

"I like swimming more than walking," Jennifer said. "I'm going to be in eight swim meets this summer when I get back home."

"You do the swimming and I'll do the walking," I said.

"There's another advantage to swimming," Allison chimed in. "Keeps kids clean."

Jennifer rolled her eyes again. "Aw, Mom. That has nothing to do with it."

We reached the surfing beach and watched the surfers catch waves and paddle back out in the foam.

"You have to be nuts to do that," I said.

"Oh, Grandpa. It's fun."

"Not for me."

We watched a female surfer dart in and out of a wave.

"That's going to be me in a few years," Jennifer said, holding her chin high.

"Pretty big wave," I said.

"Yes, but I made good progress during my first lessons. I'll be ready."

After an hour or so, Denny said, "Let's head back to the car and find somewhere to eat lunch."

My stomach growled. "That's a good idea. I'm ready for some chow."

"Aw, Dad," Jennifer said. "Do we have to leave so soon? Let's stay a few more minutes."

"Get moving," Denny said. "After lunch we'll stop farther down the road."

Jennifer sighed and turned away from the ocean.

We all walked back along the side of the

road until we reached the spot where we'd parked. No car.

"It was right there," Denny said. "I remember that curved rock."

"Yeah," I said. "I even remember it. Looks like Henry's bald head."

Denny shielded his eyes from the sun with his right hand and looked both directions along the road. "It's been stolen." He extracted his cell phone and reported the theft, reading the license number off the Avis keys.

"Now what do we do?" Allison asked.

"Wait for the police to arrive," Denny said.

Moments later, a tow truck pulled up next to us. A man with a tattoo of an eagle on his arm leaned out the passenger side. "You folks looking for your car?"

"Yes," Denny said. "It's been stolen."

The man laughed. "Not stolen. Towed. You parked in a tow-away zone."

"You're kidding," Denny said.

"Nah. Look up there." The man pointed.

Sure enough. We'd all missed the NO PARKING sign up ahead.

"We've been towing cars for the last hour. We'll give you a ride to yours."

"What is this?" Denny said. "Some kind of scam."

"The police contract with us to clear cars

away from the no-parking zone."

"But look at all those cars parked along the highway," Denny said, waving his hand.

"They'll all get towed," the man said.

Denny shook his head in disgust, and we all squeezed into the back of the truck. After maybe half a mile, the driver pulled into a grass field full of cars.

When the truck stopped, Jennifer shouted, "There it is! The red one!"

I hadn't even paid any attention to the color of the car.

Denny took care of the payment and returned to the car. "I've been ripped off, but they seem happy," he said with a scowl.

"Lucky you come Hawaii," I said.

We found a hamburger joint and after eating drove toward Ka'ena Point. Jennifer spotted some surfers and held her dad to his promise that we'd make another stop. I told them I'd stay and guard the car from any more over-ambitious towing services. We rolled down the windows and I moved to the driver's seat to get the best breeze. After the three of them had scrambled down to the beach, I closed my eyes and relaxed.

A few minutes later, there was a tapping on the side of the car and I opened my eyes to find a uniformed policeman standing there.

"Would you please step out of the car," he commanded.

"Sure, Officer," I said and opened the door.

"May I see some identification?"

I pulled my wallet out and showed him my driver's license.

He looked at it. "This expired a year ago. Driving a stolen car with an expired license. You wait right here."

I was ready to explain that I didn't drive anymore, but he had already returned to his car. At the same time, he kept an eye on me.

He spoke on a phone in his vehicle and then returned to me.

"Please place your hands on the car," he said, and frisked me.

"I'm a little old for this, don't you think, Officer?"

He handed my driver's license back. "Your name is flagged in our database as a murder suspect. You've been driving a stolen car with an expired driver's license. Care to give me an explanation?"

"Look, this car was rented by my son. If you check the rental records, you'll find that out. And I haven't been driving it."

He glared at me. "I've had enough of people arguing with me today. I'm taking you in."

"Check with my son. You'll see this is all a mistake. He's down at the beach with his wife and daughter." Then it struck me and I almost laughed. "My son reported the car stolen because it had been towed away. He forgot to call again to say he found the car."

"Come on. You're going with me."

"Let me leave a note on his car, so he'll know where I am."

"Don't give me any more lip."

I found myself in the locked back seat of a police car.

When we reached the Waianae police station, they booked me and put me in a holding cell. I grasped the bars while my cellmate — a spaced-out hippie in a tie-dye robe — snored on a cot. "Call Detective Saito of the Kaneohe Police Department. He knows who I am."

Sitting on a small stool, I looked over at my groggy companion who was regaining consciousness.

"Hey, man," he said, "can you lend me twenty dollars?"

"Why'd I want to do that?"

"I'll get you some good dope when we get out."

"No thanks. My brain's already screwed up enough."

He tried to lurch to his feet, but collapsed back onto the cot, and fell asleep again.

I'd have crooned a few bars of "Nobody knows the trouble I've seen," except I couldn't hold a tune worth a tinker's damn.

Half an hour later a police officer stopped by my cell.

"Any word from Detective Saito?" I asked.

"No. But we left a message and —"

"I have to reach my son. I should be entitled to a phone call."

He glowered at me. "What's the number? I'll dial it for you."

"I don't remember. Let me see if I wrote it down somewhere."

I rummaged through my wallet and found a scrap of paper with Denny's name, the word "cell phone," and a number written on it.

"This is a mainland number," the policeman said.

"It's his cell phone," I said. "He's nearby."

The officer dialed and said, "I have a Mr. Paul Jacobson here to talk to you."

He handed me the receiver through the bars.

"Dad, where are you? We were worried. We thought you'd wandered away."

"Just a little misunderstanding with the local constabulary. I'm in the Waianae police station. Come bail me out."

"What are you doing there?"

"The police and I have this thing for each other. I'm here inspecting their jail."

CHAPTER 19

Fifteen minutes later, Denny, Allison, and Jennifer charged into the police station. I could see them enter from where I stood in the holding cell.

"Reinforcements have arrived," I said to my cellmate, who was snoring with his mouth wide open. I considered stuffing one of the socks lying on the floor in his mouth, but decided, instead, to watch what my family would do about my incarceration.

I could hear Jennifer's voice. "You need to let my grandpa go. He doesn't belong in jail."

I heard Denny shouting about false arrest. All the turmoil was getting nowhere. I cleared my throat and screamed above the din, "Denny, show them the car rental agreement!"

There was a moment of stunned silence, then Denny raced out of the building to return moments later with a red folder in his hand.

Finally, one of my jailers ambled over and unlocked the door.

The clanging of the keys woke up my hippie friend. He rubbed his eyes and said, "Hey, man, can you lend me twenty dollars?"

"You need a new line," I said, and dropped a twenty spot on his cot.

"Thanks, man," he said. Curling up with the twenty-dollar bill, he went back to sleep.

"What'd you do that for?" the policeman who was standing there asked.

"Doing my bit to support the local economy."

The policeman led me to the lobby.

"Can you take a picture of Grandpa and me next to his jail cell?" Jennifer asked.

"No," Denny said. "This isn't Disneyland. Let's get out of here."

"Aw, Dad."

As we exited the building, Denny turned to me. "How do you get yourself into these situations?"

"Me? I was sitting in the car minding my own business. You were the one who neglected to call the police to inform them that your car wasn't stolen, after all."

"And having an expired driver's license?"

"It's only an ID. No danger of me driving."

Denny and Allison didn't say much on the return trip. Sitting next to me in the back seat, Jennifer whispered in my ear, "That was a cool jail."

I whispered back. "You wouldn't have liked it as much from the other side. I think I prefer my cell at the retirement home."

We arrived back at Kina Nani with no further "encounters of the police kind" and my family accompanied me up to my room.

"We're planning to go to Turtle Bay tomorrow and stay overnight," Denny said. "How'd you like to come join us for a little change of scenery, provided you can stay out of trouble with the police?"

I grimaced. "As long as you don't report any more cars as stolen, I'm game."

"Good. You and I can also get in a round of golf while we're there."

"Now you have my attention," I said.

"You need to retrieve your clubs and pack an overnight bag."

I looked around my dwelling. "Now that you mention it, where the hell is my golf equipment?"

"In a storage area on the first floor. When I moved you in, I stashed your golf clubs down there. Inside a bin, along with some excess junk from your condo."

"So when do we start this expedition?" I asked.

"We'll pick you up at nine tomorrow morning."

"Fine. I'll be ready with my putter and dancing shoes."

Denny opened his wallet, looked at a slip of paper, and wrote something on the notepad on my kitchenette counter. "Here's the storage location. Row seven, cage eleven. There's a lock you can open with the small brown key on your key chain."

"I'll cart the golf equipment up here after you leave."

"With your memory, Dad, how have you been doing on not losing your keys?"

"The system works. When I'm in my apartment, I keep my keys on that stretchy bead bracelet on the inside doorknob. I've been able to remember to put them back when I return, so they're always ready for me the next time I go out."

My family departed and, for a fleeting moment, I only had the memory of one day: Jennifer's enthusiasm — even wanting to have a picture taken in front of the jail cell; Denny with his quiet efficiency, except for forgetting to call the police, which led to my being locked up. Uh oh. Was he starting to have memory problems like my dad and I had? Was I passing on a defective memory gene?

No use thinking about that. I had work to do. I had to find a way to clear my name. I didn't want to end up like that hippie in jail.

The discussion with Denny rattled around in my defective brain. Then the image came back to me of the policeman unlocking the cell. He had a ring with keys. I had my set of keys on the doorknob. Keys. It clicked with what I had read in my journal. The man with the scar on his cheek had duplicate keys to my room and the trash chute. I just had to find him.

My thoughts were interrupted by the phone ringing.

"Mr. Jacobson. I'm calling to check on how you enjoyed your stay in the Waianae jail."

"Who is this?" I said, not recognizing the voice.

"Detective Saito."

"Ah. The police officer who's investigating the murder."

"The same."

"To what do I owe the honor of your call?"

"I thought your taste of jail life might cause you to admit your role in the Tiegan murder," he said.

I thought back to what I had read. "That's pretty perverse logic. Why would spending time locked up convince me to spend more time in jail?"

"If you were cooperative, it would reduce your length of sentence."

I laughed. "Detective, at my age anything over twenty minutes might be irrelevant. I could kick the bucket anytime. No. I think my preference is to clear my name and enjoy my last few days, months, or years, in the comfort and company of decrepit old people."

"Have it your own way. I'm closing in on you, Jacobson."

"Yeah. If you're done threatening me, I have some work to do."

"Actually, I'd like to stop by to speak with you in person."

"Be my guest," I said.

"I'll be over in fifteen minutes, more or less."

"Fine. I'll be in my room, or down in the storage area retrieving my golf clubs."

"Aren't you kind of old for golf?"

"Nah," I said. "I still like to whack things with my clubs."

After I hung up, I looked out my window at the fading light of dusk. There was one thing you could say for Detective Saito. From what I had read, he was persistent. I just didn't want to end up like one of the butterflies in his collection with pins through my wings.

I strolled to the elevator and after waiting long enough that I could have walked down and back up three times, it arrived to transport me to the first floor.

"Where's the storage area?" I asked the receptionist.

"Back of the building by the service entrance."

"Is it locked?"

"Yes. But your room key will open the door."

I found it, let myself in, and entered a cavernous dimly lit warehouse with two levels of cages. My footsteps echoed and I sniffed the aroma of old furniture mingled with dust and mildew. The place reminded me of a setting for a gothic drama.

Coming to a stop, I spotted numbers on the end of the aisles. I heard a scraping sound somewhere in the room. I listened again, but heard nothing.

I located row seven and found cage eleven up on the second level.

I heard a sound again.

"Hello?" I said, and heard the quaver in

my voice.

No answer.

The place gave me the creeps. I could just imagine what you could find in some of these cages.

Looking around for a means to reach the second level, I spotted a gurney with ladder attached. I wheeled it over and climbed up to unlock my bin.

Inside, stacked, were my golf clubs, some dusty suitcases, two old lamps, and some unlabeled boxes. I extracted my golf bag, put the lock back on the bin door, and navigated my way to level ground.

I looked up at the ceiling. I half expected to see bats hanging there.

Heading up the aisle, I heard a crash, a scream, and a thud coming from the back of the room.

With my golf bag on my shoulder, I moved as fast as I could toward the sound.

I peered into each aisle I passed, until I reached one where I spotted another gurney ladder.

My eyes scanned downward.

A man sprawled on the floor with a pool of blood around his head.

CHAPTER 20

I bent over to examine the injured man, who was lying on his back. One of my golf clubs slipped out of the bag, clattered to the cement floor, and splashed some of the blood onto my pants and shoes.

Taking my golf bag off my shoulder, I scrutinized the injured man more closely. Didn't recognize him. Local man in his thirties with a goatee and dark hair. He didn't move.

My heart was racing faster than when I was with Marion. The man needed help fast. I lurched up the aisle, out of the storage room, and stumbled to the front desk.

"There's an injured, unconscious man in the storage area. Get some help."

"I'll page Doc Fry and call an ambulance," the woman at the desk said.

A few minutes later, a man in a white coat raced down the stairs. He carried a medical bag. I led him into the storage area.

In the distance, I heard a siren. Soon, two paramedics arrived with a stretcher. The doctor had stemmed the bleeding, but the man was still unconscious. Then a short stocky man in a dark suit showed up. He watched the proceedings.

"Who found the injured man?" he asked.

"Me," I said.

He eyed me. "Well, Mr. Jacobson. At the scene again."

"Who are you?"

"Detective Saito. I was coming to see you, remember?"

"Yeah. I didn't recall what you looked like."

Detective Saito bent over the body while the doctor continued to minister to the man's head.

"What's the prognosis?" Detective Saito asked.

"Head trauma. He's unconscious but breathing."

The paramedics lifted the injured man onto the stretcher and carried him out of the storage area.

Saito turned to me. "Know who that was?"

"No," I said. "Should I?"

"He's the one you're always telling me to go after instead of you. It's Moki."

I flinched. "I didn't recognize him."

"I know," Detective Saito said. "Your defective memory. This your golf club?"

"Yeah. I was getting my bag out of a storage locker when I heard a noise. I came to investigate and found Moki lying on the floor."

Saito removed a pair of rubber gloves from his pocket and slipped them on. "Blood on the golf club. Were you and Moki having another argument, Mr. Jacobson?"

"Wait a minute. That club fell out of the golf bag. Moki was already on the floor."

"You have some blood on your clothes," Saito said, as he pointed to my pants. "You and I spoke a little while ago and you indicated you were going to 'whack something with your golf clubs.' Was that something Moki?"

"Look, Detective, I'm going to Turtle Bay tomorrow with my family. My son invited me to play golf, so I retrieved my clubs from a storage cage. I don't know what Moki was doing here. I thought he was a night watchman."

The receptionist who had come into the storage room after all the commotion spoke up. "That's right. He's not on duty for another five hours."

Detective Saito ignored her and leveled his gaze at me. "Awfully convenient that you and Moki both happened to be here at the same time, given your previous encounter. Did you set up the meeting?"

"Are you kidding? It was a coincidence."

"I don't believe in coincidences," Saito said.

"Give me a break. I just spoke with you on the phone. Knowing you were coming over, would I pick that time to whack Moki over the head?"

"You probably already had it planned."

"When Moki regains consciousness, why don't you find out why he was here? I've told you what I was doing."

"I'm taking the golf clubs in for lab analysis," he said.

"And how am I supposed to play golf with my son if you're confiscating my equipment?"

"That's your problem. Right now this is evidence. One more crime on your growing list, Mr. Jacobson."

"Yeah, right. And you'll find my fingerprints on the clubs, because I'm the only one who uses them."

"And I need to take your pants and shoes."

"Why?"

"Because they have blood on them."

"You want me to strip down right here?"

"No. We can go up to your room."

"Great. Any other possessions you'd like me to donate?"

"You have a stamp collection?" Saito asked.

He accompanied me up to my domicile, and I changed my pants and shoes.

"Anything else I can do for you, Detective?"

He shrugged. "You could confess and make all our lives easier. Remember that Waianae jail. You ready to come clean about this crime spree of yours?"

"I'm only guilty of being in the wrong place at the wrong time."

"You and every other criminal. I should take you in."

"Why don't you talk to Moki when he regains consciousness? He's not going to say he was hit over the head with a golf club."

"We'll see, Mr. Jacobson. We'll see. Remember my warning. And don't leave the island."

"I'll be at Turtle Bay for the next two days, Detective."

After Saito left, I looked at my watch and decided it was time for some dinner. I found Meyer and Henry already eating.

Without looking up, Henry said, "You smell musty."

"What's that supposed to mean?"

"And you have dust all over your shirt."

"Crap. I've been rummaging around our storage area. What do you expect?"

Henry said, "Trying to hide from the police?"

"No. Just finding more bodies. You could be next, Henry."

He looked up with eyes as wide as saucers and started chewing like a mulching machine.

The next morning, thanks to my journal, I was ready when my family came to pick me up.

"I get to go surfing, Grandpa," Jennifer informed me as we sat together in the back seat of the once "stolen" rental car.

"And I'm going to play golf," I said.

"Why didn't you bring your clubs, Dad?" Denny asked.

"It's a long story. I'll spring for rental clubs."

"There's a neat surfing spot right next to the hotel," Jennifer said. "I researched it on the Internet."

"You're a wealth of information," I said.

"And you'll be able to watch me," Jennifer said.

"I'd like that, as long as I can do it from

solid ground."

After we arrived at Turtle Bay and checked in, we were led to adjoining rooms. Jennifer came bouncing through the connecting door from her room into mine. "Look at the cool view, Grandpa."

I gazed out the sliding glass door to see a white sand beach below, with people swimming in the calm water. "I don't see any surfers."

"That's because the surfing is on the other side of the hotel."

"I'm glad you know where things are."

"I'm going to put my bathing suit on and catch some waves."

"I'm ready to come watch you," I said. "Just point me in the right direction."

After Denny rented a surfboard for Jennifer, he, Allison and I sat in lounge chairs on a bluff overlooking the ocean. We watched Jennifer paddle out and join some other surfers waiting on their boards.

I leaned over to Denny. "It's amazing. I'd be scared shitless to be out there, and my granddaughter is in the middle of the ocean with no concerns."

"She's a good swimmer. Been competing in swim meets since she was seven."

"This is a good spot to watch," Allison said. "Usually you're looking straight out from a beach, but we're on this peninsula right alongside the surfers."

Jennifer caught a wave and balanced on her board as she headed toward shore. We all clapped, even though she was too far away to hear us.

Later, when Jennifer took a break and returned to where we were sitting, I said, "Weren't you scared out there?"

She looked at me like I had motored in from another planet. "Of course not."

"What about other things in the ocean with you?"

"Oh, Grandpa. That doesn't worry me."

"I guess I'll do all the worrying for both of us, then. You'd never get me out there."

Later, Denny and I played nine holes of golf. I upheld the family honor by only feeding two balls into water traps. With some creative scorekeeping, I broke fifty for the nine holes.

After my golf exploits, we had a pleasant dinner, and Jennifer and I sat by the pool while Denny and Allison had a nightcap.

"How will you know where you are in the morning, Grandpa?"

"That's a good question. When I wake up, I will have forgotten all the events of today and coming here."

"There must be something we can do to

help your memory."

Besides Marion, I had no other suggestions. "I'll have to write a note to myself and leave it in a place where I'll read it first thing tomorrow."

"But what if you forget to read it?"

"That's a problem," I said.

"You should do what I do. I put a sticker on my chin."

"How does that help?"

"When I wake up, I feel the sticker on my chin and know I have something to remember," Jennifer said.

"Kind of like tying a string around your finger?"

"I've never heard of that."

"What we old folks used to do," I said. "Trouble is, I don't have any stickers."

"But I do. I have stars and kittens and bells and . . . all kinds. I'll give you some when we get upstairs."

"I don't know if it will help me."

"Give it a try, Grandpa. It can't hurt."

Before Jennifer went to bed, she brought me a strip of stickers. After I wrote up the day's events, I considered what she had said. What the hell? I stuck a teddy bear on my chin. It was no dumber than anything else in my life lately.

■ ■ ■ ■

Where was I? It was dark. I fumbled around and found a lamp by my bed and turned on the light. I was in some strange room. Looked like a hotel. Getting up, I found my robe and put it on. I looked out the window. A sliver of moon hung in the sky and reflected on the ocean. What was I doing in a hotel by the ocean? Where could I be?

Opening the door to my room, I peered outside and spotted a newspaper lying on the carpet across the hall. I had no clue what day it was. I stepped out and reached for the paper. There was a click behind me.

Horse pucky. The door had locked. I was stuck outside my room. I wandered down the hallway and found a staircase which I descended to a deserted lobby. Damn. I hadn't even noticed what my room number was, or what floor I was on.

No one seemed to be around, so I climbed the stairs again. I thought I had come down two flights. I tried to retrace my route as best as my foggy memory could reconstruct it. This could have been the right floor. I wasn't sure. Wandering down the hallway, I looked at room numbers. Fiddle fart. I should have paid attention before. Then I came to an ajar door. A book propped it open. What the heck? I pushed it open. A woman lying in bed was reading. She looked my way, her eyes went wide, and she screamed.

I raced out the door. I heard continued screaming as I reached the stairway and descended to the lobby again. I sat in one of the wicker chairs there.

Tightening my robe, I stared at an antherium in a green vase on the table in front of me. At least it wouldn't scream at me. My eyes closed and I was ready to doze off when someone shook my shoulder.

My eyes popped open. A security guard stood there.

"May I see some identification please," he said as he narrowed his eyes.

I patted my robe pockets. "My wallet seems to be in my room."

"Room Key." He held out his hands, his fingers motioning toward his palms.

"I'm locked out of my room."

"Come with me."

I struggled to my feet and followed him.

He motioned for me to go behind the check-in counter. We walked down a hallway and entered an office.

"Wait here."

After he left the room, I heard the sound

of the door locking.

The windowless room had several chairs, a desk, a computer and a file cabinet. What was going on here?

Shortly thereafter, another man entered. He wore dark pants and a blue aloha shirt. Stood my height with neatly trimmed dark hair.

"Your name please," he said, tapping his fingers on the desk.

"Paul Jacobson. Who are you?"

"Peter Nakamura. I'm the night manager. Mr. Jacobson, we had a complaint that a man with a deformed chin, who was wearing a robe, entered a woman's room on the third floor."

"I don't know where I am. I was wandering around and found an open door and looked in. A woman screamed. I don't know about a deformed chin."

"What's that on your chin?"

I put my hand to my face, peeled off a teddy bear sticker, and said, "What in blazes is this?"

"Good question. Are you a guest here, Mr. Jacobson?"

"I think so. I woke up in a room. I can't remember how I got here. What is this place, anyway?"

He stared at me like I was some kind of

pervert wandering around with a teddy bear sticker on his chin. "You're at Turtle Bay."

"This is all very confusing."

"Let me check the registration to see if your name is shown."

He strolled over to the computer on the desk and clicked the keys, turning periodically to keep his eyes on me.

"No Paul Jacobson shown. I see a Denny Jacobson with two adjoining rooms."

"That's my son! My son must be here."

"I'll call and have him come down."

I sat with my head bowed. Ten minutes later, Denny stormed into the office. He didn't look awake.

"What's going on, Dad?"

"You Denny Jacobson?" Nakamura asked.

"Yes."

"Your father has been wandering around the hotel and intimidating a guest."

"Wait a goddamn minute," I said. "I was lost and didn't know where I was. All I did was look in a room and a woman screamed. That's all."

Denny smiled at the hotel guy. "This is easily explained. My dad has short-term memory loss. He forgets things."

"That doesn't excuse going into someone's room uninvited," Nakamura said.

"Give me a break," I said. "The door was

open. I was trying to find where I belonged."

Nakamura unfolded a sheet of paper. "Here's the statement from Mrs. Hughes. 'I couldn't sleep as I felt warm. I opened the sliding glass door and the room door to get a cross breeze. I was reading in bed when this crazy man charged into my room. He was wearing a robe, had wild hair and a deformed chin.' "

"That what happened, Dad?"

"I entered a room with an open door," I said. "As far as wild hair, it might be that way from sleeping."

"Mr. Jacobson had this on his chin." Nakamura held up the teddy bear sticker.

"Looks like one of Jennifer's stickers," Denny said.

"I have no idea what it was doing on my chin," I said.

"Maybe Jennifer knows. She should be up soon." Denny turned toward Nakamura. "This all seems to be a misunderstanding."

"You may be right," Nakamura said. "I still need to file a report with the police. Mrs. Hughes is threatening to sue the hotel."

"Just because a menopausal woman lets her imagination run wild?" I said.

Denny put his hand on my shoulder. "Enough, Dad. Let's get you upstairs."

Inside Denny's room it was light, and the commotion had awakened Jennifer.

The first thing she said to me was, "Did the sticker help you remember, Grandpa?"

"The house dick busted me for wandering around," I said. "I had a sticker on my chin. What was I supposed to remember?"

"You wanted to remember to read what you wrote in your journal."

"What journal?"

"You keep notes about what you do every day," Jennifer said. "To remind yourself." She walked into the adjoining room and returned with some note paper. "Here's what you wrote last night."

I sat down and read that I had watched Jennifer surf and had played a round of golf. "I live a pretty quiet life from what I wrote," I said.

Jennifer shook her head and then leaned over and whispered in my ear, "I've read the rest of your journal. You're a murder suspect and have a girlfriend."

"What?"

"Sshh." Jennifer put her index finger to her lips. "All the things I read are our little secret."

"Now I'm really confused."

"Come with me for a walk on the beach, Grandpa. I'll help remind you what's been going on in your exciting life."

I dressed and followed Jennifer downstairs and out onto the sand.

As we walked along the shore, she recounted some of my exploits.

"This has all happened to me?"

"Yes, Grandpa. But you're going to find the real murderer."

"I can't even remember who I am. How am I possibly going to clear my name?"

"You have lots of help. Meyer and me."

I bent down, picked up a cowry shell, and handed it to Jennifer.

"See, Grandpa, it's like finding a shell on the beach. You need to find the man with the scar on his cheek who stole the stamp collection."

I thought of Mrs. Hughes reporting me as someone with a deformed chin. "If only it was that simple," I muttered.

Denny and I played another nine holes of golf before we headed back to a building I had never seen before.

"What's this place?" I asked, as we pulled to the curb.

"This is where you live, Grandpa," Jennifer said.

I stared at a group of old biddies sitting on benches in the front of the building.

"It's full of old people," I said.

"You're no spring chicken yourself," Denny said.

"I like being around young people like all of you."

Jennifer whispered in my ear. "Marion's old, but she's nice and you like her."

I shook my head in amazement. My own granddaughter knew more relating to my life than I did.

"Be sure to keep writing in your journal," Jennifer reminded me, wagging her finger as if I were a naughty child.

"Yes, ma'am," I replied.

They led me up to what appeared to be my apartment. Didn't look the least bit familiar, except for some of the old furniture and pictures.

Denny looked at his watch. "We need to head to the airport."

We said our good-byes. They were flying to Kauai for a few days at Poipu Beach, before returning to the mainland.

Jennifer had tears in her eyes as she gave me a hug.

"Write a letter once in awhile," I told her. "I want to hear how all your activities are going."

"It would be easier to send an email, but I will write."

After the door closed, I sank into my easy chair and was seized by an empty feeling. My whole family had left. Here I was, no brothers or sisters, no other close relatives, and my family — Denny, Allison, and Jennifer — wouldn't be back to see me for probably half a year.

I took a deep breath.

It had been quite a visit. I would miss them. The only good news was that tomorrow I wouldn't remember that they had been here and that I had felt sad when they left.

My phone rang and it was a wrong number. A little while later, my phone rang again. This was like a Jerry Lewis telethon. "Paul, this is Marion. I know your family left today and wanted to invite you to a picnic tomorrow."

"Sure. What are the particulars?"

"A bus will pick us up in front at eleven. We're going to Ho'omaluhia Botanical Garden."

What a busy social life I was leading. No blank spots on my dance card.

The next morning I read a note I'd left for myself. It told me I was going on a field trip and to look at the picture on my dresser so I'd remember what Marion looked like.

At breakfast, I was reacquainted with my two buddies. Meyer waved his arms around and knocked over the salt shaker.

"You seem pretty hyper," I said.

"This is a special day. I turned eighty-five at five A.M. this morning."

"Hot damn," I said. "This calls for a celebration. I'll take you and Henry out for some puu puus and a drink before dinner. You up to that Henry?"

Henry nodded and continued to attack his pancakes.

"I'll line up a cab and we'll meet in the lobby at four this afternoon," I said.

At eleven I spotted Marion in a crowd of gabby women, waiting in front of the prison. She wore slacks and a gold blouse. Classy looking old broad. She gave me a hug and we climbed on the bus.

The driver clicked on a microphone. "Good morning, folks. We have a short drive today. It'll only take us ten minutes to get to the Ho'omaluhia Botanical Garden. I want you all to be good. No rowdy behavior on the bus."

There were a few chuckles.

When we stepped off the bus, the driver unloaded the picnic materials. After stuffing our faces with hamburgers and hot dogs,

Marion and I strolled along a path that had small signs identifying the variety of plants nearby.

"Did you ever garden?" she asked me.

I thought back to the distant past. "Not much. I planted vegetables a few times. Never could get the corn to grow, but the zucchini went nuts. I'd drop some seeds in the ground and by the end of the season, these oblong dark green blobs had taken over my yard."

"I grew some zucchini, too," Marion said. "I had a little cock-a-poo that growled and attacked some zucchini I left on the patio. He must have thought the zucchini was an alien life form."

"My dad had a saying regarding gardens," I said. "Tend your garden like you would live forever and live your life like it was your last day."

"Seems appropriate advice, particularly at our age."

"Yeah. But I never followed it."

We continued the conversation and then out of the blue Marion said, "Paul, I've been thinking of you and your memory problem."

"Have you figured out a cure for me?"

She laughed and held my arm. "No. I've tried to imagine what it would be like if we had some sort of more permanent relation-ship."

The hair on my arms shot up like I was in an electrical storm.

"What do you have in mind?" I asked, afraid of what I'd hear.

"You know. Living in the same apartment. We could save money that way. But I have to be honest with you, as you have been with me. I'm not sure I would like that you don't remember me from day to day."

I stopped walking, turned toward Marion, reached out to hold her hands, and looked into her blue eyes.

"I wish I didn't have this messed-up memory," I said.

"You seem better some days than others. I recall you remembering the circumstances of us being intimate. And that was the day after."

We were getting into dangerous territory. "There are rare days when I can remember things from the day before. But most of the time it's a blank."

"So if we lived together, you wouldn't recognize me most mornings?"

"That's it."

"I wish there was some medication that could help you."

I thought of saying "Viagra," but decided

now was not the time to be flip. "The doctors have pumped me full of pills. Nothing seems to work."

"I don't know if I would like being a stranger to you most mornings."

"Yeah. I don't particularly like it, either."

Her look softened. "At least you won't get tired of me."

"That's true. You're an exciting person to me every day."

"I don't know whether I like that or not," she said. "I'll have to consider this some more."

I gave her hand a squeeze. "I wish it weren't so, but I do have this problem. I think we should keep things the way they are. You don't deserve the hassle of dealing with my memory problems all the time."

"Oh, Paul. It's not that."

I held my hand up. "I know. But at this age we have enough to take care of for ourselves. You don't need the additional burden. And besides, we can continue to see each other. Now let's explore the rest of the garden."

We walked on in silence, admiring the rhododendrons planted along the path.

Later that afternoon, after my kickboard laps, I put on a wild aloha shirt to wear for the celebration of Meyer's birthday.

Meyer and Henry arrived as the cab pulled up. We piled in the back seat.

"Pearl's in Kailua," I told the driver.

"No problem," he answered.

Pearl's was a mob scene. We finally found a small table that we squeezed around, each of us defending a small space from the boisterous youngsters around us.

"What's the occasion?" I asked the waitress in her short black skirt.

"Friday afternoon. It's always like this. What'll you boys have?"

"I don't usually drink," Meyer said.

"Hey, this is a special event," I said. "Have one drink. I'll take care of getting you home afterward."

Meyer and I ordered glasses of wine, Henry a beer, and then we asked for the biggest puu puu platter they had.

"If we stick to these drinks, they won't have to kick us out for drinking too much," I said, sipping my Merlot.

The waitress delivered the food and we started to fill plates with buffalo wings, fried cheese, egg rolls, calamari, and beer-batter zucchini.

A man bumped into our table and almost landed in my lap. He grappled with the edge of the table and extracted himself without an apology.

Once we sorted out our plates, Henry pointed at my plate and said, "I want that piece."

"Are you nuts?"

He pointed again. "I want that buffalo wing."

"What's wrong with the piece on your own plate?"

"Too small," Henry said.

I pictured throwing the buffalo wing at his face, but it was Meyer's birthday.

"Your mother must have spoiled you as a child, Henry," I said, and switched plates with him.

Henry munched on the food.

"How's it feel to be even farther over the hill?" I asked Meyer.

"Except for not being able to see and that one other problem, not bad."

"Stay away from excessive liquid refreshment and you'll be fine," I said.

Henry had ripped through his plate of food when all of a sudden he said, "I don't feel good." He placed his hand on his stomach and toppled over, knocking plates, glasses, and calamari to the floor.

I knelt down beside him. He was unconscious. "Someone call 9-1-1," I shouted.

CHAPTER 21

There was a sudden silence in the restaurant, and then I heard the beeps of someone punching in numbers on a phone.

The paramedics arrived in five minutes and started giving Henry oxygen. Then they lifted him onto a stretcher and carried him toward the door.

"Where will you be taking him?" Meyer asked one of the paramedics.

"Castle Hospital," he called over his shoulder.

"That's the same place I visited you," Meyer said to me.

It took us half an hour to get a cab. When I told the driver our destination, he didn't say, "No problem."

"I don't know what we can do," I said to Meyer, when we arrived at the hospital.

"He has no relatives in the islands, or friends for that matter. He should have someone with him."

I thought back to what I had read about how Henry had acted. No wonder he had no friends. Still, he didn't deserve to be abandoned in an impersonal hospital.

After a half hour wait, we were directed to a room with two occupants. Henry lay motionless on one of the beds.

"Henry, this is Meyer. Paul and I are here."

No reaction.

I looked at the blank walls and beige curtains separating Henry from the other occupant. What a place to spend your last hours or days.

"Hi, Henry," I said. "You need to pull out of this so you can teach me some more baseball statistics."

At that moment a young kid in a white coat came in and checked Henry's pulse. The kid nodded to us, then tested Henry's reflexes, and looked into his eyes with a penlight.

"How's he doing, Doc?" I asked.

The kid pursed his lips and slicked back his brown hair. "He's in a coma. Not much we can do."

"Chances of survival?"

"Fifty-fifty. We'll know in the morning."

"We have to stay here with him," Meyer

said to me.

"Why not? I can't think of a better thing to do than watch someone die. Although, I could use some dinner. I never had much of a chance to eat the puu puus with Henry keeling over."

"Go grab a bite in the cafeteria," Meyer said. "I'm not hungry."

"I'll be right back."

"While you're gone, I'll have someone call Kina Nani to let them know what happened and where we are," Meyer said.

I ate a turkey sandwich, washed it down with an iced tea, and returned to the death watch.

Henry lay there, unchanged, while Meyer paced back and forth.

"Ever consider how you'd like to die?" Meyer asked.

"No," I said. "I kinda focus on how I'd like to live."

He broke into a wan smile. "Now that I'm losing my sight, I've been thinking more about my quality of life. I've always wanted to live to be a hundred. Now I'm not so sure."

"Since I wake up each morning in a brave new world, I can't remember giving the matter any thought. I don't seem to be bored. It took me most of today to get oriented. Then I ended up at a picnic, with Marion hinting about living together."

"You sly dog." Meyer punched me on the shoulder.

"I couldn't foist my memory problem on her."

"You'd have someone to be with."

"I'm having enough of an adventure just being with myself."

"You should consider it."

"Right now, let's consider how Henry's doing."

Around nine P.M. a nurse came in and said, "Unless you're family, you'll have to leave now."

"We're all the family he has," Meyer said.

The nurse shrugged and left the room.

We pulled our chairs up and sat next to Henry's bed. He remained immobile.

"I'm still worried that I may soon need to move into a care home," Meyer said.

"What?"

"If my eyesight deteriorates and my incontinence problem doesn't improve. . . ."

"You'd desert me?"

"That's why it would be good for you to get together with Marion."

"We've already discussed it. But if you leave, my main memory crutch besides my journal would be gone."

He smiled. "I'm glad you think of me in such a positive light."

"I might not remember who you are each morning, but by the end of the day I appreciate what you're doing for me. Besides, you can't bail until the murderer calls to answer the stamp ad."

"Yeah, if he ever calls."

We continued our watch, but there was no change in Henry. I finally tracked down some paper and pen and documented the day's events for my journal.

"What the hell?" Jolting up from sleep, I found myself sitting in a chair. I was in a hospital room. An old guy with a white beard was snoring in a chair next to me and another guy was stretched out in bed.

"Where am I?"

The guy in the chair blinked his eyes and came to. "Paul, you must have dozed off."

"You were sawing z's pretty hard yourself. Who are you and why do you know my name?"

He stretched. "I'm Meyer, and we're here because Henry's sick." He pointed to the stiff in the bed. "You need to read those sheets of paper on the table."

I picked up a handful of pages, wondering

if this guy Meyer was nuts or not, and began reading.

"Holy shit. We've been here all night, watching this guy Henry who might die."

"We should be able to get some breakfast in a half hour or so."

"Are we homeless or do we live somewhere?" I asked.

"You live in a beautiful retirement home."

"I'm confused."

"You have a memory problem, Paul. You forget things when you go to sleep. That's why you write down what happens each day."

A gurgling sound came from the bed. Meyer and I both looked over at Henry. The body shook, and his eyes opened.

"Henry's coming to!" Meyer shouted.

He fumbled around, finally latching onto a cord, and pushed a button on the end. An alarm bell rang. Moments later, a nurse rushed in, followed by a kid in a white coat.

"He's conscious," the kid said. He took Henry's pulse and checked his eyes. "The worst is over. I need to ask you gentlemen to leave while I run some tests. It will take several hours."

Meyer headed out the door, and I followed him.

"Now what?" I asked.

"We'll go to the front desk and have someone call a cab for us."

When we were settled in the cab, I said, "Did you see that look on Henry's face when he opened his eyes?"

"No. I can't see well enough to notice more than general shapes."

"He looked as contented as an angel."

"Now don't get weird on me, Paul."

We arrived at this building I had never seen before, then entered a large dining hall, and ate some breakfast.

"Doesn't seem right without Henry here," Meyer said, as we chowed down on fried eggs.

"I don't remember."

"Do you remember Marion?"

"I read about her. We apparently have something going. What's she look like?"

"You're going to find out. Here she comes."

An attractive old lady hobbled toward our table. She put her hand on my shoulder. "I'm sorry," she said. "I just heard that Henry's hospitalized."

"We had a pretty tough night," Meyer said.

"Not as rough as Henry's," I added. "But he's pulling through."

■ ■ ■ ■

After breakfast, at Meyer's insistence, I went up to the apartment he directed me to and found a journal by the bed. I spent part of the morning catching up on my life and adventures.

Late that afternoon we returned to Castle Hospital to visit Henry. We had been the only visitors from Kina Nani. From what I read, I could understand why none of the women came.

Henry's son, Ralph, was there, having flown in from Portland. He even seemed like a normal person.

When Henry fell asleep, Ralph started talking to us. "Dad never was interested in playing baseball when I was growing up. But what a mind. Because of him, I knew more baseball facts than any kid in my school."

"How did he and your mom get along?" Meyer asked.

"They had a strange relationship," Ralph said. "She was a warm person. She took care of all the emotional support in the family. Dad was the breadwinner and kept to himself. Somehow they seemed to complement each other."

302

"I wonder how they hooked up in the first place," I said.

Ralph laughed. "That was one of the family mysteries. All I know is they met at a mathematics symposium. Mom was coordinating the event and Dad was one of the speakers. Maybe within a group of mathematicians, Dad appeared normal."

"When was he diagnosed with Asperger's syndrome?" Meyer asked.

"When I was a teenager," Ralph said. "I always knew my dad was extremely single-focused. I'd visit other families and see how my friends' dads acted, and I realized something was different. Mom dismissed it as 'the mind of a mathematician.' But, clearly, it was more than that."

As it approached dinner time, we caught a taxi home.

When I returned to my cell at Kina Nani, I pondered my existence. How soon before I'd end up like all the vegetables in the hospital? I seemed healthy, but you never knew when your clock would stop ticking. Or the murderer might get me. And if I survived that, what was in store for me? Living in this rat hole by myself? Still, I had to be fair. I lived on a beautiful island. I had my eyesight and could look out at the trees and mountains of Hawaii. I wasn't stuck in some devastated city, desert, or gloomy plain. I was just feeling sorry for myself after visiting the hospital. But why couldn't I enjoy each day as it came? Waking up was an adventure for me. Why not relish each new day? Because I couldn't remember shit from the day before. You could say all you wanted in relation to living the moment, but there was something to be said for continuity.

Then there was Marion. From what I read, a hint had been dropped regarding living together. I seemed to like her. But it wasn't right to burden her with my leaky memory.

So, what were my options? I could jump off my balcony and make a statement on the pavement below. That wasn't my style. Things weren't bad enough to resort to that.

I could mope around and say, "Woe is me." That would be pretty stupid, although there were a lot of old people doing that.

I could suck it up and accept my fate. Realize I'd been dealt a mixed hand. Accept the crap with the crapola.

Or I could try and do something about my situation. My memory wasn't going to get any better, but I could get involved in something. I could become part of the Kina

Nani welcoming committee and greet new residents: "Hi, I'm Paul. Welcome to Kina Nani. This is a great place, if you like being around old people. Please join me at a meal. Experience the old fogies chewing, drooling, and farting. You can have your own cane or walker. Medical care? Don't have a clue since I can't remember. Meal hours? Got me. They should be written down somewhere. Activities? I'm sure there's something other than eating, sleeping, and peeing. Friendly staff? Yeah, this nice young girl stopped by and crammed pills down my throat this morning. She seemed to be okay."

I thought of taking a nap but rejected that idea because I'd forget how miserable I felt. I enjoyed wallowing in my misery too much.

CHAPTER 22

The next morning I was back to reading the notes by my bed.

At breakfast Meyer and I stared at each other.

"Henry should be coming back today," he said.

I shrugged. "This is all a new experience for me, with or without Henry."

The corner of Meyer's mouth turned up in an ever-so-faint smile. "What a life you live, Paul. You don't have to struggle with unpleasant memories."

"I have to struggle with figuring out where the hell I am every morning and who everybody is."

"I have an idea — a little diversion for you."

"What do you have in mind?"

"My daughter and one of her sons are visiting today," Meyer said. "We're taking a tour of Doris Duke's estate this afternoon.

Since my other grandson's not coming, we have an extra ticket. Would you like to join us?"

"Let me check my busy social calendar and see if I'm free." I closed my eyes and put my hand on my chin for a moment. "Looks like I have an opening."

"Good. I'll give you a call when they get here. It should be right after lunch."

"I can remember that," I said.

"You better get your memory revved up right now. Here comes your girlfriend Marion."

I saw a winsome old dame approaching.

"How are you boys this morning?" she asked.

"Just peachy," I replied.

"We'll have our full trio back together today," Meyer said. "Henry's recuperated."

"That's good to hear," Marion said. "Everyone should be glad, except for Alice."

As Meyer and I walked out of the dining room, he said, "I've been thinking about your investigation."

"You've figured out who murdered Tiegan?"

"No, but I've been wondering. You said that there might be some additional litigation against you, that a lawsuit might be filed claiming you stole the stamp collection."

"Yeah, I read that this morning. But no recent update mentioned in my journal. I think I'll call my lawyer."

Back in my apartment, I found the phone number and called Frederick Kapana, my slimebag lawyer who was protecting me from Tiegan's slimebag lawyer.

"Any news of another lawsuit?" I asked.

"Nope," came the booming voice. "You're clean for the moment."

"But I thought Tiegan's attorney was threatening further legal action."

"He was, but it must have been a bluff. Nothing's happened."

"I guess that's a relief," I said and hung up.

Henry was back at lunchtime. To celebrate, Meyer, Henry, and I ate outside on the patio.

Marion stopped by our table. "There's a man inside asking questions about you, Paul."

"I can barely make out a shape by those ladies near where we usually sit," Meyer said.

I looked through the window and saw a short bulldog of a man in a dark suit. He stood near three seated ladies. One of the women was waving her arms like an animated scarecrow.

A few minutes later, the man in the suit came strolling out the door to where we sat. He looked like a diminutive weight lifter, taller than Henry, but shorter than Meyer or me.

He pulled up a chair. "Mind if I join you?"

"No problem," I said.

He gave me a long, thoughtful look and then sighed. "I want to make sure you know who I am, Mr. Jacobson."

"Blinky the clown?"

He started to reach for his identification.

"That won't be necessary," I said. "I've already figured out who you are, Detective Saito."

"You've been busy in the last few days, Mr. Jacobson."

"What's that supposed to mean?"

"It seems wherever you are, people are killed or hurt. You were sitting at a table with Henry Palmer here when he was poisoned."

"Poisoned?" I said. "I thought he had a heart attack."

Meyer jumped in. "What are you implying, Detective? Paul and I were with Henry when he got sick. We also spent the night with him at the hospital."

Saito shook his head. "It's amazing that Mr. Palmer survived, with Mr. Jacobson in the room. I talked to two people who overheard Mr. Jacobson threaten to poison Mr. Palmer."

"What!" I shouted.

Saito looked at me. "In addition to your other crimes, I have enough evidence to lock you up on suspicion of an attempted homicide."

"This is bull," I said. "I have no idea where this poisoning crap is coming from."

I started to rise from my chair. Meyer put his hand on my arm. "Calm down, Paul." He turned toward Saito. "I think I can clear this up, Officer. I know what you're referring to. Henry is a little different. He suffers from Asperger's syndrome and says some pretty obnoxious things at times. Don't you, Henry."

Henry looked up briefly, didn't answer, and then went back to eating.

"You see, Detective, sometimes Paul says things to get back at Henry," Meyer said.

Detective Saito looked at his notes. "I quote from what Mr. Jacobson said. 'You better be careful, Henry. I might poison your food.' "

"I remember when Paul made that comment," Meyer said. "Henry had been insulting Paul, so Paul scared him a little. Henry gets pretty intense at meals. He wants food his way. At Pearl's he insisted on getting a buffalo wing from Paul. . . ."

Meyer stopped with his mouth wide open. "Wait a minute. Just before Henry got sick, he traded plates with Paul. If the food was poisoned, then it was meant for Paul, not Henry."

"I don't buy that," Saito said.

"Well, you better look into it, Detective," Meyer said. "I was there. Paul was getting ready to eat the food on his plate when Henry insisted on switching."

"Mr. Jacobson could have poisoned it after the plates were switched," Saito said.

Meyer shook his head. "That's not possible. Henry grabbed the food and pulled it over, right in front of him. When Henry eats, it's like a junkyard dog guarding a prize bone. No one gets near his food."

"What about it, Mr. Palmer? Did you see Mr. Jacobson put something in your food?"

Henry looked up like a startled rabbit and blinked. "He's a criminal, but he didn't do anything to my food."

Saito scowled. "So if the poison wasn't meant for Mr. Palmer, why would someone be trying to poison Mr. Jacobson?"

"The same reason someone conked him on the head and left him in a ditch," Meyer said. "Whoever killed Tiegan wants to get Paul out of the way."

I thought back to what I had read in my journal. "Meyer, do you remember at Pearl's? A man crashed into our table?"

Saito looked at me. "I thought you had a memory problem?"

"I do, but I don't have a reading problem."

Meyer paused for a moment. "You're right. A guy bumped into you."

"Did you get a look at him?" I asked.

Meyer wrinkled his brow. "It all happened so fast. With my eyesight, I didn't see much anyway."

"Tall guy who had a scar on his cheek," Henry chimed in.

I jumped up from the table and waved my right index finger at Saito. "There you go. Find a tall man with a scar on his cheek. He's the one who killed Tiegan, stole the stamp collection, and poisoned Henry."

"Seems like another convenient diversion," Saito said.

"Have it your own way," I said. "You're wasting your time accusing me. Go find this guy. If I were you I'd start with Moki, the night watchman. He might be the link to the murderer."

"Speaking of Moki, he regained conscious-ness an hour after that little incident with you in the storage area. He's recovered and back at work."

"Did you speak with him? Verify that I didn't hit him over the head?"

"I interviewed him. He said he couldn't remember what happened. I wasn't able to confirm or refute your alibi."

"*My* alibi? You should be checking out his alibi. What was he doing in that storage area?"

"He said it was all a blank, and he didn't know why he was there, Mr. Jacobson. Between you and Moki, memories are pretty sparse. It's interesting that you can speak to occurrences of a week ago when you claim you have such a bad memory."

"I can't remember, but I keep a journal. That helps me refer to past events."

"You're a suspect in quite a list of crimes, Mr. Jacobson. Mr. Palmer's poisoning, as well as the Tiegan murder and the theft of money from the Kina Nani business office. I'm still not convinced you're not the cause of the suspicious injury to Moki. Also, I received a report that you had intimidated a guest at Turtle Bay."

"That was a simple misunderstanding," I said.

"You're this close to getting locked up for good." Saito held his thumb and index finger a quarter of an inch apart.

"Paul, you need to get a good lawyer," Meyer said.

"I don't need to involve a lawyer in this. I haven't done anything wrong."

Saito closed his notebook and stood up. "Is there anything else you want to tell me, Mr. Jacobson?"

I remembered reading that the stamp store owner had seen the man with a scarred cheek, but decided to keep that to myself. Saito might try to use that against me somehow. No, I needed to clear this up myself first.

After lunch I put on a clean polo shirt and a pair of brown slacks. When Meyer called, I went up to his apartment. Inside with him stood a teenage boy and a pretty woman in her early fifties, sporting a short brown pageboy cut and wearing large oval glasses.

"Paul, meet my daughter Harriet and grandson Brad."

Harriet smiled warmly. Brad gave me a sullen nod.

"I've heard so much about you," Harriet said.

I looked at her clear complexion and small

nose and caught a whiff of perfume. Trying to find a resemblance to Meyer, the only connection that struck me was the intensity of her bright eyes.

"I try to entertain your dad and keep him out of trouble," I said.

Her eyes twinkled. "Sounds like you're enmeshed in a few problems here."

"Nothing that couldn't be fixed if I could remember what happened to me the day before."

Brad perked up. "You have memory problems?"

"Yeah," I said. "My brain does a reset overnight."

"I studied the brain in school this year," Brad said. "Your synapses must be misfiring."

"I think my synapses have all gone out on strike."

"We better get going," Meyer said, looking at his watch.

"You're always so concerned about time," Harriet said.

"I'd rather be early than miss the bus," Meyer said.

We all headed down in the pokey elevator and approached a white Toyota Camry along the curb in front.

"Can I drive, Mom?" Brad asked.

"No. The rental contract doesn't allow it."

"Aw, Mom."

Harriet turned toward Meyer and me. "Brad has his learner's permit and has been driving every time we get in our car in Hilo."

"So what's the plan for this expedition?" I asked, after Meyer and I slid onto the back seat.

"We're going to the Honolulu Art Academy," Harriet said. "There's a short introduction and then we'll get on a bus that takes us out to Black Point and the Doris Duke home."

"I remember reading about Doris Duke when I first came to Hawaii," I said.

"I thought you had a memory problem," Brad said.

"You remind me of my granddaughter. Nothing gets by her. I remember squat from yesterday, but can still remember details from ten years ago."

"Cool," Brad said.

"Not exactly," I said.

We settled in for the ride through the Pali Tunnel. I looked at the back of Brad's head. Long hair, but not greasy. I should fix him up with Jennifer . . . in twenty years.

We arrived at the Honolulu Academy of Arts and after a movie and short delay sitting on stone benches, we were ushered into a mini-bus.

Harriet handed each of us a water bottle.

"Thanks," I said. "You're taking good care of your three kids."

"Stay on your side of the seat and don't start poking my dad," she said with a smile.

"You don't have to worry about me," I said, "but he's already fidgeting."

"I get restless when I'm sitting," Meyer said, crossing his arms, "and we were already on the bench too long."

"How was it growing up with a hyperactive dad?" I asked Harriet.

"It was a unique experience. Let's just say I was prepared for sons."

We drove behind Diamond Head, into the residential neighborhood of Black Point with all its well-manicured lawns and hibiscus hedges, down a winding tree-lined driveway, and arrived at a rather plain-looking house. Inside, it was anything but ordinary, having been designed and stocked with every imaginable form of Islamic art: tapestries, intricate tiles, woodwork, an interior garden, carved wooden doors, stained glass, and inlaid mother-of-pearl chests.

I stared in amazement at an estate that certainly earned its name: Shangri La. Tobacco heiress Doris Duke became hooked on Islamic art during her honeymoon in the 1930s. She built this place and then wandered throughout the world purchasing works of art, before her death in 1993.

We entered a room with a view through one whole glass side looking out toward a guest house.

The tour guide was describing the huge glass wall that was electronically operated to open and close, a marvel for the 1930s, when a wooden, carved box next to a large sofa caught my eye. I thought: *expensive box,* then *money,* then *money box.*

In that strange way that misfiring synapses work, my mind made a connection with something I'd read in my journal that morning — the theft out of the cash box in the business office at Kina Nani.

I had picked the box up in my hands at the request of the office manager. She called out a greeting to Moki, who happened to be passing by. Yes, that was it. Moki had seen me holding the box. He had a set of master keys and could get into the office at night. After everyone else was asleep, he could easily have gone into the office, put on gloves, broken into the box, and removed the money. With my fingerprints on the box from handling it earlier, I'd be set up as the suspected thief.

The guy with the scar had killed Tiegan, stolen the stamps, conked me on the head by the ditch, and attempted to poison me, almost killing Henry instead. But the theft was committed by Moki. Did the two of them work in cahoots, or were their actions unrelated? And what had Moki been doing in the storage area while I was retrieving my golf clubs?

"Paul, are you going to join the tour or not?" Meyer called from the next room.

"Just lost in thought," I said.

After meandering through the next room, we came out onto a patio that overlooked the ocean. Surfers caught waves at the end of Diamond Head, some bailing out with their boards shooting into the air. A small boat harbor built of volcanic rock jutted out from the shore just below. A group of local boys were diving off the jetty into the backwash.

"I wish I was out there surfing," Brad said, as he hung over the railing.

"I don't. Being out in the ocean scares the piss out of me."

Brad regarded me like I was from another planet. "Really? You don't remember stuff and you don't like the ocean?"

I shrugged. "I guess I'm like the wicked

witch and water shrivels me up."

"I love the ocean." Brad spread his arms wide, as if giving tribute to the Hawaiian version of Poseidon. "The excitement of catching a huge wave."

"Aren't you concerned about what's out there with you?"

"You mean the wahine surfers?" he said with a smirk.

"No. Things in the ocean that bite and chew."

"Nah. I've only seen a shark once and I think it was more scared of me. It's kind of peaceful out there, sitting on a surfboard, waiting for the perfect wave. Sometimes I point my board out to sea and watch the sets of waves form."

"Maybe it's a generational thing. My granddaughter is interested in surfing, too."

"No way," Brad said. "This lady, Doris Duke? She surfed and hung out with the beach boys in Waikiki."

"I guess you're right," I said. "If she were still alive, she'd be older than me."

"It's your attitude," Brad said. "You need to think positive about the ocean."

"You planning to be a psychiatrist when you're grown?"

"Nah. Lawyer like my grandpa."

Brad jogged ahead to catch up with the

rest of the tour. I took one last look at the ocean. You'd never get me out there.

CHAPTER 23

As Meyer and I sat together on the bus on the way back to the Academy of Arts, I said, "I've been thinking what I need to do to clear my name from the most wanted list."

"I thought you were enjoying all your visits with Detective Saito," Meyer said.

"I figure it's time to let him work on some other crimes, like poi heists and tourists having their pockets picked. We have to find the guy with the scar on his cheek."

"We'll see if anyone responds to the ad I placed."

"That's the first step," I said. "I also need to figure out how Moki ties in. I'm convinced he stole the money from the cash box in the business office. He's been up to some strange activities."

"You'll need to find some evidence linking him to the theft. Right now you're the only suspect they have."

"Well, thanks for believing in me."

Meyer shrugged. "You'll come up with something."

Later that afternoon, my phone rang.

"Hi, Grandpa."

"This a representative of the Mainland Surfers' Association?"

"Oh, Grandpa. It's Jennifer."

"It's good to hear your voice."

"I called to say how much I enjoyed visiting you and to find out how you're doing."

"I'm getting by," I said. "I'm still alive."

"And how are your friends?"

"They're still alive, too. Aren't you supposed to be in school?"

"Nope. It's still summer vacation. I'm learning how to skateboard. It's almost as much fun as surfing. And Dad's going to take me skiing next winter."

"You're becoming a triple threat athlete."

"Yes, but I want to come back and visit you again and do some more surfing," she said.

"Meyer's son was here today. He's a surfer. Maybe he could show you some surfing spots next time you're here."

"Cool. Have you found the man who stole the stamp collection yet?"

"No, but we're advertising in the newspaper."

"Oh, Grandpa, that's so old fashioned. You should use the Internet."

"The Internet?"

"Sure. There are probably all kinds of stamp collection web sites. You could post information and see who responds."

"I have no clue how to do that."

"But I do."

I thought for a moment. "We used Meyer's phone number in the ad. Let me get that for you." I put the receiver down, looked up Meyer's phone number in the Kina Nani directory, and read it to Jennifer.

"Okay," she said. "I'll get on my computer right now and see what I can do."

After I hung up, I sat there staring at my hands. I didn't even know which end of a computer to turn on, and my granddaughter could do all this stuff. It made me feel even older.

An hour later the phone rang again.

"Hi, Grandpa. It's all set up."

"What did you do?"

"I found three stamp collecting web sites and posted messages offering to buy a Swiss stamp collection in Hawaii. If I get a response, I'll email the phone number you gave me."

"Thanks," I said, wondering at the world of modern youth.

"No problem," Jennifer replied.

I now needed to act on one specific thing if I were going to be allowed to continue to live in this garden spot.

Reading through my journal, I verified my suspicions. Then I took the elevator from molasses hell down to the front desk.

"When's Moki next on duty?" I asked.

The woman behind the counter stuck a pencil behind her ear and thumbed through several sheets of paper on a clipboard. "Looks like tonight. Starts his shift at ten."

Next, I called Meyer. "You up for a little adventure?" I asked.

"What are you setting me up for?"

That night we waited inside Meyer's apartment.

"Why can't we do this in your apartment?" he asked.

"Because Moki knows who I am. He won't be suspicious of you."

"I don't know if this is such a good idea." Meyer paced back and forth.

"Hey. What's the worst that could happen?" I glanced at my watch. "He starts his rounds at the top. He should be here in fifteen minutes."

"There's no one else on this wing who

stays up this late, so his should be the only footsteps we hear," Meyer said.

At ten-fifteen I heard the sound of a door rattling, then creaking shoes moving toward Meyer's apartment.

"Okay," I whispered. "Show time."

We stood in Meyer's kitchenette with the louvers above the door open, so the sound of our voices would carry out into the hallway.

"What are you doing with ten thousand dollars in cash in your room?" I said, cupping my hands around my mouth and aiming my voice toward the louvers.

"I cashed a check today." Meyer spoke loudly toward the door. "I'm buying a beautiful set of jewelry for my daughter. Trouble is, the guy only takes cash."

I heard the footsteps stop outside the door.

"Seems like keeping ten thousand dollars in cash here is pretty risky," I said.

"It's only for one night. I meet the guy at eight in the morning."

"Where are you going to store that much cash?"

"I have a cash box tucked under my bed. It'll be safe there."

"I guess you know what you're doing," I said.

The footsteps started again, and I gave

Meyer the thumbs-up sign. We talked of other things for awhile. When we were sure Moki had moved to another floor, we stuffed a bunch of Meyer's clothes and a spare pillow under the covers of his bed.

"It looks like someone sleeping," Meyer said, stepping back to admire our work.

We took two wooden chairs from Meyer's living room and placed one in the closet and the other in the bathroom. Meyer owned a digital camera so we designated him the official photographer for the upcoming event. He sat down on the chair in the closet with the camera in his lap. Then I turned out the lights and adjourned to the bathroom to wait.

Stay awake, you old poop. Every so often I pinched myself to keep from nodding off. This was no time to fall asleep, reset my memory, and wake up screaming and wondering where the hell I was.

It must have been two hours later that I heard a key scraping in the lock. I was suddenly one hundred percent alert.

I cocked my head to the side.

The door creaked open. I listened as faint footsteps passed through the kitchenette.

The sound of breathing was discernible above the gentle hum of electrical equipment far below.

I could imagine Moki down on his hands and knees, reaching under the bed.

The cash box rattled, followed by a creaking sound. He had it open.

Time to make our appearance.

I stepped out of the bathroom and turned on the hall light.

Meyer almost bumped into me as he shot out of the closet.

Moki stood there with a stack of money in one hand and the metal cash box in the other.

"You're busted, asshole," I said to him.

Meyer pointed his digital camera at Moki, and a flash lit up the room.

Moki's eyes widened, and his head ping-ponged from side to side, looking for a way out. He dropped the box and money, turned, and ran toward the door. His elbow clipped the vase, and it twirled off the table.

"Not Martha!" Meyer shouted. He lunged forward.

Too late.

The vase crashed to the floor, shattering and sending ashes spewing across the room.

In the meantime, Moki had disappeared.

I called 9-1-1 to report the attempted burglary and asked to have Detective Saito contact me.

As I hung up the phone, I heard a car start

and then race down the driveway. The police could bring in Moki later.

Meyer sat on the couch with his head in his hands. "What a way for Martha to go," he said. "Her remains are scattered all over the room."

"I hate to tell you, Meyer, but she's already gone. Don't take it so hard. Maybe Martha didn't want to be in that vase. We'll get her cleaned up after the police come."

Fifteen minutes later a policeman arrived. He was in his late twenties, clean-cut, and efficient. "Your call indicated an intruder and attempted burglary."

"He escaped," I said. "But his fingerprints are all over that cash box and the stack of money."

"I took a nice picture of him," Meyer said, showing the image to the policeman.

Shortly, a bleary-eyed Detective Saito arrived.

"You weren't trying to get some sleep were you, Detective?" I asked.

"Not any more. What did you two do?"

"We caught the guy who's been stealing things from around here," I said.

Saito stared at the scattered powder. "Looks like you've been dusting for fingerprints."

"We saved that for you, Detective. It's

Martha."

"Who's Martha?"

"The remains of Meyer's wife. He kept her in the vase that Moki knocked over."

Detective Saito looked upward as if he were pleading with some of his long dead relatives. He put on rubber gloves and placed the cash box in a large paper bag. Then he lifted up the stack of bills.

"What's this?" he asked.

"That's the simulated ten thousand dollars Moki thought he was stealing," I explained. "Fifty dollar bills on each end and cut paper inside."

Saito shook his head. "Maybe I should start dealing with criminals in preschool rather than this place."

"Aw, you'd miss us, Detective," I said.

After Saito left, I looked around at the mess in Meyer's apartment. I could imagine Rhonda and Martha getting a kick out of what we two old farts had done. And by tomorrow I would have forgotten it all anyway. Did I want to remember? Sure. I'd take any memories I could dredge up.

Meyer stared at the mess on the rug.

"That's the calmest I've seen you today." I put my hand on his shoulder.

He pursed his lips. "There's Martha

spread out all over the rug. I'm still trying to take all of this in."

"Tell you what. You shouldn't have to deal with this. Why don't you take a little walk? I'll clean up everything and put Martha in that Tupperware container on the sink."

"Martha hated Tupperware."

"Then a plastic bag? It's only temporary, until you can buy a new vase."

"Take a look in my closet," Meyer said.

There I found a dust pan, whisk broom, and Long's Drug Store bag.

Within fifteen minutes of Meyer leaving for his walk, I had most of Martha safely stowed.

The next morning I dutifully reviewed my journal before heading down to breakfast.

I identified Meyer as the white-bearded guy and the bald-headed squirt as Henry.

"From what I read, we had quite a night," I said to Meyer.

He frowned. "I'm getting a new vase for Martha today."

"I must have had a good time with your family yesterday," I said. "I wrote a lot about Harriet and Brad in my journal."

"Good. They enjoyed meeting you, as well." His head bobbed up. "It looks like we have a visitor."

An attractive woman who I recognized as Marion from the picture on my dresser and the notes in my journal stopped in front of me.

"I didn't see you around yesterday afternoon," she said.

"Meyer kidnapped me."

She lifted her eyebrows.

"Paul joined me on a family outing," Meyer said.

"Well, Paul, if you're not busy today, you'll have to stop by to see me later."

"Sure thing," I replied, as Meyer winked at me.

Later that morning someone pounded on my door. It was Meyer, and he was bouncing up and down. "It's happened. Someone called about the stamps."

"Who?"

"It's the strangest thing. A man called and said he found out that I was interested in buying a Swiss stamp collection. I asked him if he had seen the ad in the newspaper and he said no, that he found out about it on the Internet."

I mentally reviewed what I had read in my journal. "I forgot to mention something to you. My granddaughter Jennifer put out some message on her computer. It must have worked."

Meyer slapped me on the back, probably leaving a hand print. "That explains it. Anyway, he said he had a Swiss stamp collection to sell. I'm sure it's the guy we're looking for."

"Did you plan a meeting with him?"

"You bet I did. It's all set for two o'clock this afternoon at Star Stamp and Coin in Kailua, as we planned. I told him we needed to get an appraisal."

"Did you get his name?"

"No. He said he'd prefer to remain anonymous until we met in person. He did ask my name. I told him Adrian Penniman."

"Where'd that come from?"

"It was the name of my first client when I became an attorney," Meyer said.

"We have to think through how to trap this guy," I said. "First thing is to find out who he is."

"We'll stake out the stamp store. But I won't be any help since I can't see much."

"I'll be the eyes."

"But we need some way to follow him."

I thought back to my journal. "I used a cab to visit all the stamp stores. Had a cooperative cabbie. I might have his card somewhere."

Searching though my nightstand drawer, I

found the card. Then I called the number and spoke to Ray Puhai. "Pick us up at one-thirty, and I'll pay for several hours of driving."

"I'm your man, braddah," he said.

I saw a large chunk of my retirement funds flying away, but I would have been wasting it on car maintenance and insurance if I still had my old Volvo.

CHAPTER 24

Just before we were to meet the cab downstairs, I phoned Star Stamp and Coin. "There will be a gentleman asking for Adrian Penniman this afternoon. Please tell him Mr. Penniman had a family emergency and had to cancel the meeting."

Meyer and I arrived in front of Star Stamp and Coin at one-forty-five. The taxi driver parked so I could watch the entrance from the cab window.

Precisely at two, a gold Lexus pulled up in front of us. A tall, muscular man got out and glanced around. He looked strong enough to have thrust a body into a trash chute.

I spotted a scar on his left cheek.

He headed toward the store, carrying a package under his arm.

"That's him," I said, and wrote down the license number.

Five minutes later he walked back to his car. He looked angry.

"Follow him," I told the cab driver.

"No problem," the cabbie said.

Here we go again, I said to myself.

The gold Lexus shot away from the curb, and Ray stomped on the gas to keep our target in sight. We settled in at a safe distance, close enough for us to see the car, but far enough away to not be obvious.

"You're pretty good at this," I told Ray.

"Sure," he replied. "Watch a lot of cop shows on TV."

The Lexus pulled into the driveway of a large condominium in Kailua, drove into a parking structure, and disappeared.

We parked by the curb in the driveway, and waited. After two minutes, the tall man strolled up the walkway. I noted his dark hair and the distinct scar on his cheek. He proceeded into the building.

I exited the taxi and shuffled as fast as I could to the door. It was locked and required a card to enter.

"Great," I said when I returned to the cab. "A twelve-story building with hundreds of residents."

"No problem," Meyer said with a smile. "I'll have one of my contacts trace the license plate number."

Ray drove us back to Kina Nani. He seemed disappointed that we hadn't been out long enough to pay for his daughter's college education, but as we left the cab he said, "Call me any time."

"Bet your ass, braddah," I said.

That evening Marion and I went to a movie that was being shown in the lounge. Several old ladies served miniature bags of popcorn, and we settled in to watch an old Cary Grant movie on a large television screen. We held hands, just like teenagers.

Afterwards, I accompanied her to her apartment. She offered me a drink, which I used to surreptitiously swallow a Viagra without choking. Then before I knew it we were entangled, our clothes came off, and my medical assistance kicked in.

I performed adequately for a geezer.

At breakfast the next morning, Meyer caught on right away.

"No questioning who I am or where you are this morning, Paul."

"Nope. Clear as a sunny day at the beach."

"The wonders of the testosterone-filled brain," he said with a smile.

Later that afternoon, I heard pounding on

my door. When I opened the door, Meyer raced inside like a cat that had caught a mouse.

"Calm down," I said.

"We found him," Meyer said, as he bounced up and down like an eighty-five-year-old Tigger.

I stepped over to guard my precious antique lava lamp, then placed my hand on his shoulder to rein him in. "Okay, tell me everything."

"My contact tracked down the owner of the car we followed."

I wiped the spittle off my face. "Easy, Meyer. Take a deep breath. I don't want you having a heart attack."

He smiled. "Okay. Here're the facts. He lives in apartment 910 at the Windward Passage condominiums. That's where we saw him go in. I even have a phone number."

"You've forgotten one important fact," I said. "His name."

"Harrison Young."

I reeled. My stomach felt like it was trying to jump out of my throat. "I read that name in my journal. That's . . . that's the name of Tiegan's lawyer."

"Do you suppose it's the same Harrison Young?"

I thought for a moment. All that I had

read in my diary swirled in my head. *Think. Put the pieces together.* "Yes. It's all starting to fit. He stole the stamps and killed Tiegan. He knew that I was linked to Tiegan. He set me up for the murder he committed. Your boys did a good job of tracking him down from the license plate."

"With computers, all you need is access to the right database. I owe an old friend big-time for this."

"You can invite him over for an all expenses paid lunch at Kina Nani, after we nab Harrison Young."

"Don't you mean after we turn this over to the police?"

"Not so fast," I said. "I'm not convinced Detective Saito will believe us. He'll consider this another of my 'diversions.' From what I've read, he doesn't seem to buy anything I tell him."

"But this time I'll support you as well," Meyer said.

"It'll probably get you locked up as my accomplice."

Meyer had stopped bouncing. That was good because I didn't need an eighty-five-year-old pogo stick destroying my apartment.

"I have another thought," I said.

I rummaged through my nightstand

drawer and found the copy of the Kina Nani visitors' log. I pointed to the illegible name. "This person signed in the night of the murder. Could be the signature of Harrison Young."

"Can't help you with that," Meyer said. "I could only read it with a magnifying glass."

"We're quite a pair of detectives, with my memory and your eyesight. Between the two of us, we don't even make one lame-ass amateur."

"But think of all the life experience we've had," Meyer said. "A young kid like Detective Saito can't match us."

"Somehow that doesn't give me a sense of confidence," I said.

Meyer looked thoughtful. "So we either turn it over to Detective Saito or we try to do something ourselves."

I sat and tried to think up a good plan. There appeared to be no other alternative. "All right. Here's what I need to do. First, I'm going to pay Harrison Young a visit."

"Won't that be dangerous?"

"Probably. You don't have to come. This is my problem, and I need to step up to it."

Meyer regarded me with his fuzzy stare. "Give me a break, Paul. I'm in this with you."

I shrugged. "Okay. We'll put both our

asses on the line, then. If we confront Harrison, we may get him to admit what he's done. In fact, if we have a hidden tape recorder, we can collect some convincing evidence for Detective Saito."

"What's to keep Young from overpowering both of us?"

"We outnumber him. We'll have to be smart and light on our feet."

Later I caught the van over to the shopping center and bought a small tape recorder with cord-attached miniature microphone accessory. When I returned to Meyer's apartment, he looked like a caged tiger pacing back and forth.

"I don't know if this will work, Paul."

"I don't either, but I need to give it a try. As I mentioned before, you don't have to come with me."

"We need some kind of backup plan," Meyer said.

"Such as?"

"We need to let someone know where we're going, just in case we have a problem with Young. That person could alert Detective Saito, if necessary."

"What about Henry?"

Meyer smiled. "Sure. I'd feel better if Henry were our backup. Let's go talk to him."

■ ■ ■ ■

"You're both nuts," Henry said, after Meyer explained the plan. "Let Paul hang for what he's done."

"But he hasn't done anything," Meyer said. "We need to prove that Harrison Young is the murderer. I'm taking my cell phone along. I'll call you as we're going up to Harrison's apartment. Then you can notify Detective Saito."

I gave Henry a slip of paper with Saito's phone number.

Henry shook his head. "Two pissants."

Next, I called Harrison's number from Henry's apartment.

"Yeah?" a gruff voice answered. I hung up.

"He's there. Time to go."

I called a taxi, placed the tape recorder in my pocket, and with a strip of duct tape attached the microphone inside my aloha shirt.

As we rode toward Windward Passage, I said to Meyer, "All we have to do is stay alive for half an hour."

"That's encouraging."

"We get him to talk, then Detective Saito

shows up. Harrison Young wouldn't kill us in his own apartment. It would be too risky for him."

The cab dropped us off in front of Windward Passage. I looked up at the twelve-story building, the tallest in Kailua, as Meyer pulled the cell phone out of his pocket. He had it in a Ziploc bag.

"Why the protection for your phone?" I asked.

"So it won't get ruined if I get caught in the rain." He dialed Henry. "We're here. Call Saito."

Meyer resealed the phone inside the plastic bag and thrust it back in the pocket of his khaki pants.

I switched on the tape recorder I had hidden in my pocket. "Show time," I said.

We waited until a resident opened the door, tailgated into the building, and then took the elevator to the ninth floor.

As we walked along the hallway, I looked down at the gray carpet and wondered what the hell we were doing. Taking a deep breath, I rang the doorbell of apartment 910. Our fate was sealed tighter than the cell phone in Meyer's Ziploc bag.

I stepped to the side, out of view, per the plan Meyer and I had discussed. When the door opened, Meyer said, "Mr. Young. I'm

343

here to see you regarding a stamp collection."

"Who are you?" he said.

"I'm Adrian Penniman."

"The guy who stood me up?"

"I apologize," Meyer said. "I had a family emergency."

"That's what the stamp store owner told me."

"I'd like to see the Swiss collection."

"Would you now?" Harrison Young said. "Why not?"

Meyer started into the room, and I followed. Harrison had turned his back and was lifting a stamp album off a shelf.

"Say, how did you know where I lived?" Harrison spun back around. Our eyes locked, and his brow furrowed. "Well, if it isn't Paul Jacobson. What brings you here?"

I saw his set jaw and the one-inch scar on his cheek. I gave him my most deprecating smile. "Just checking out stamp collections."

His eyes narrowed. "How did you figure this out?"

"You're a guy who attracts attention, Harrison," I said. "First you knock off Tiegan; then you steal his stamp collection. A typical lawyer."

"You got something against lawyers?"

"I don't like them much. Particularly the

344

murdering kind," I said. "So, how'd you get into the robbery and murder racket?"

He looked at me, and a smile crept across his face. "Just supplemental income to support my family."

"You don't strike me as a family kind of guy."

His gaze hardened. "You know nothing about me."

"Other than being a scumbag lawyer, that's true," I said. "Just trying to get to know my neighborhood murderer a little better."

"These stamps will assure a good life for Ali."

Meyer said, "Who's Ali?"

Harrison turned toward Meyer. "Kid I adopted from Afghanistan. When I was stationed over there, I found a boy living in the streets. Brought him back to the states and fattened him up."

"Sounds like Hansel and Gretel," I said. "You going to eat him?"

Harrison Young laughed. "You're a real comedian. Maybe you'll soon be a dead comedian."

"Hey, I try to please," I said. "Where is good old Ali?"

"He's visiting my brother's family in Miami. But I support him." Harrison glared

345

at me. "And you aren't going to get in my way."

"You're quite the role model for little Ali."

"I don't care what you think. When I sell Tiegan's stamp collection, I'll get close to half a million bucks. That'll get the kid through college."

"I can just see it. He gets a check from home. Courtesy of murder and rape incorporated."

"I've never raped anyone."

"Well, that's one on your plus side, Harrison."

"You always yammer this much?" he asked.

"Only when I'm around murderers."

"Maybe you better back off a little, Paul," Meyer said, his gaze darting from side to side.

"Yeah, yeah," I said. "I know. Don't get the murderer riled up."

I thought back to an incident described in my journal. I pointed at Harrison Young. "After you whacked Tiegan over the head with a bottle, you must have used a master key to get in my room to leave the murder weapon and a Swiss stamp."

A wide grin spread across his face. "That was fun. I had to think on my feet. See, I was going to steal the stamps from Tiegan, but he woke up. Had to kill him and did that ever give me an unexpected thrill. Then I came up with the idea of framing you. I knew you lived in the same building. After I planted the bottle and stamp, I placed an anonymous call to the police suggesting the murder weapon and some stolen property were in your apartment. And I bet the police have been trying to nail you for the murder."

"No, Harrison, they're going to get you. And you were the one who hit me over the head with a bottle and left me in a ditch."

"You must have a hard head. I thought I took care of you, like Tiegan. After doing it once, I enjoyed trying again. With your defective memory, I didn't have to worry that you would identify me."

"I've been wondering," I said. "How did I end up in the ditch?"

He chuckled. "I found out from a stamp store guy that you had been snooping around. You were butting in where you didn't belong. Came up to your apartment to have a little friendly chat."

"Hell. It couldn't have been friendly if you whacked me over the head."

"After a little man-to-man persuasion, you accompanied me to my car," Harrison said.

"You mean you gave me a free ride in your beautiful gold Lexus?"

"I thought you couldn't remember stuff."

"I don't remember your car from that experience, but I've seen it since."

"You been playing amateur cop?"

"Something like that. And then you tried to poison me at Pearl's."

Meyer gasped.

Harrison smiled. "I never did understand how you survived that. I figured a little arsenic on the buffalo wings would take out an old guy like you."

"Nah," I said. "I'm too tough. Besides, the wrong person ate the food."

"Too bad," Harrison said.

"I'm curious," I said. "How'd you happen to be at Pearl's that night?"

"When I found out the knock on the head didn't work, I bought some poison and followed you. Pearl's seemed to be the perfect place. Big crowd and confusion."

"Does Ali know his adoptive daddy is such a bastard?"

"Ali must be so proud," Meyer said.

"Leave Ali out of this." Harrison's eyes narrowed.

"Hey, you're the one who brought him up as the reason for all of this," I said.

Meyer looked at his watch. "We should get going, Paul. My water aerobics class will start soon."

"Shit," I said. "This is more fun than swimming."

"You don't like swimming?" Harrison asked.

"Nah. I hate the ocean. Being in it, that is. I like looking at it. Meyer here is a good swimmer, but I sink like a rock."

"Really?" Harrison's eyes lit up. "I have an idea of just the place for you."

CHAPTER 25

I looked at Harrison Young. "I get the impression you have something in mind that won't make little Ali proud."

"Enough talking," he said. "Let's head down to the car."

"On second thought, I like it here," Meyer said.

Harrison reached in the top drawer of his desk, pulled out a handgun, and pointed it at Meyer's forehead.

Meyer's eyes bulged.

"I wouldn't do anything stupid, Harrison," I said. "We're old and almost dead anyway. Also, the police will be here any moment."

"That so?" he said with a sneer. He pointed his gun toward the door. "Move."

"I don't know if that's such a good idea," I said. "The place is probably swarming with cops by now."

"Yeah, right. They don't care about sorry

old wastes like you two." He waved his gun at us. "Let's get going."

He jabbed the gun in my back, and I stumbled toward the door. Then we were in the hallway and moving toward the elevator.

I was hoping to see some other people, but we had the elevator to ourselves.

Once downstairs, Harrison put the gun in his pocket and steered us into the parking structure. When we reached the gold Lexus, he beeped the doors open.

"You drive," he motioned to Meyer.

"That wouldn't be such a good idea," I said.

"Don't give me any lip, old man."

"You can have it your way," I said. "It's just that having a half-blind guy drive might cause some problems."

"All right. You drive." He pushed me toward the driver's side.

I tested the steering wheel while Meyer struggled into the passenger side with the gun-toting Harrison Young behind us.

"This will be interesting," I said. "I haven't driven in five years."

"It'll come back to you," Harrison said. "Now, let's get started."

I fumbled with the key he had given me, trying to waste as much time as possible, but the car started the first time. I tried to back out, but the car wouldn't budge.

"Release the parking brake," Harrison said in a cold voice, as he pushed the gun into my shoulder.

"Yes, sir. Where is it?"

"On the left."

I tapped the pedal and we lurched backward. I found my driving legs and aimed us out of the parking structure. As we drove past the front of the building, I surveyed the turnaround circle. No Detective Saito. The one time I wanted to see him.

We came to the street.

"Turn left," Harrison said.

I jerked the steering wheel and stomped on the accelerator. We shot around the corner.

"Drive normal," Harrison said, pushing the handgun into the back of my head.

"That's as normal as it is for me. I'll try to get used to the car." We turned left on Kailua Road and headed across Ku'ulei Road. Then I noticed Meyer squirming in his seat. "Uh oh," I said.

"What's the problem?" Harrison said.

"Just a little DNA evidence being left on your seat," I replied.

Meyer didn't say anything.

"It's not a good idea to kidnap old guys,"

I added.

"I'm not kidnapping you," Harrison said. "We're going for a little one-way ride."

"I don't like the sound of that," Meyer said.

"If I'm not going to live much longer, anyway," I said, "how did you get keys to my apartment and the trash chute?"

"Easy. Moki. I found out he was a guard at Kina Nani. I bought him drinks at a bar and offered to take him back to his apartment. When he passed out, I copied his keys."

"And I bet you even signed in to Kina Nani earlier in the evening of the night you bumped off Tiegan, later recognized your mistake, and came back to steal the page."

"No way. No one at Kina Nani has ever seen me. Except for Tiegan, who's dead, and Moki, but he wouldn't remember anything, given how drunk he was. I used Moki's copied keys to get in the service entrance."

"So now all you have to do is get rid of us and sell the stamps," I said.

"That's right. Third time's the charm. Knocking you off, I mean. You're going to be very dead; then I'm heading to the mainland tomorrow morning. Get away from this place and sell the stamps. Park up ahead."

I pulled in and managed to not hit the curb.

"Out," Harrison said.

Meyer slid out, and I looked at the wet spot on the seat where he had been.

Harrison Young opened the trunk and retrieved a coil of rope and a small tool kit. He motioned toward a boat anchored along the side of a canal just ahead. I helped Meyer in and then stepped in myself. Harrison hopped aboard, untied the line, and started the engine. He spun the boat around and pointed it down the canal. I estimated that we had an hour of light left.

"Where you taking us?" I asked.

"We're going on a little cruise," Harrison said.

"I'm not much of a swimmer," I said.

"Swimming won't help you," Harrison said.

The canal emptied into Kailua Bay, and once we were in open water, Harrison gunned the engine. We powered along the nearly empty beach — only a woman walking a black dog, several kids still splashing in the gentle waves, and a man packing up his windsurfing equipment.

My stomach tightened the farther we traveled from shore. I took deep breaths trying to think of something pleasant, like being on land again.

Fifteen minutes later we passed Popoi'a Island. I watched a flock of seagulls rise from the small flat rock surface. I wished I could fly. In the distance, a car traversed the point between Kailua and Lanikai. Unfortunate that nobody knew we were here.

It would have been an enjoyable boat ride at dusk, except I hated being on the ocean and knew that Harrison Young didn't plan to take us back to shore alive.

I looked over at Meyer. The blood had drained from his face, and he was rocking back and forth.

I kept hoping a police patrol would come charging after us, but no other boats were in sight.

We headed toward the Mokulua islands, and Harrison steered for the left island. He cut the engine. We drifted into a spit of sand and scraped to a stop.

Unfortunately, we had the island to ourselves.

"Everybody out," Harrison said.

Both Meyer and I struggled out, our legs stiff from the cramped ride.

Harrison pulled the boat up farther on

the sand and grabbed the coil of rope and toolkit.

"Walk over those rocks," he said, giving us both a not-too-gentle shove.

I stumbled, regained my balance, and followed his directions.

After a short hike, Harrison said, "Stop right here." He extracted a knife from his tool kit and cut a section of rope.

"Put your hands behind your back," he told Meyer, then tied Meyer's hands together with the rope.

"Do the same," he said to me, and then bound my hands with the other end of the rope. Meyer and I were now both connected, with a short tether between us. From the tool kit, Harrison extracted a hammer and something else I couldn't see.

"Now comes the fun part," Harrison said. "It's swimming time."

I looked down at a rock shelf that dropped off into deep water.

"How are we going to swim with our hands tied?" I said.

The question was rhetorical, but Harrison said, "You're not going far."

"I'm not going in there."

"Get in the water."

We edged onto the rock shelf. Small waves lapped at our feet. My heart thumped double time. Harrison gave Meyer and me a shove, and we tumbled into the water.

I came up spluttering and Meyer cried out. Then Harrison jumped in, grabbed the rope, and unceremoniously pulled us along the rocky coastline. I tried to tread water and struggled to keep my head above the waves. Damn. If only I didn't float like a rock.

He dragged Meyer and me toward an opening in a rocky abutment and pushed us inside. I found that we were in a long narrow cave. Now my stomach really tightened.

"All the way to the back," Harrison said.

I barely kept my head above water and heard Meyer gasping. My feet finally hit bottom, and I staggered up a small sand beach at the back of the cave. Meyer and I collapsed in a heap. I tried to control my breathing, struggling to overcome the panic that seized my every muscle.

As we lay gasping, Harrison grabbed the length of rope between us and started hammering.

"There," he said. "You're securely attached."

I tried to lean forward and found that I couldn't. "What did you do?" I asked, unable to see in the dark cave.

"I've fastened you to the cave wall. Now

you can slowly drown as the tide comes in. It gets you out of the way even better than how I took care of Tiegan."

I felt drops on my forehead and didn't know if it was ocean water or sweat. What could be done? Only one thing seemed to have any impact on Harrison Young.

"This isn't a good idea, Harrison," I said, shaking my head.

"And why is that?"

"Some kid, like Ali, is apt to swim in this cave tomorrow. Some innocent kid will find two old, fish-nibbled bodies. It's liable to scar him for life. You wouldn't want that to happen to your Ali."

I heard a laugh. "No fear of that with him safely off in Miami. Nice try, but you're fish food. I'll check back on your dead bodies first thing in the morning, before I head to the mainland. Have a good end of your life, boys."

He splashed into the water and swam out of the cave.

So much for an appeal to his sense of decency.

A few minutes later, I heard the sound of an engine starting and then the change of pitch as the boat moved away from the island.

"We've had it," Meyer said.

I needed to get my mind around the situation. With an effort, I tried to push the rising panic away. "Don't give up so fast. It wasn't easy for Harrison to get my hands tied using only one end of the rope. There's some slack in it. If we both move up the sand close to where he attached the rope, you can get your hands on the knot around my wrists.

We adjusted our positions.

"I have the rope," Meyer said.

I flexed and relaxed my hands, trying to increase the slack in the rope.

"There's a little loop I can feel," Meyer said.

"Good. Try to pull it over my wrist."

He grunted and tugged.

"It budged a little, Paul, but not enough to come free."

"Keep trying."

Sea water covered my feet. The light at the cave opening had disappeared with the setting sun. I shuffled to give Meyer a better grip. My neck ached, and my arms were sore.

Meyer tugged at the rope again. "It's close, but I still can't get if off. My fingers are cramping."

"Rest for a minute."

I heard some deep breaths.

"I'm sorry I got you into this, Meyer."

"What a way to go." He sighed. "I always thought it would be cancer or a heart attack."

"Maybe you can still wait for that. I don't intend to let Harrison have the satisfaction of us dying here. I'm stretching the rope. Try again with the knot."

I felt his fingers fumbling with the rope.

He tugged and the rope gave.

"One loop's off!" he shouted.

There was more slack in the rope, and I flexed my wrists to open more space.

"I need to rest," Meyer said.

The water lapped at my waist.

"Take a short break," I said. "But we don't have much time."

After several minutes, Meyer tugged on the rope again. He pulled, and I stretched. I felt like a calf that had been hog-tied.

"I've got another loop off," he announced.

I felt the rope giving way. I twisted my wrists as far as I could and one hand broke free.

I brought my arm around in front of me, pain shooting through my shoulder. Turning my body, I unwound the rope from my other hand. Then I shook both hands to get the circulation going and to loosen up my stiff arms.

"I'm too old for this crap. Meyer, you don't mind if I swim out of here, do you?"

"What!"

"Just testing your sense of humor. Give me your hands so I can untie you."

I worked at it in the dark. Harrison had tied Meyer's wrists with no slack. I was able to slide my end of the rope through the u-shaped metal piece that Harrison had driven into the wall. Then I worked on getting a knot loosened and slid the whole length of rope through the knot.

As the water reached my chest, I undid another knot and pulled the rope free.

"We need to get out of here," Meyer said.

Only a foot of space remained between the waterline and the top of the cave.

"I'm scared," I said.

"So am I, but we can't stay here. Keep your face close to the ceiling." I felt him brush past as he moved toward the cave entrance. "Put your hand on my shoulder."

We paddled toward the cave entrance. A wave surged in and banged my head against the top of the cave. I lost contact with Meyer's shoulder and started thrashing. I went underwater. I clawed at the cave wall in panic. My lungs were ready to burst. Then I felt Meyer's hand on my shirt.

I came up spluttering.

"Easy does it," Meyer said.

I spit water out. My heart was pounding. All I could taste was salt.

"Hold on," Meyer said. "We're almost out of the cave."

I struggled forward. I didn't remember the cave being so long. Where was the ocean? How much farther?

My one-arm stroke and kicks propelled me forward, as I maintained a death grip with my other hand on Meyer's shoulder. *Breathe, dunk, stroke, kick. Breathe, dunk, stroke, kick.*

My arms felt like they were going to fall off when I looked up and saw a partial moon. We were bobbing in the open ocean.

"Let's get up on the island," I said.

A wave hit Meyer, and he crashed into a rock. He screamed.

I grabbed the rock shelf and boosted myself part way up. Another wave struck and lifted me up on the land. Once I had a good grip, I grabbed Meyer's hand and helped him get his footing.

We scooted out of the reach of the waves and sat there gasping for breath. It took several minutes before we could speak.

"I thought our number was up," Meyer said.

"Me too. Thanks for helping me out of

the cave."

"Looks like we're stuck on this island for the night," Meyer said. "My shoulder really hurts."

"We need to reach Detective Saito right away. Harrison will think we're dead, so this is the time to apprehend him."

"I have my cell phone," Meyer said.

A spark of excitement went through my wet body, then reality set in. "But after all the time in the water. . . ."

"I sealed it in a Ziploc bag. Let's see if it stayed dry. He reached for his pocket and winced in pain. "You'll have to get it out. I can't move my arm."

I extracted the bag from his pocket, opened it, and turned on the phone. "Power's on . . . damn, out of cell range."

"See if you can get any reception by moving."

I limped around to see if I could get a better signal. All I succeeded in doing was almost tripping over a piece of coral.

"No friggin' luck," I said. "We need a way off this rock."

Meyer shook his head. "My shoulder's too injured to swim. I'll wait for someone to find us. There's bound to be some boats in the morning."

"We can't wait that long. Harrison's coming back first thing tomorrow to verify that we're dead."

"What choice do we have?"

"I don't know, but let's look around."

He followed me over the rocky terrain until we reached the pebbly beach that faced Lanikai. I saw something white in the dim moonlight. I bent down to find half of a foam boogie board. Looking across the water to the lights along the shoreline, I gauged the distance. Couldn't be more than a mile. Might as well have been halfway to the moon.

Myer collapsed on the sand, groaning in pain.

I stared at him writhing there, holding his arm, and then I lifted my head again to squint at the pockets of light across the abyss of ocean. Part of my mind said: *You need to get over there, you old fart. Some way. You've got to get help for Meyer and reach Saito.*

Another part of my brain made my throat tighten and screamed: *You can't go in the ocean. It's dark and full of creepy things that will grab you. You swim like a lead weight. Sit down and wait for someone to rescue your sorry ass.*

Images replayed. A little boy thrashing in a swimming pool. An instructor fishing him out of the water. The other kids laughing and calling him "sinker" for months afterward.

What to do?

"How are you feeling, Meyer?"

"Not good. I'm in a lot of pain."

"We have to get word to Saito."

"I wish the cell phone worked. If only I could move my arm, I could swim to shore."

"But you're out of commission. That leaves me."

"I know how you feel about the ocean, Paul. Lie down, and we'll wait out the night."

That would have been the easy path, the sensible thing. But even if we didn't die, Harrison Young would get away.

In the dim light I could see Meyer grimace again. I had to do something.

Chapter 26

I took a deep breath. My heart pounded, and my stomach turned into a hard knot. "I'm going to have to paddle to shore," I told Meyer.

"Are you nuts? You're over eighty years old. And you hate swimming."

"I know," I said. "It scares the piss out of me."

"And look how far it is."

I narrowed my gaze at the lights across the water. He was right. It seemed much farther away than before.

"I have to try it. I've been using a paddle-board in the swimming pool. This shouldn't be that different."

Right. Brave words. I'd been using a flotation belt around my waist. Here I'd be out in the middle of the ocean with just a hunk of foam to hold onto.

Meyer stared at me with his mouth open.

"I'll reseal the cell phone and call 9-1-1

when I get to the Lanikai Beach," I said. "Someone will come get you."

I put the phone in my pocket and discovered the tape recorder. It wasn't running.

"Damn. I wonder if the tape captured everything Harrison said." I placed it on the sand beside Meyer. "You keep this."

Pacing back and forth, I weighed the foam board in my hands, assessing how solid it was. Would it support me enough to get to shore? Would I be able to paddle that far?

If only I were younger. If only I could swim well. If only I could shut off my brain in connection with what was in the ocean. The good news was that I wouldn't remember any of this a few days from now. But I'd have to get through it first.

I kicked off my waterlogged shoes, tiptoed into the water, and grasped the hunk of foam board. It seemed solid. It didn't submerge. It might be able to hold some weight.

But would I be able to get across the ocean at night?

I shivered. The trade wind felt like an arctic blast.

I squinted again at the lights of Lanikai across the black expanse of ocean.

Crapola. I had to do something.

"I'm going to try this," I said to Meyer.

He groaned. "You don't have to."

"I know, but I will. You take care of this island for me, and I'll get someone to come back for you."

Yeah. Right. Who was I kidding? I was scared shitless. No, I was too scared to even shit.

Wading in, I felt the water seize my legs like I was imprisoned by a liquid snake. My right foot scraped a rock and I almost fell. I righted myself and limped farther into the water.

A deep breath and I propelled myself forward. I felt the shock of being immersed again. I clutched the board. I was moving! Then my feet sank beneath me. I started kicking.

"Good luck, Paul," a plaintive voice sounded from behind me.

I was grateful that Meyer didn't say to watch out for sharks.

I shoved the foam board ahead and kept kicking. *Don't even think about sharks.* Nice of my mind to dredge that up.

I needed to get the old legs in gear.

My feet started flapping faster than two broken windmills. I managed to get up a head of steam and surged forward. Or, at least, I thought I was moving.

Where was the moon? Damn. It must have

set over the mountains. Or was it behind clouds? In the dark, who could tell if I was moving or not?

I hoped my thrashing wouldn't attract sharks.

Hell. Thinking of sharks again. With my weird memory, I couldn't remember last week, but I suddenly remembered reading about a boy killed by a shark in these very waters in 1957. He had been paddling along on a surf mat and a shark snagged him.

I kicked harder. *Calm down,* I told myself, *and remember you've been doing this in the swimming pool.* But I had a long way to go. I took a deep breath and focused on the twinkling lights of the Lanikai shoreline. *Kick. Breathe. Kick. Breathe.*

Small waves pushed me forward. As they passed, my view of the shore momentarily disappeared. When the next wave lifted me up, I could see the lights again.

My shoulder ached, my legs felt like jelly, and I gasped for breath. But I kept kicking. The sooner I reached the shore, the sooner the discomfort would end.

I needed to keep my mind off sharks.

I had to think of something pleasant. Like I did when I took walks. I tried to recount positive parts of my life. Meeting Rhonda. It had been right at the beginning of the war. I had just graduated from UCLA. Had a job with Lockheed. Went to a dance with two friends. Nothing much happened until I spotted this beautiful girl in a white frock. She was talking to two other women. My two friends and I walked over, and the rest was history. Rhonda and I were married. Then I enlisted. I spent two years in Washington, our extended honeymoon, and then England, where I handled supply logistics for Operation Overlord.

Now I was going to make my own landing. I looked over my shoulder. Couldn't see the island in the darkness. Lights ahead still a long way off. *Kick. Breathe. Kick. Breathe.*

Good thing I'd been walking to stay in shape. As long as my old legs didn't give out and the sharks didn't sense my fear. . . .

Think positive. Like after the war. Started my own business in Los Angeles. Sold auto parts. Had twenty employees, treated my customers fairly, made a good living. Never rich, but Rhonda and I managed. Saved enough to put Denny through college. Was able to retire in Hawaii. Not bad for a geezer. But what was I doing out in the middle of the ocean at night? You'd think I'd have learned better by my age.

A wave surged and smacked me in the

back of the head, and my face went under. I came up spluttering and spit water out of my mouth. *Keep your yap closed. Kick. Breathe. Focus. Move ahead.*

The waves seemed to push me forward, or that's what I hoped was happening.

Uh oh. Don't even consider what's in the water.

Hell. When I needed my memory to blank things out, it wouldn't.

I shivered, even though the water was warm. The hairs on my arms prickled as the gentle evening breeze periodically blew past.

My stomach tightened. How was I going to get across this huge distance? I struggled to look back. Couldn't see a damn thing. A feeling of panic gripped me. I was all alone in the middle of the ocean. What if the currents carried me out to sea?

I stuck my head up to see if the lights were getting closer. Couldn't tell. At least they were still there.

Get control of yourself.

I kept kicking. *Push. Kick. Breathe.* Head toward the lights. Was I making any progress?

How much longer would I have to keep kicking? Would my old legs or arms give out, first? Would a shark get me before I had a heart attack?

Had to get my mind off the situation.

I remembered a day in the desert of Southern California with Rhonda. Hot and dry. Boy, I wanted water then. Now I had enough water to last three lifetimes.

What if the foam board became water-logged? I'd last ten seconds. I clenched the board tighter.

What if I cramped up?

Keep kicking. Had to get to shore.

Another surge.

Lights were still there. What a relief.

Why did I do this? I could have stayed on the island and taken care of Meyer and his injured shoulder. Waited to be rescued in the morning.

No. Harrison would be back. I had to get to Saito and stop Harrison before he left the islands.

But was this just a stupid idea?

What if I didn't get to shore? Then Harrison would find Meyer, kill him, and leave for the mainland anyway.

What was I doing out here?

I felt something swoop by.

I cringed.

Just a seagull. Probably thought I was dinner.

I had to piss. Just let it loose in your pants.

I let go. Ah. A sense of relief.

Uh oh. I wondered if sharks could smell human pee?

I had to get to shore. *Kick. Breathe. Move those ancient legs, you old poop.*

A wave lifted me up.

Uh oh. Where were the lights?

My stomach tightened again. On the next wave, I turned my head back and forth. Where were the lights? There. Off to the right. I corrected my course and kept kicking.

My legs were tired. Would something suddenly grab them from the depth of the ocean and drag me under?

I couldn't think of a worse way to die. I didn't want to drown.

Got to get to shore. How much farther? Would I last?

The aroma of steak filled my nostrils. I was hungry. Was this coming from a backyard barbecue that was close ahead? I sniffed again. Now only the smell of salt water.

Keep kicking.

What if the current carried me to either side of Lanikai Beach and I reached shore where it was rocky? What if the waves dashed me into the rocks? What if my legs gave out?

I wanted out of this damn ocean.

Kick.

How much longer? Why did I do this? Was this worth dying for?

Come on you old fossil. You don't have much time left, anyway. You need to keep kicking and use those old legs. They aren't good for much else anyway, so you might as well get to the beach and nail Harrison.

If I were just able to reach shore. How much farther?

Another wave and I popped up briefly, saw the lights ahead. Crap. So far still to go. *Kick.*

What else was in the water with me? What else wanted to get me? Was there a shark circling, waiting to strike?

Had to think positive. Had to take my mind off my fears. Count ten kicks. *One, two, three . . . ten.*

Now what?

Count again.

A wave caught me unaware and water spilled over my head. I came up, spitting water out. *Keep your mouth closed!* I expelled more salty water.

My hands were cramping. Couldn't lose hold of the foam board, whatever I did.

What if it were torn out of my grip? I'd be stuck out in the darkness. I'd never make it.

Would I make it even if I kept holding the board?

I imagined something brushing against my leg. The hair on my head would have stuck straight up except for being waterlogged. I shivered. Maybe I was developing hypothermia. Would my muscles quit? Would I fall into a coma and slip into the depths?

I was in warm Hawaiian waters.

Get a grip.

I had run all the possibilities through my defective mind: sharks, other fish out to get me, current carrying me away, losing my foam board, cramping, passing out.

Maybe I'd be hit by a meteorite. Damn. Maybe I'd even make it to shore.

On the next crest, I peered ahead. Lights still there. Maybe even closer. I could do this!

Then my right calf seized up in a cramp. I stopped kicking and my feet immediately sank. I reached down with my right hand to massage my calf.

A wave hit me and my left hand slipped off the foam board.

My chest tightened. I started thrashing.

Where was the board?

Another wave surged by and in the dim light I saw the reflection of white three feet away.

I kicked and threw my arms toward it.

Seizing the board, I brought it under my chin like the lifeline it was.

Don't do anything stupid!

My cramp had turned into pain. I gritted my teeth.

Keep kicking, you old fool.

Would I make it? People swam out here all the time. I remembered years ago, sitting on the beach in the early morning after the sun had peeked above the horizon, watching a person in a bathing cap stroking along the shoreline some fifty yards out.

Yeah. But that person was a good swimmer with consistent, strong strokes — like a machine. And it was daylight. Here I was in the dark, flailing, inefficient — a sinking machine.

Keep kicking.

On the next wave, the lights looked a little closer. Was there a chance I'd make it?

Then my leg cramped up again.

Uh oh.

I moved my foot around in a circle trying to shake the cramp loose. I didn't dare let go of the board again.

My leg felt a little better. Then my side started to ache. I tried to stretch. *Ouch.* I felt a twinge in my neck. The old body was protesting.

Keep kicking no matter what.

I felt something brush against my arm. I jerked to the side, my heart pounding. Just some seaweed.

How much longer?

I could actually see a faint outline of the beach ahead.

Just needed to be like Peter Pan. Think happy thoughts.

There! I could make out a boat up on the sand. How shallow was the water below me? Could I touch? I stopped kicking and let my feet sink.

Nope. Not shallow enough.

I resumed my sporadic kicking. One more wave pushed me. I tried again. There. My feet were on sand and I could walk with my head out of the water.

I stumbled forward. I pictured emerging from the ocean like a Japanese horror movie monster with baby sharks and moray eels attached to my clothes.

I staggered up the beach and collapsed on the sand.

So tired. . . .

CHAPTER 27

My eyes popped open. I had dozed off. Then, faint memories came back to me. I had been kidnapped. Meyer was still stuck on Mokulua. I shook my head to clear the cobwebs. It was fortunate that Marion and I had been together last night or my defective brain would have been zotto. As it was, things were woozy enough.

The phone. I needed to call Detective Saito. I extracted the still-dry phone from the Ziploc bag and dialed 9-1-1.

"My name is Paul Jacobson and I've escaped from a kidnapping," I said. "I'm lying on Lanikai Beach. Please get word to Detective Saito. Tell him Harrison Young murdered Marshall Tiegan and kidnapped me. Also, my companion is still on Mokulua. . . .

"No, I am not drunk, just exhausted from paddling to shore. Call Detective Saito."

After I put the phone down, I lay on my

back and looked up at the stars. A wisp of cloud momentarily blocked part of my view, then blew past.

I couldn't move. My legs ached and when I tried to lift them, they felt like they were trapped under logs. The sand, still warm from the day, cushioned my sore body.

Some time later, I heard footsteps and turned my head to see a dark shape emerging from the shadows and heading toward me. For a moment my mind played tricks on me. I imagined Harrison Young returning, but at closer range, I saw a uniformed police officer.

"You call 9-1-1?" he asked.

"Yes. I'm the one."

"Are you injured?"

"Just tired. You need to get a boat out to Mokulua. My friend Meyer needs to be rescued."

"Is he injured?"

"Hurt his shoulder, and he's out there all alone!"

The cop held his hand up. "Calm down. Let's go to my squad car and you can make a statement."

I couldn't stand on my own. He helped me to my feet, and I staggered until I could get my wheels going. Still limping, I followed him along the sand and through the narrow public right-of-way between a brick wall and a wire fence, leading to the road. After I recounted the events, I said, "Has Detective Saito been informed?"

"Yes. He's asked me to bring you in to the station house."

"Fine. Is someone going to get Meyer?"

"A police boat has been dispatched from the Kaneohe yacht harbor."

"That seems like a long way to go," I said.

"It's the closest place a boat is kept."

The policeman drove to the Kaneohe police station, and I was led to a room. "Please wait here, Mr. Jacobson," he said.

After he closed the door, I stared at the blank walls for a few minutes. I closed my eyes but was too tense to fall asleep. Weird images of sharks swimming in the Kina Nani pool swirled in my head. Then someone shook my shoulder.

"Mr. Jacobson?"

I blinked.

"Ah, Detective Saito," I said to the short, stocky man who had awakened me. "For once I'm happy to see you."

"I thought you couldn't remember who I was?"

"I can't. But you're wearing a nameplate today."

He looked down at his chest, then back up at me, and smiled. "I understand you've had quite a night."

"You bet your sweet ass. Have you arrested Harrison Young yet?"

"Hold on. Let's go through everything that happened."

"It's real simple. Meyer Ohana and I visited Harrison —"

"And why were you going to see him?"

"We found out he had a Swiss stamp collection to sell."

"You should have informed me."

"Well, Detective, I would have, but you never seem to believe anything I say."

He shrugged. "Go on."

"Did you get a message from Henry Palmer that Meyer and I were visiting Harrison Young?"

"I received a strange telephone call. To paraphrase, 'If you want to find two idiots trying to get themselves killed, go to Harrison Young's apartment in Windward Passage.'"

"Nice to know we had such solid backup," I said. "Did you ever go over there?"

"I was in the middle of another investigation on the far end of Kaneohe. By the time I arrived at Mr. Young's apartment, there was no one there."

"Meyer and I suffered through all of this because you were busy?"

"That's the risk of amateur sleuthing. You could have informed me ahead of time."

"Would you have believed me?"

"I don't know." He gave me a half-smile and opened his hands. "Guess it was kind of a Catch-22. Now, tell me about Mr. Young."

"Harrison kidnapped Meyer and me. The scumbag was Tiegan's lawyer, killed Tiegan, and stole the stamp collection." I reviewed our night's activities.

"So you drove around with an expired driver's license," Saito said.

"Give me a break. I was being kidnapped."

"Probably not worth adding to your list of suspected crimes." Saito smiled.

"Thanks for being so understanding, Detective. Have you rescued Meyer yet?"

"Yes. He's on his way here. He had a short stop at the hospital, where his shoulder was taken care of."

"Good. He can independently confirm everything I've said."

"We'll see if your story checks out," Saito said. "And your memory problem?"

"Once in awhile my memory gets jump-started, but most days it's as solid as yogurt. Meyer also has a tape recorder. If the tape can be dried out, you'll have some interesting statements from Harrison."

"You're not off the hook yet, Mr. Jacobson. I'll need you to stay here until I've talked to Mr. Ohana."

"All right," I said. "Arrest Harrison Young before he destroys any evidence."

"In due course."

"Harrison's planning to leave for the mainland in the morning."

"You're a wealth of information."

"Just trying to help, Detective."

After he left, I closed my eyes again, but stayed awake.

I heard a sound and opened my eyes. Detective Saito shut the door and sat down across the table from me.

"Mr. Ohana is back safely, and I've had a chance to talk to him," Saito said. "There are a few more things I need to ask you."

"Fire away," I said.

"Describe the car Mr. Young kidnapped you in."

"It's a gold Lexus. Front passenger side smells like pee."

Detective Saito actually smiled. "Mr. Jacobson, for a man with a poor memory, you remember the most interesting things."

I shrugged. "I do what I can."

"Mr. Ohana gave us the tape player, and we've been able to listen to the tape."

"It worked! I taped our encounter with the illustrious Harrison Young. He confessed to bumping off Marshall Tiegan."

"Sound's not all that clear in spots, but we could decipher the gist of what he said."

"Did you find the stamp collection?"

"A search warrant is being issued. We'll check his place for it."

"Fiddle fart," I said. "What you have to do around this place to get criminals off the street."

"Cheer up. You're not my prime suspect anymore."

"Great. I'll feel a lot better when you have Harrison behind bars."

"I also wanted to let you know that we arrested Mr. Maurice 'Moki' Iwana two hours after he left Mr. Ohana's apartment."

"Good work," I said.

"He broke down and confessed to stealing money from the cash box in the Kina Nani business office, as well."

"Imagine that."

Saito stared at me and laughed. "You old fraud."

"Just trying to do my part to make Kina Nani a safer place to live."

"And there's another question he cleared

up," Saito said.

"He didn't admit stealing some of my brain cells, did he?"

"No, but he confessed that he had been breaking into the storage lockers in his off-hours. Seems he raided stuff that had been stored there, figuring most people never claimed items before they died anyway. That day you found him unconscious on the floor, he must have been breaking into a storage bin, fallen, and hit his head."

"There you are, Detective. I knew my golf swing wasn't good enough to knock him out. I hate to be rude, but I'm kind of tired. Any chance I could get a lift back to my humble abode for a little shut-eye?"

"Sure. I'll have an officer take both you and Mr. Ohana back."

A baby-faced policeman gave us a ride back to our chateau.

Meyer had his arm in a sling.

"All the girls back at Kina Nani will fuss over you with that war wound," I said.

"I'm ready for a calm few days," Meyer said.

"Not you. You'll be up pacing the hallways tomorrow."

Meyer put his good hand on my shoulder. "That was a pretty amazing thing you did, Paul, as much as you hate the ocean to swim across to Lanikai Beach at night."

"My once-in-a-lifetime experience. I'll never do that again."

"I would have understood if you waited until someone came to rescue us," Meyer said.

"But Harrison might have returned first, and we needed to get word back to Saito."

"Still, that was really something. You managed to overcome your fear."

"Nothing's changed. I'm sure I'll have nightmares, but I won't remember the details after a good night's sleep or two."

He punched my arm. "That's the advantage of your rotten memory. You don't have to relive painful situations."

"I'll write it up in my journal and be able to read it later as if it happened to someone else. Just don't expect that I'll swim with you and your lady friends in your water aerobics class."

"And I thought you were going to become the instructor," Meyer said.

I looked out the window at a used car lot as we zipped along Kamehameha Highway.

"Could you turn on the siren?" I asked the driver.

He gave me a brief sideward glance that communicated: "Are you nuts?"

"Just kidding," I said.

"Quite a night," Meyer said.

"It goes to show that my dislike of lawyers was justified, present company excepted."

"We've definitely had our experience escaping all types of sharks," Meyer said with a twinkle in his eyes.

"Yeah. Not bad for two old fogies."

"We escaped from the bad guy and we're no worse for wear, except for my shoulder. I know you hate the ocean, but I may never go near it again either."

"Cheer up," I said. "You won't be around that long, anyway."

He smiled. "Speak for yourself. I'm planning to live to be a hundred and ten."

"Right. Pacing around blind and pissing in your pants. Give me a break."

Inside my apartment, I found my second wind, so I wrote in my journal.

Later I tossed and turned, but finally zonked out at daybreak.

When I awoke I had a vague memory of an island. It felt like a dream until I read my journal. I spent a few minutes matching the hazy memories with the written account. Yup, it had all happened. By concentrating, I could even bring up a faint image of Harrison Young, scar on his cheek, dark intense eyes.

Not someone I wanted to encounter again.

Just then the phone rang.

"This is Detective Saito," the voice on the other end of the line said.

"Hello, Detective. I was reading what happened to me yesterday."

"I need to warn you. Harrison Young wasn't in his apartment. We've been unable to find any sign of him, his car, or the stamp collection."

"So why call me?"

"There was an article in this morning's newspaper reporting Meyer Ohana's rescue from the Mokulua islands. An overeager reporter on the police beat managed to get some of the information and wrote it up."

"So?"

"When we searched Young's condo, a newspaper lying on his table was open to that page," Saito said. "I called Mr. Ohana, but there was no answer. I've sent an officer over to Kina Nani. In the meantime, don't let anyone into your apartment."

CHAPTER 28

As I looked up Meyer's apartment number in the Kina Nani directory, I felt a gnawing concern in my gut.

In front of his apartment, I heard a voice coming through the louvers above his door. I turned the handle and slowly opened the door.

A voice from around the corner and out of view said, "And what did you tell the police?"

A gasping voice said, "I told the police that I had been kidnapped."

I took a step forward.

A man with his back to me was pointing a gun at a white-bearded guy lying on the floor.

Within my reach stood a colorful vase on a high three-legged table. I quietly picked it up, raised it above my head, and brought it crashing down onto the head of the man with the gun. The vase shattered into a thousand pieces. Gray powder billowed around the room.

Meyer gasped, "Not the vase."

The man with the gun slumped forward and collapsed onto the rug.

"My vase," Meyer said with a sob.

"My ass," I said. "If he had shot you, the vase wouldn't have done you any good."

"I don't know how many more incidents like this Martha can take," Meyer said.

I heard footsteps and a policeman burst into the room.

"Here's the guy you're looking for, Officer," I said.

"I know you from the last time I was here," he said.

I shrugged. "Can't say as I remember you."

"Yeah. Just like before. Gray powder all over the room."

"We old guys are in kind of a rut," I said.

As the police officer cuffed Harrison Young, Meyer paced the room.

"We can't keep treating Martha like this," he said.

"Think of it as her doing her part to save your life," I replied.

He smiled wanly. "I guess you're right, but I've lost two vases now."

■ ■ ■ ■

Detective Saito arrived as Harrison Young was regaining consciousness.

Saito read Harrison his rights.

Harrison glared at me. "I should have stuffed you down the trash chute with Tiegan."

"That would have been kind of cramped," I said.

He lunged toward me, but the police officer pulled him back like a dog on a leash.

"Go lock him up," Saito commanded.

After the policeman had led Harrison away, Saito put on rubber gloves, took a pen out of his pocket, lifted the revolver by the trigger guard, and dropped it into a paper bag.

"Seems like every time I come here, Martha's been spilled," Saito said.

"Martha wanted to get some fresh air," I said. "Do you have all the evidence you need, so I can help Meyer clean up?"

"Yeah. But I need to get a statement from each of you."

Saito asked me to wait outside while he interviewed Meyer.

I walked into the open-air hallway. Leaning on the railing, I looked at the green hillside. I could hear roosters. Out in the wilds of Kaneohe. I imagined being young again and hiking through the jungle of trees and vines.

My reverie was interrupted by Saito, who asked Meyer and me to trade places. I walked inside to give my statement.

"So exactly what happened?" Saito asked.

"Simple. After you called me, I got concerned about Meyer and went to his apartment. I heard a voice inside questioning Meyer, so I sneaked inside. Saw Harrison waving a gun, and I whacked him over the head with Martha."

"Pretty reckless thing to do, Mr. Jacobson."

"It was what jumped into my defective brain at the moment, Detective."

Saito closed his notebook with a snap. "That should do it for now."

"Although I've enjoyed our frequent meetings, am I clear now to complete the rest of my short life unmolested by the police?"

"Yeah. We have the right guy now."

"Aren't you going to apologize for suspecting me?"

He shook his head. "Nah. You were a good suspect."

That was as much of an apology as I was going to get.

"I'm glad I was able to give your work some meaning," I said. "Now, if we're finished, I'll help Meyer clean up."

With no further words he turned and headed out the door.

I cleaned up Martha for Meyer, as his wounded wing was still bothering him. Admiring the glass jar in which I had stored Martha's remains, I said, "All recovered. She's none the worse for wear. But you need to buy an unbreakable vase. Get a metal one and put a stopper in it. Then you'll be ready for anything."

"With you around, Paul, that's a necessity."

"Hey, I only try to keep your life interesting. Without me, you'd be pacing the floor and staring at all the vegetables."

I took the plastic bag containing broken pieces of vase and emptied it into the trash chute. There was no body blocking the chute this time.

Later that morning, as I walked past the front desk, the receptionist called to me, "Oh, Mr. Jacobson."

"Yes?"

"We found the missing page to the visitors' sign-in log you were looking for."

"Is that so?"

"Yes. It must have been accidentally torn off and mixed in with some receipts."

"Imagine that."

"One other thing," she said. "That name you were trying to identify."

I thought back to what I had read in my journal. "The indecipherable signature with an 'H.' "

"Yes, that one. We know who it is. She visited again this morning and signed in with the same signature."

Obviously not Harrison.

"It was a Harriet Bowers visiting Mrs. Chang in room 704."

"Well, that explains the mystery," I said. "Thanks for the update."

"No problem."

No, it wasn't a problem. I smiled at the receptionist.

I had one other piece of business to conduct. I found the office I was looking for and knocked on the door that had a sign: DIRECTOR FARNS.

"Come in."

"You a mortician or the guy who runs this place?" I asked the stiff behind the desk. This guy made me want to puke. Slimy. I wouldn't want him standing behind me with a knife. You had to give this place credit, though. Farns was the perfect overseer for this nuthouse. I sure wouldn't want the job.

"Yes, Mr. Jacobson. What can I do for you?"

"A few weeks back you told me to pack my bags and leave on the next boat."

He adjusted his spectacles and cleared his throat. "Ah . . . that was all a little misunderstanding."

"You must have assumed I was part of the Hawaiian mafia."

"When the evidence for murder and theft pointed to you, I thought it was best to allow you to . . . er . . . reside somewhere else."

"As I said, you tried to kick my ass out of here. Just want to set the record straight. I'm not all that fond of this place, but I think I'll stick around for awhile."

"At some time you might need additional care because of your memory," Farns said.

"This a sales pitch for your care home facility?"

"No," he said, adjusting his tie. "Just one of the options for the future."

"I guess I'll tough it out for the time being. By the way, I hope you do a better job of selecting employees in the future. You won't have to suspect your paying clients if you don't have people like Moki on your payroll."

Farns started twitching, and his eyes

flicked from side to side like he was looking for an escape path.

"That's okay," I said. "I'm not going to sue your ass or anything. Just stay out of my way."

I turned and sauntered out of his office. I wished I had a smoking gun so I could blow on the end of the barrel.

Returning to my apartment, I sat in my armchair and looked at a picture of a purple and white orchid on my wall. I contemplated what I wanted to be when I grew up. Now that I was stuck in this place, couldn't remember squat, but had survived a near-death experience, what was I going to do?

Well, I guessed I would go on living day-to-day. I would wake up, and my life would be a brand new adventure every morning. I had friends like Meyer and Marion, as long as there was a way to jog my memory. Harrison Young and Moki were locked up. Life was good. Sort of.

The next day I slept late, read my journal to reacquaint myself with my recent activities, and then looked out my window at the mountains, glistening after a rain shower. I felt like a gutted fish. Empty inside. Sure, I had accomplished something. I had overcome my fear of the ocean. Well, not overcome it, really, since I would never go in again. But I had stepped up to the plate and done what I needed to do. And it should have given me solace that my good name had been cleared. After all, Saito had wanted my scalp and thought me a murderer.

I tried to reach deep down inside for that feeling of pride and accomplishment. I remembered that high when I closed a business deal many years ago. The special warmth I'd felt when Denny hit a home run to win a little league game in Torrance one time.

But now? Nothing. Maybe my defective memory erased part of my pleasure mechanism. Or maybe I was getting too old to care. This was the pits. Would I turn into a wrinkled old vegetable who didn't care about anything? No highs? No lows? Just sitting there?

How did I feel now?

I pinched my arm.

Ouch. I was still alive.

Taking a deep breath, I slowly exhaled. I felt alone. Just me and my defective memory. A pretty exciting crowd.

Still, I was alive, had a solid appetite — enjoyed a good meal as much as the next guy — and could read a book. And, thanks to Jennifer, I was sticking to short stories, so I could complete a story in one sitting. I had lived a good life. That I could be thankful for.

I had never been too much of a jerk, never cheated my customers, never been like Harrison Young. So why not take each day as it came? Since each new day was an adventure for me, why not just play it out?

I stood up, walked toward the window, and watched a car pull up into a parking space in front of the building. Hey, at least I wasn't looking out at a slum tenement.

A few minutes later my doorbell rang.

"Who are you?" I said to a man built like a fire hydrant holding some golf clubs.

"I'm Detective Saito, Mr. Jacobson."

"I've read all about you. Lately, you've been busy getting criminals off the street."

He handed me the golf clubs. "Just returning your property. By the way, thank you for your assistance in solving the Tiegan murder and the thefts."

My mouth must have dropped open.

Saito smiled. "Don't look so surprised."

"It's just that after all the crap from you, I'm flabbergasted."

He shrugged. "It was nothing personal. Everybody's guilty in my book until I arrest the culprit."

I thought for a moment. "I guess you have

to be that way to get your job done."

"There was another crime on your list. A Mrs. Hughes accused you of entering her room at Turtle Bay."

"Yeah, I read that."

"You're off the hook," Saito said. "Apparently, she had such a good round of golf yesterday, she forgave you and the hotel and decided to drop charges."

"Will wonders never cease!"

"And some final news for you. We recovered Tiegan's stamp collection. It was in the trunk of Mr. Young's car. Found something else. Relates to the lawsuit brought by Tiegan against you for stealing some stamps."

"Yeah," I said. "I remember reading that."

"Turns out there was a pocket in the back inside cover of Tiegan's stamp album. We found an envelope wedged in there. Contained the missing stamps."

"So I'm not a thief *or* a murderer," I said.

"That's it."

I thought back to something else I had read in my journal.

"Say, Detective. That stamp collection. Is it really worth half a million dollars?"

Saito laughed. "That's what Mr. Young must have thought. The stamps might have been bought for that if they were all unused. Turns out the collection was primarily used stamps, which would have put the buying price at around two hundred thousand dollars. But the real grabber is that there's a huge difference between the buying and selling price. A dealer would have paid Mr. Young thirty cents on the dollar, so maybe sixty thousand dollars, max. That's how dealers make their money."

"That explains why he was interested in selling directly to a private party," I said.

"Yeah. He thought he might be able to get something substantial, but he never would have been able to get the amount of money he thought he was murdering Tiegan for."

"Must be the impact of inflation," I said. "Crime doesn't pay what it used to."

"Not on my watch, anyway. One other thing we found on Mr. Young — a set of keys."

"Conveniently duplicated from Moki's set," I said.

"Exactly. But missing a key. The one to the trash chute."

"I guess that wraps up everything you've been investigating here."

"It does," Saito said. "I've also given up smoking again, after seeing all the people with oxygen tanks around this place."

"See, Detective? I've been a good influence on you."

He forced a wan smile. "And since we won't be seeing each other again, I brought you a little present."

His eyes danced at my look of astonishment. He handed me a brown paper-wrapped package.

"Should I open this now?"

"Sure. Go ahead."

I removed the brown paper covering and found a wooden box with a glass cover. Inside were six yellow and black monarch butterflies, neatly mounted with pins through their wings.

I laughed. "I'm glad I didn't end up like that. It will be nice not having you breathing down my neck anymore, Detective."

He smiled and opened his hands toward me. "You're clean, for now. Keep it that way."

I saluted him. "Will miracles never cease. Now I can go back to being an absent-minded geezer."

He gave me a half-salute in return, turned, and strolled out of my apartment.

I guessed I'd miss Detective Saito . . . if I had been able to remember him.

I admired the butterfly collection and set it on my bookshelf. It would be something to show to Jennifer on her next visit.

So here I was, in my luxury resort, without a care in the world. Except, I was hungry.

Rather than chewing on a magazine, I decided it was time to hit the chow hall. See what gourmet meal was in store for me.

CHAPTER 29

I found a bald-headed runt chomping away at a hot dog. I stood in front of him and poked him in the chest. "From what I read, you weren't very convincing in getting Detective Saito to come rescue Meyer and me."

"You two nutcases deserved whatever happened," Henry said.

"Fortunately, we're fine, but no thanks to you."

"The whole thing wasn't my idea," Henry said.

Just then a white-bearded guy showed up and pulled me away. "Take it easy, Paul," he said.

"I'm pissed that Henry wasn't more help."

"We're fine now," Meyer said. "Cool your jets."

I sat down, and then it all hit me. I started laughing and Meyer joined in.

"What a place," I said. "This guy cares

more about his hot dog than saving his buddies."

"He did make the phone call," Meyer said.

We chatted for a while, then Meyer leaned
close to me.

"I've made a decision," he said.

I sensed something monumental. "What's
that?"

"It's time for me to move to a care home."

"And break up our trio?"

"I've been trying to put this off, but it's
inevitable. I woke up this morning in a
puddle. I can't see well enough to even
clean it up effectively anymore."

"Too bad we couldn't combine your
problems and mine in just one of us. Then
the other could still be a functioning human being."

"That's the crapshoot of aging, I guess,"
Meyer said.

"Without you, I'll really have to follow my
instructions every morning when I wake
up."

"That's why I think you should get together with Marion. She'd be able to remind
you."

"I read that we had discussed this hypoth-
esis of yours," I said, "but I still can't accept
the idea of foisting myself off on someone
else."

"I think she'd willingly accept it."

"I don't know. From what I read, we discussed it once and she had her doubts."

He threw his cloth napkin on the table. "It's your life, Paul. What's left of it. If I were you, I'd try to talk her into it. You can live out a lonely existence or be with someone who cares about you."

I took a sip of coffee. "You may be right, but I know what it's like being me every morning. I still can't bring myself to impose that on Marion."

"It's your choice. Still seems like a wasted opportunity."

"So, how are you going to afford the new place?"

"It's less expensive than the care home here at Kina Nani. Not quite double the independent living fees I'm paying now."

I whistled. "That's a big bite."

"I don't have any other expenses. My pension covers it. That's one of the benefits of having been a judge."

"I wondered where all my tax dollars went."

"You should come with me," Meyer said. "Maybe we could swing a package deal."

"I'm not ready for that. And my financial adviser might not approve. From what I read, I can just afford the Kina Nani rent.

I'll wait until I really need a care home. How soon are you planning to move?"

"Next week. You'll have to come visit me, Paul."

"Maybe we can meet for lunch at a neutral site."

"Just write it in your journal so you'll remember."

"No sweat," I said. "A note to myself to call the white-bearded freak."

He grasped my hand, then leaned forward and gave me a hug.

I watched as he turned and shuffled away.

After lunch my telephone rang.

"This is Barry Tiegan. I was informed that you helped find my uncle's stamp collection. I want to apologize for accusing you of stealing it."

"No problem," I said. "But, Barry, I have some advice for you. Stay away from lawyers and other denizens of the deep."

Later my doorbell rang. It was the woman whose picture I had in my bedroom.

"We need to talk," she said.

"Sure. Come in."

We sat on the couch together.

"Meyer is going to move to a care home," I said.

"Yes, I know. With all the changes taking place here, I've been contemplating some of my own."

"Oh?"

"I've been thinking about the conversation we had at Ho'omaluhia Botanical Garden," she said.

"Us living together?"

"Yes. I care about you, Paul, but I don't know if I'm ready to deal with your poor memory all the time."

I took a deep breath. "You have become important to me, Marion."

She gave me a hug. "Thank you." Then she stepped back and looked at me. "I'm moving to California. My daughter has a cottage above her garage that I can move into."

I looked at her in disbelief. "Leave Hawaii?"

"Yes. I think it's time for a change."

"Seems like a lot of turnover around here."

"That's the nature of a retirement home," she said.

"I'm planning to stay here, but it will be lonely without you."

"I'll be back," she said, giving my hand a squeeze. "I know I'll miss you and want to see you again."

My heart felt heavy. "I'll miss you, as well.

Don't stay away too long."

After she left, I felt empty. I was losing my friends, but it was hard to feel much, knowing them only through what I had read that morning. I cared for Marion, but it was like I had just met her for the first time. Would I miss Meyer? He and I had been through a lot together, but by morning I wouldn't even recognize him. And Henry? Just a name.

CHAPTER 30

A week later I sat at breakfast by myself. Marion had moved back to the mainland. She'd left me a note that I had found with my journal. I also read that a friend of mine named Meyer Ohana had moved to the Hale Pohai care home several miles away. A notice on the bulletin board had informed us that Henry Palmer had been hospitalized with a heart attack. It would only be a matter of time for me. I'd either kick the bucket or require additional care myself. A toss of the dice, one way or the other.

Here I was sitting alone like the last cactus standing in the desert. What did I want? It would be nice to be surrounded by family and friends. But my wife was gone, my son and granddaughter lived on the mainland. I'd like to see them more, particularly Jennifer. What a spitfire.

I guess I missed Meyer, but what a weird relationship that must have been. He had continuity, but I had to start over every day. In the morning he was a stranger, but from what I read, by the end of the day, he was a true friend. How absurd to have to repeat that every day.

And Marion. How could you be intimate with someone you didn't recognize the next day, unless you had sex the night before? That wasn't much basis for a long-term relationship.

How would I have felt if it were the other way around? I'd hate to have a friend or lover who didn't know who I was each morning. It was the shits.

I took a bite of omelet. Food really wasn't bad here.

So what were my choices? For now, I'd sit here, stare at the other inmates, and feel sorry for myself. Nothing like the satisfaction of self-pity.

Back in my apartment, I settled down to read the newspaper.

There was a knock on my door.

"Come in," I shouted. "It's unlocked."

A smiling young woman in a neat black skirt and flowered blouse entered. She shook her right index finger at me. "Mr. Jacobson, you snuck away this morning before I could give you your pills."

"I wanted to get downstairs early."

"Well, you'll have to take your pills now."

"You must really like me, giving me all this attention," I said.

"Oh, Mr. Jacobson. You're one of my favorites."

"Then why don't you give me liquid medicine rather than these huge pills?"

"They're not that big. See?"

I looked at three golf ball–sized horse pills. "Maybe to you they seem small."

I struggled to gulp them down with the cup of water she offered. Good thing I didn't remember *this* happening every morning.

"Oh, I meant to remind you," she said. "There's a special party for you tonight."

"Special party?"

"Yes. Because of how you helped solve the murder of poor Mr. Tiegan. And thank you for donating the reward money to the employees' fund."

"I did that?"

"Yes. Thanks again." She gave me a kiss on the cheek, turned, and left my room.

Once again my crapola memory was to blame. I guess I forgot to write it down in my journal. Imagine that.

After lunch, as I sat in my living room

contemplating the wonders of still being alive, my telephone rang. I picked it up and was greeted with, "Hello, Grandpa!"

"This someone I know?"

"Oh, Grandpa. It's me. Jennifer."

"I have a granddaughter named Jennifer."

"That's me."

The image of a six-year-old came to mind.

"How are things on the mainland?" I asked.

"They were pretty good until I sprained my ankle. I have to use crutches and keep my foot up a lot."

"What happened?"

"I stepped on my skateboard wrong, and my ankle twisted. The doctor first thought I might have broken it. I even had an X-ray."

"Sounds like a dangerous sport," I said.

"Nope. I just put my foot in the wrong place. So as long as I'm resting today, I decided to call to say hello."

"Well, hello to you too."

Then I remembered what I had read about her most recent visit.

"You coming to see me again to rescue me from Nurse Ratched?" I said.

"No, Grandpa. I told you before. Your nurse is nice. I think we're coming again sometime during Christmas vacation. I can't wait to go surfing again . . . and see you."

"I'll be here waiting."

"And Daddy told me you solved the murder."

"Yes. It was the man with a scar on his cheek who did it. He also stole the stamps."

"I told you so," she said.

I thought back again to what I had read in my journal that morning.

"And you were the one who helped solve the crime," I said.

"Really?"

"Yeah. The bad guy phoned Meyer as a result of what you did with your computer."

"It worked! I got an email about stamps and sent the phone number you gave me. I even remember the email address — ali-dad at hotmail.com."

"What a memory."

"I don't have any problem remembering things," she said. "What happened after he called Meyer?"

"We tracked him down. He's behind bars, and I'm no longer a suspect."

"I knew you didn't do it, Grandpa."

"But the police weren't sure."

"How did you catch the criminal?"

"It's a long story, but when you come out at Christmas, I'll let you read my journal

. . . the censored version, that is."

"How are all your friends?"

I paused for a moment. "Not good. Marion moved back to the mainland. Meyer's in a care home, and Henry's in the hospital."

"You must be lonely."

"It's not bad," I said. "Nurse Ratched visits me every day."

"Oh, Grandpa. Melanie is nice."

"I don't know. She's still trying to kill me with those huge pills."

"You have to be brave," Jennifer said.

"You're right again."

I thought for a moment. If I could survive getting kidnapped and being tied up in an underwater cave, I guess I could handle some pills.

"The biggest problem with having a sprained ankle is I can't go to swim practice," Jennifer said.

"When you recover, keep up your swimming. You never know when it will come in handy."

"And, Grandpa, I've made a decision."

"Oh?"

"Yes. When I went to the hospital because of my ankle, there were all kinds of people bleeding and hurt, waiting there. It was pretty gross. I've decided I don't want to be a doctor, after all."

"You have years before you need to make a career decision."

"But I have a new plan now," she said. "I remember talking to your friend Meyer while I was in Hawaii. What he did before he retired sounded kind of cool and . . . guess what, Grandpa?"

"What?"

"I'm going to be a lawyer."

After I hung up, I sat there thinking. My own granddaughter going over to the dark side and becoming a lawyer. Oh, well, she'd probably change her mind a dozen times over the next ten years. I still couldn't believe it. My own flesh and blood liking the ocean and wanting to be a lawyer.

I looked at the picture of Jennifer on my dresser. I could only remember a six-year-old, but her voice was definitely older. Would my defective memory ever be able to process new memories? Probably not.

Later the phone rang again. What a popular guy I was.

"Paul, this is Meyer."

"I was just telling Jennifer that you bailed out on me."

He chuckled. "You can come join me any time you're ready. There's one thing that you'd like about this place where I'm living."

"What's that?"

"It's a single story building. No trash chute."

ABOUT THE AUTHOR

Mike Befeler turned his attention to fiction writing after a career in high technology marketing. His short story "Never Trust a Poison Dart Frog" was published in the mystery anthology *Who Died in Here?* and was submitted for Edgar Award consideration. He holds a Master's degree from UCLA and a Bachelor's degree from Stanford. He lives in Boulder, Colorado, with his wife, Wendy.

If you are interested in having the author speak to your book club, contact Mike Befeler at mikebef@aol.com.

The employees of Thorndike Press hope you have enjoyed this Large Print book. All our Thorndike and Wheeler Large Print titles are designed for easy reading, and all our books are made to last. Other Thorndike Press Large Print books are available at your library, through selected bookstores, or directly from us.

For information about titles, please call:
(800) 223-1244

or visit our Web site at:
http://gale.cengage.com/thorndike

To share your comments, please write:
Publisher
Thorndike Press
295 Kennedy Memorial Drive
Waterville, ME 04901

Praise for
Last Chance for Justice

A delightful blend of healing, new beginnings, and the simplicity of the love that shines for a new season. *Last Chance for Justice* tugs sweetly at the heart with delicious hope for tomorrow.

—Janet Perez Eckles, author of best-selling *Simply Salsa: Dancing Without Fear at God's Fiesta*

Kathi Macias writes a hometown tale reminiscent of *Anne of Green Gables*, yet with a modern-day twist. She masterfully weaves a tale of mother-daughter love, complete with small-town gossips, a sweet romance, and a bit of mystery. I was enamored by the uplifting story, endearing characters, and the snuggle-down tale of loss, love, redemption, and discovery.

—Susan G. Mathis, author of *The ReMarriage Adventure* and *Countdown for Couples*

Kathi Macias's new book *Last Chance for Justice* is as inviting as Bloomfield, home to the annual Spring Fling Festival and lots of characters who will feel like old friends. You'll want to meander down Main Street and stop for lunch at Bert's Barbecue. And of course you'll cheer for Lynn Myers, the widow who returns to her old hometown and gets a fresh start in the old house next to the cemetery.

Last Chance for Justice is a delightful read you won't be able to put down. If you love stories that entertain and capture your heart, this one hits the spot! Can't wait for the next Bloomfield book!

—Kathy Howard, author of many books, including *Unshakeable Faith* and *Fed Up with Flat Faith*

Last Chance for Justice is a masterful story that blends the most important issues of life, love, and faith into one compelling contemporary novel. With realistic characters and a great plot set in a small town where life moves at a slower pace, the dialogue alone will keep a reader turning the page.

—Rita Gerlach, author

Once again, Kathi Macias hits her target square in the center! *Last Chance for Justice* strays a bit from her usual deeper, darker subject fare, but it surely doesn't lack in reader satisfaction. Rather, it has the perfect blend of mystery, sweet romance, and inspiration. As always, Macias delivers a fine, compelling story to capture a reader's heart and full attention. Couldn't put it down!

—Sharlene MacLaren, author and speaker

Last Chance for Justice is a lovely story about coming home and connecting to community. Mrs. Macias brought out some crucial and universal questions. How far do we go to honor the wishes of a departed loved one and how might that be part of God's plan? *Last Chance for Justice* explores honor and love in relationships from families to the delight of budding new love, a book you won't want to miss. (You won't want to miss any books by Kathi Macias!)

—Angela Breidenbach, speaker and author of
A Healing Heart

Love, mystery, and friendship are blooming in Bloomfield! In *Last Chance for Justice*, Kathi Macias weaves a refreshing and often humorous tale of a mother and daughter's journey home.

The deeply connected people and simpler pace of Bloomfield made me want to pack a bag and pay the small town a visit of my own.

—Julie Carobini, author, *The Otter Bay Novels*

Last Chance for Justice is a wonderful addition to the Bloomfield series of novels. It's homey and heart-warming with a touch of mystery. The cast of unique characters quickly made their way into my heart. And the setting of Bloomfield expanded to include even more of the town and countryside. A delightful and insightful read.

—Lena Nelson Dooley, multi-award-winning author of McKenna's Daughters, including the recently released *Catherine's Pursuit*

Pleasant characters, a cozy little mystery and a love story to boot. Kathi Macias's *Last Chance for Justice* lets us walk alongside Lynn as she wrestles with the death of her husband, her reluctance to embrace change and the hesitant but brave return to the hometown she left behind years before. As God unfolds His plans for her, for her daughter Rachel, and for some of the people of her quaint old hometown, it becomes wonderfully clear that His plan is bigger than her fear of change and her fear of what others might think put together. Deliciously heartwarming, *Last Chance for Justice* left me with a smile and a sigh—and a major craving for some sun tea.

—Rhonda Rhea, humor columnist, radio personality, and author of ten books, including *Espresso Your Faith* and *Get a Grip*

Last Chance for Justice

KATHI MACIAS

A Bloomfield Novel

Last Chance for Justice

PUBLISHING GROUP

Nashville, Tennessee

978-1-4336-7717-5

Published by B&H Publishing Group
Nashville, Tennessee

Dewey Decimal Classification: F
Subject Heading: MYSTERY FICTION \ LOVE STORIES \
INHERITANCE AND SUCCESSION—FICTION

1 2 3 4 5 6 7 8 • 17 16 15 14 13